ANGEL RISING

ANGEL RISING

Christopher Nicole

This first world edition published 2008
in Great Britain and the USA by
SEVERN HOUSE PUBLISHERS LTD of
9–15 High Street, Sutton, Surrey, England, SM1 1DF.

British Library Cataloguing in Publication Data

Nicole, Christopher
  Angel rising
  1. Fehrbach, Anna (Fictitious character) - Fiction 2. Women
  spies - Fiction 3. World War, 1939-1945 - Secret service -
  Germany - Fiction 4. Suspense fiction
  I. Title
  823.9'14[F]

ISBN-13: 978-0-7278-6681-3   (cased)

Except where ac... historical event ...ters are being
described for the ... and purely ...
publication are f... and any resembl... g person...
is purely coincid...

All Severn House t... ...printed on acid-free...

Printed and bound in Great Britain by
MPG Books Ltd., Bodmin, Cornwall.

Prologue

*W*e drove into the hills behind the Costa Blanca resort of Javea, to visit the historic site of Guadaliest, where some centuries ago a fortress town had been split asunder by an earthquake. I was not sure this was a journey we should risk, because although the ruins are spectacular, viewing them involves a good deal of walking, either uphill or down again, and my companion was in her late eighties. But she pooh-poohed the suggestion that it might be too much for her.

This attitude was typical of Anna Fehrbach, alias the Countess von Widerstand, alias the Honourable Mrs Ballantine Bordman, alias Anna Fitzjohn. Her ebullient confidence had carried her, when hardly more than a girl, through the horrors of the Second World War, not to mention the traumas of trying to survive afterwards, which for her had been greater than for most, as she had remained for too long the most wanted woman in the world.

I had been fortunate in coming into her life as she had been realizing that the time was approaching when she should be preparing to leave it. She had closed the book on her career several decades ago, when circumstances had led to the decision that the time had come for her to disappear, and by which time she had achieved the immense wealth that had enabled her to do so, completely and without trace. Her vanishing act had caused many people to wonder if she was dead, or had ever existed, or merely been a figment of frightened men's, and women's, imaginations. But after having withdrawn for so many years entirely from the life she had once lived, and understanding that even her retirement was drawing to a close, she had felt the urge to leave behind some proof that she had been, that she had played so important a part in history, had, indeed, influenced the course of those tumultuous years. And while she was in this retrospective mood, who should appear but a journalist who had spent many years of his own life tracking her down.

Of course Anna Fehrbach was well aware that there were quite a few people, principally resident in Moscow, interested in *discovering whether she might still be alive, and thus she had regarded me with suspicion when at last I had traced her to her secluded villa situated high on Montgo, overlooking Javea. And when I had first called upon her, having by then learned enough of her from guarded references in autobiographies and other memoirs, the descriptions of her as the most beautiful but also the most deadly woman of her time, I had had no doubt that I was taking a considerable risk. Anna's skills were immense, but they, and her survival, had rested on a single supreme characteristic: when she felt it necessary, or herself to be in danger, she acted without hesitation, and with tremendous speed, and her actions were always lethal.*

But her perception of the world, governed by her genius – as a girl she had had an IQ of 173 – had taken her no more than a few seconds to discern that I was too young and too innocent to have ever been an enemy, and that I was suffering almost an obsession with this nebulous figure I had sought for so long. And Anna, whatever her reputation for cold-blooded ruthlessness, remained essentially a woman, and thus susceptible to flattery.

So we had struck up a strange relationship, almost that of mentor and pupil, with the pupil falling more and more under the spell of the mentor as she had told me her story. Much of it was disturbing, certainly amoral, but when one was in the company of Anna Fehrbach morality was irrelevant. Thus I could glance sideways at her as we followed the winding road, and picture what had been. She remained tall, only an inch beneath six feet, and slender, although her full shirt still suggested what might lie concealed. Her legs were long. I had never seen them, as at her age she always wore pants, but her feet and ankles, exposed by her sandals, were exquisite. As was the bone structure of her face. The skin was now drawn a little tight, but the beauty was untarnished. The whole was set off by the jewellery she was never without, the little gold bar earrings, the huge ruby solitaire on the forefinger of her right hand, the gold Rolex on her left wrist, and of course the gold chain that disappeared, enticingly, into her shirt front and from which, I knew, was suspended the crucifix which was the only reminder of her Catholic childhood. Only her hair, now quite white and cut short, where once it had been pale gold and brushed her thighs, definitely established her age.

After what she had told me, it was simple to see beyond this elderly but still entrancing mask, and picture the seventeen-year-old Austro-Irish schoolgirl, arrested with her family in Vienna in March 1938 because her father was an anti-Nazi journalist. Or the innocent who, because of her beauty and her intelligence, as well as her athletic skills, had been sent to an SS training camp, taught to seduce and then to kill, and inducted into the SD, the Sicherheitsdienst, the most secret of the Nazi secret services, and thus become the mistress as well as the private assassin of Reinhard Heydrich, Hitler's Hangman, compelled to obey his every command because the Nazis held her parents hostage for her loyalty.

I could imagine her, if I dared allow myself, being strapped naked to a bar in a Gestapo torture chamber to be punished for a breach of discipline, or rolling in the arms of Clive Bartley, the MI6 agent who had 'turned' her, and to whom she had given all her angry, youthful, loyalty.

I could imagine her suspended naked by her wrists in a cell in the Lubianka Prison in Moscow, being tortured by the NKVD with jets of water after her failed attempted – as ordered by Heydrich – assassination of Josef Stalin, just as I could imagine the Angel from Hell, as she often described herself, committing a terrible vengeance when the American, Joseph Andrews, had secured her release.

I could see her again avenging herself, and thousands of Nazi victims in concentration camps, by master-minding and completing the assassination of Heydrich in Prague in 1942, just as I could see her undergoing the humiliation of sharing Hitler's bed in order to place the bomb that would blow him to perdition . . . and had not done so.

And most of all, I could see her, when the Americans had allowed themselves to be convinced by their then Soviet allies that she was too dangerous to be allowed to live, killing the old friend they sent to 'eliminate' her, after he had made the fatal mistake of attempting to enjoy her beauty before completing his mission.

But she had survived all of that, and even, in the collapse of the Third Reich, managed to extricate her parents from their prison, and get them to the supposed safety of England, and herself to a new life, hopefully free of the traumas of the past. But . . .

I pulled into a parking spot in the little town beneath the ruins. We had had a splendid lunch at a delightful restaurant called El Riu, but in the last stages of the drive she had been pensive, as she often was when considering her past. I had not wanted to disrupt her reverie, but now I ventured, 'When last we talked,

*you suggested that things did not work out quite the way you had
hoped, when the shooting stopped.'*

   *She seemed to awake with a start. 'Do you really suppose the
shooting has ever stopped?' She still spoke English with the soft
Irish brogue she had inherited from her mother. 'Certainly for
me. There were just too many people who wanted me, for too
many reasons. Did not someone once say, once you climb on
the back of a tiger, you can never get off. I was just coming up
to twenty-five years old when I fled Nazi Germany. And do you
know how many people I had killed by then, either for the SD
or for MI6? Or,' she added, 'simply to stay alive?'*

   'I have been keeping count,' I admitted. 'Fifty-three.'

   'Fifty-three,' she mused.

   *'But,' I pointed out. 'As you once told me, you were fighting
a war. Had you been a fighter pilot you would have received the
Victoria Cross.'*

   *'It is still quite a burden to carry to one's grave, even had it
stopped then. I so wanted it to stop then, to turn my back on my
past . . .' Another gentle sigh. 'You know –' and I felt now she
was talking to herself rather than to me – 'with perhaps six
exceptions, they were all guilty men, and women, if only by
belonging to such horrendous organizations as the SS and the
Gestapo or the NKVD, or trying to betray me. But . . .'*

   'They wouldn't let you retire.'

   *She made a moue. 'Clive had planned it all so carefully. I
was supposed to have died along with most of the others, when
the Russians stormed Berlin. But I had made the mistake of
trusting people.' She brooded for several seconds, and I knew
she understood that had been her greatest, indeed, her only,
weakness, caused by the extreme loneliness of her profession,
the urgent necessity of a very young woman, as she had then
been, to find a friend in whom she could confide, on whom she
could rely.*

   'You are thinking of Henri Laurent?'

   *Her mouth twisted. 'Henri didn't betray me, then. He intended
to, but Clive scared him off. As a reputable Swiss banker, had
it become known that he had been secretly laundering money
for Himmler his career would have been over. That he reappeared
in my life was because of Katherine.'*

   'Your sister, who was captured by the Russians.'

   *'But they released her, and then –' for a moment her expres-
sion hardened, before relaxing again – 'but Birgit, and Stefan
. . . Birgit had been my maid for five years. She had been with*

me in Moscow, in Washington, and in Prague, and every time had been pretty traumatic. But always I had had her unquestioning support. I actually thought that she would follow me to hell and back. And Stefan . . . he had been my personal trainer for four years. He worshipped me. He said so, and I believed him. What had never occurred to me was that they were giving me their entire support as the Countess von Widerstand, the Fuehrer's favourite woman, not as Anna Fehrbach. When I told them I was abandoning the Reich, they refused to follow me. I should have shot them both. I think they expected it. But I thought I had turned my back on killing. So I let them go. To buy their own salvation, as they supposed, by telling their eventual captors that I was alive.'

Another brood. I rested my hand on hers. 'But there were compensations, weren't there? Like ten million dollars? When you could get to it.'

Anna Fehrbach smiled.

The Pursuit

Lavrenty Beria was a very large man. Tall and powerfully built, his size was accentuated by his great hairless head and bland features, in the centre of which the delicate pince-nez seemed out of place. And, of course, there was his aura. As commander of the NKVD, the Narodny Kommissariat Vnutrennkh Del, the Russian secret police throughout the recent war, he was the second most powerful man in the country, after Premier Stalin himself. And now that the NKVD had been reconstituted as the Ministerstvo Gosudarstvennpy Bezopasnosti, or MGB, that is, from being the Commissariat for Internal Affairs to being the Commissariat for State Security, he was more powerful than ever. There could be no appeal from his decisions, and to be accused by him was to be condemned: he told the courts what sentences to pass.

Thus Nicolai Tserchenko trembled as he entered the office. A heavily built man himself, but overweight and with a somewhat sleepy expression on his broad Tatar features, he had not been here for a year, had hoped he had been forgotten. But whatever the reasons for this summons, he could take comfort from the fact that if he had failed in his primary duty of delivering the Countess von Widerstand alive to this prison, to be tortured into confessing before being placed before a public tribunal and condemned to death for her attempt on the life of Premier Stalin back in 1941, he had at least seen her to her grave. To all intents and purposes. So the reason for this peremptory summons was a mystery.

And Beria was looking genial enough, at this moment. 'Comrade Colonel,' he said. 'Sit down. What have you been doing with yourself, since the shooting stopped?'

As if he did not know. 'I have—'

'Yes, yes,' Beria said. 'But you must have been enjoying a considerable amount of satisfaction at having brought the business of the Countess von Widerstand to a satisfactory conclusion.'

'Well, Comrade—'

'Even if you did not actually do that.' Beria's voice suddenly cracked like a whip.

Tserchenko winced. 'Well, Comrade—'

'I would like you to tell me again, Comrade, exactly what happened that night in Germany.'

'I submitted a full report . . .'

'I read your report, Comrade, and I accepted it as representing the facts. Now I would like to go through it again. Acting on information received from one of our agents in Berlin, that the countess had been authorized to leave the capital before it was entirely surrounded by our forces, and was planning to do so within twenty-four hours, you thrust an advance guard of our people forward to block the Berlin–Magdeburg road as this was the escape route you had been told she would probably take. And, unsuspecting that she had been betrayed, she blundered right into your arms. But yet you could not hold her.'

'As I explained in my report, Comrade Commissar, I cannot account for what happened. She tried to drive through our road-block, and we opened fire. Her driver was killed, and the car went into a ditch. We arrested her and her maid, and took them to our temporary headquarters. We could not get them out that night, as there were Germans all around us, but we radioed for assistance, and were told that we would be relieved the next day. All we had to do was hold our ground. So this we did. Both the women were securely bound, and I placed them for the night in a room, guarded by Major Morosawa. You may remember,

Comrade Commissar, that you yourself appointed Major Morosawa to be my aide on this mission, because she had dealt with the countess before, in 1941, and knew all about her various tricks and abilities.'

'Olga Morosawa,' Beria remarked, 'was a very competent officer. So, you left her alone, in charge of the prisoners.'

'Well, Comrade Commissar, I felt it was proper. Both the prisoners were very handsome women, and I felt it might lead to impropriety were they left in the hands of male soldiers.'

'Did you not even trust yourself?'

Tserchenko licked his lips. 'I . . . well . . .'

'I see.'

'And, I may say, sir,' Tserchenko hurried on. 'Major Morosawa was absolutely confident that she could take care of the situation. Besides, there were two armed guards in the outer room.'

'And now she is dead. As well as the two guards.'

'Well, sir, she also was armed, and as I said, the two women had their hands securely bound behind their backs . . . and yet they got out, somehow, stole a truck, and escaped.' He frowned as an idea occurred to him. 'You do not suppose that Major Morosawa untied the countess to . . . well . . . the countess was a very beautiful woman.'

'I think you can assume that she still is a very beautiful woman.'

'Sir?'

'So she escaped your custody, after shooting Major Morosawa and the two other guards . . . but you say she had no weapon and was bound.'

'She must have had help, from somewhere, somehow . . . those guards were shot with a Luger pistol, and one of them had been robbed of his tunic and his side cap. Major Morosawa was armed with an American Colt automatic. But she also was shot with a Luger. There must have been someone . . .'

'And with all this information, you still confidently reported her as dead.'

'Well, sir, she fled to the north. Not the south as I would have expected. Therefore she could only have been returning to Berlin. And when the city fell, I searched everywhere for her body.'

'But you did not find it.'

'There were so many bodies . . .'

'And you found no one to confirm your conviction that she had returned to the city and perished there. Perhaps you did not look hard enough, Comrade.'

'Sir, I spent two months in that dreadful charnel house . . .

and if I may remind you, the British Government, who seem also to have been looking for her, announced officially that she was dead.'

'The British Government,' Beria said thoughtfully. 'Who are becoming increasingly hostile to us. They are, as always, following some devious plan of their own. However –' he picked up a photograph from his desk and held it out – 'tell me who this is.'

Tserchenko took the photo, cautiously, as if expecting it to bite him. He gazed at the woman depicted, and frowned. 'But this is the countess's maid. The other woman we arrested.'

'Ten out of ten: Birgit Gessner.'

Tserchenko continued to stare at the photograph. 'I do not understand. She escaped with the countess, and . . .'

'Returned to Berlin? Where she died, with the countess?'

'Well, sir . . . when was this taken? She looks, well . . . not very well.'

'That was taken two months ago, that is, in January of this year, which, if I may remind you, is nine months after the fall of Berlin. And she wasn't very well, when it was taken. She had spent those nine months hiding in various cellars and living off scraps, and she had just spent the previous several hours being interrogated by Military Intelligence. I'm afraid their methods are somewhat rough and ready. But she eventually told us what we wanted to know. The countess did indeed flee north after escaping from you. And she did indeed have help. There had been four people in that car you stopped. The driver, who, as you say, was shot, the countess and her maid, and another man, one of her lovers. This man escaped in the darkness and confusion, but managed to follow your people, and the countess, back to your post, where he rescued the countess and the maid, killing Olga Morosawa and two of our people while doing so.'

'This man—'

'His name, according to the maid, was Stefan Edert. She does not know what happened to him, and he seems to have entirely disappeared, so very probably he is dead. The point is that while the countess did indeed drive north after leaving you, it was not to return to Berlin, but to rescue her parents from the village of Grozke, where apparently they were being held in an SS training camp; the maid does not know why they were under arrest. Having done that, she went south, to Switzerland. When they discovered that she intended to abandon the Reich, both Edert and this woman Gessner, who seem to have been fanatical Nazis, refused to accompany her. So she abandoned them and continued with her parents. That is the last known sighting of her. But at least we know that she did not die in Berlin, and that she did get to Switzerland. That was in March last year. A year ago, Tserchenko.'

'A year,' Tserchenko muttered. 'But . . . what can we do now?'

'You,' Beria said, 'are going to continue your search, and find this bitch.'

'But Comrade Commissar, after a year . . . she could be anywhere in the world. She will undoubtedly have changed her name. She could have changed her appearance.'

'Unless she has had a face lift, and I doubt that any woman possessing so much beauty would go as far as that, I am sure you will remember her when next you see her. Because you are going to sniff her out. By using another bitch, eh?'

'Sir?'

'Have you forgotten what happened in Warsaw, in September 1944? You learned that the Countess von Widerstand was on a visit to that city, which was still in German hands, and you led a picked squad to infiltrate the enemy lines and seize her?'

'And kidnapped her sister by mistake,' Tserchenko said ruefully. 'At a cost of six lives. Don't you think that episode will haunt me to my grave?'

'That is bourgeois thinking,' Beria pointed out 'I will admit that it was a costly error, less because of the men who were killed than because the monster slipped through your fingers. But it was an understandable error. This Katherine Fehrbach may lack her sister's beauty, but there is, or was, a considerable resemblance.'

'All but two years ago,' Tserchenko muttered. 'Two years—'

'That she has spent in a gulag.'

'Being raped or beaten every day.'

Beria checked a note on his desk. 'Number Forty-One. She will not have had a happy time. But when I sent her there, I issued specific instructions that she was not to be executed, or even crippled by mistreatment, I felt sure that one day she might prove useful. You will go to Camp Forty-One and make sure that she is well. Then you will remove her from the camp, feed her and groom her back to her best health, fit her out with a wardrobe of good clothes, convey her to Switzerland, and turn her loose.'

'I do not understand, sir. She will be—'

'Somewhat upset, of course. But you will explain to her that now the War is over, the search for her sister has been

abandoned, and that all we wish to do is make it up to her for
our error in arresting her at all. You will supply her with a Swiss
passport, arrange for her to receive, on a regular basis, sufficient
funds to support herself, and to travel if she wishes, and wish
her farewell and good fortune. Now, Nicolai, put yourself in her
shoes. You are twenty-four years old, you have had a quite horrendous experience, but you are now suddenly free and relatively
wealthy. But you are all alone in the world, and the world you
once knew, the world of Nazi Germany, no longer exists. What
would you do?'

'Well . . .' Tserchenko scratched his chin.

Beria sighed; he had forgotten this man's total lack of imagination. On the other hand, Anna Fehrbach had killed his only
sister; he had to be dedicated. 'You would seek to find something, or someone, from that world, to whom you could relate.
We know that both her sister and her parents got to Switzerland.
Make sure that she knows that too, and she will start looking
for them.'

'You think they are still in Switzerland?'

'No, I do not. But I think the young lady will do everything
she can to find out where they are, and indeed, get to them.'

'They could have separated.'

'Nicolai, if Katherine Fehrbach can locate her parents, that
should be all you need to locate the countess.'

'Me?'

'You are going to track her every inch of the way, wherever
she goes. You will not let her know this, of course. Take whatever
people you require to carry out a round the clock surveillance
of her, and you may also call on our embassy staffs when she
is located. But bring me the Countess von Widerstand. And
Nicolai . . .' Beria spoke quietly. 'You really need to bear in mind
that our search for the countess has so far cost us seventeen lives:
two, including your sister, when she broke out of this prison,
six when we tried to arrest her in Washington, six when you
tried to arrest her in Warsaw, and three when you actually did
arrest her in Germany, including one of my best aides. And she
is still at large. This is your very last chance. Bring her back or
you will wind up in a gulag yourself.'

Tserchenko swallowed. 'Yes, sir. But may I say . . . well, as
you have just pointed out, the countess's record is, ah, disturbing.
If I had been allowed to shoot her on sight . . .'

'You did have that authority, then, Colonel. But you elected
not to use it, because you wanted the prestige of bringing her

back alive. Now that authority has been withdrawn. Now you must bring her back alive.'

'Just so that she can be publicly tried and executed? And when it may cost several more lives?'

'I am certain that you will make sure that none of those lives is your own. It so happens that since we have had access to the Nazi archives in Berlin, we have gleaned a great deal of information concerning the countess's last mission for the Reich. I am not going to tell you what it was, but it is essential that we learn more about it. And she is the only person who can tell us, because she is the only survivor of that mission. So, I want her alive, standing where you are now. I will wish you good fortune, Comrade Colonel.'

Tserchenko stood up, saluted and left the room, and a few minutes later was replaced by a female secretary. 'Comrade Kamarov is here, Comrade Commissar.'

Beria had been staring at the wall, drumming his fingers on the desk. Now he seemed to notice her for the first time. 'Show him in.'

The secretary stood aside to allow the little, sharp-featured man into the office. 'I saw Tserchenko on the stairs.' Kamarov moved, and spoke, with a confidence Tserchenko entirely lacked. This was because he had spent almost his entire adult life in this building, and was indeed spoken of as Beria's possible successor when the commissar moved on to better things – as was known to be his ambition, in the course of time.

'I am giving him another chance.' Beria held up a finger. 'I know. You do not think he is worth a damn. But he has a personal stake in this business, not to mention his career. I think he may bring it off, this time.'

'You may not need him,' Kamarov said. 'We have just received a radio message from London. The man Andrews is back in England.'

Beria leaned back in his chair. 'You think he is after her?'

'We know he was once. And failed. But we also know that if she is alive, as the British are claiming that she is dead, she is almost certainly in their custody, somewhere in England. It makes sense.'

'Perhaps it does. But why should Andrews assume she is alive? We have not revealed the existence of the woman Gessner to anyone in the West.'

'But we also do not know what information the West may

have gleaned from other survivors. I think it is worth following up.'

'Even if he does have information that she is alive, what makes you think he will be able to find her and we cannot?'

'There can be no doubt that it was British Intelligence who got her out of Switzerland. Presumably this was because she has secrets they would not like to see divulged to the world, or during a public trial. Therefore it is British Intelligence who are holding her, somewhere in England. Andrews has links with British Intelligence.'

'Who also know that the Americans promised us they would eliminate her in 1944. They failed. If the British do have her, do you suppose they would allow him near her now?'

Kamarov shrugged. 'Who knows what goes on behind the scenes in the West? If the British did engineer the countess's escape from Germany last March, they have held her now for a year. They will certainly have finished interrogating her.'

'In which case they may well have shot her.'

'But you do not believe that, sir. Or you would not still be trying to find her.'

Beria studied him for several seconds. 'It may well be that your brains will one day prove too sharp for your well-being, Comrade Kamarov. But you are right. I believe the woman Gessner is telling the truth, that she got out of Germany, and that she is still alive.'

Because, Kamarov thought, that belief is controlled by your dick. He knew that his boss had never actually laid eyes on the Countess von Widerstand, but he also knew that he kept a photograph of her in his desk drawer; so great an obsession with having her back in one of his cells had to be sexually motivated. 'And if she is alive, Comrade Commissar,' he said, 'and they have obtained everything they can from her, they may have decided to hand her over to the Americans. After all, she can hardly be anything more than an embarrassment to them if it becomes known that they are concealing such a woman.'

Beria stroked his chin. 'It is a long shot.'

'Can it be any longer than using that idiot Tserchenko to find her?'

Beria sat up. 'You are right, Comrade. Tell London to place Andrews under round-the-clock surveillance. But no action is to be taken until he actually makes contact with the countess. If he does. Thank you, Kamarov. This could be the break we are looking for.'

*   *   *

Belinda Hoskin opened the door of her London flat in answer to the bell. A small, dark woman in her early forties, she had attractively sharp features and shoulder-length wavy black hair. Italian by birth and origin, she had lived in England for thirty years, and had adopted the surname of her step-father; her Italian father had been murdered by Mussolini's blackshirts, which was why his widow had fled to England with her little daughter.

Belinda had prospered, at least in her professional life, and was now fashion editor of a leading London weekly; she had in fact just returned from her day at the office, still wore her smart suit and high heels, although she had removed her hat. Personally, her life had been a roller-coaster ride, her long standing on-off affair with Clive Bartley, which had actually led to her becoming involved in his undercover work as an MI6 agent, being further complicated by her relationship with the operative he controlled, the fabulous Anna Fehrbach, so-called Countess von Widerstand. Not that it mattered now, she supposed.

But the eagerness with which she had opened the door had been because she anticipated that it might be Clive; she did not see him all that often nowadays. When she recalled that once he had proposed marriage, and she had turned him down, being at that time more interested in her career in fashion than in domesticity! Now . . . she peered at the tall, thin, hatchet-faced man standing in the doorway. 'May I help you?'

He raised his hat. 'Miss Belinda Hoskin?'

It was a slow, southern drawl. 'Yes,' she acknowledged, cautiously.

'Joseph Andrews.' He held out his hand.

Belinda considered. 'Do I know you? You're an American.'

'I guess I am. You make me sound like an alien from Mars. We have never met, but we have several mutual acquaintances.'

'Oh? Well . . .' she squeezed his fingers.

'Do you think I could come in?'

Another consideration. 'I suppose so,' she said at last, released his hand and stepped away from the door. 'I was just about to pour myself a drink. Would you care to join me?'

Andrews closed the door behind himself. 'That depends on what you're planning to drink.'

'I only drink Scotch whisky.'

'That's fine by me.' He took off his topcoat and hung it behind the door, together with his hat; he was wearing a double-breasted grey suit. Then he walked into the centre of the little lounge, looked around himself.

Belinda went to the sideboard. 'I take mine neat.'

'Ah . . . sure. A little ice would be nice.'

'Ice? With Scotch?'

'Ah . . . maybe not.'

Belinda poured. 'Are you looking for something? Or someone?'

'I was just wondering . . . you don't seem to have any photographs.'

'Photographs belong in albums. Frames have to be dusted.'

'Interesting point.'

She gave him his glass. 'You may sit down, if you wish.' She sat herself, on the settee, crossed her knees. Andrews chose a chair opposite her. 'What do you Americans say?'

'Happy days?' He sipped, appreciatively. 'Good.'

'Johnnie Walker Black.'

'Yeah. Nearly as good as Chivas Regal.'

Belinda regarded him as she might have done a beetle. 'You said something about a mutual acquaintance?'

'Yeah. I guess you see a lot of Clive Bartley.'

'Is he our mutual acquaintance?'

'One of them.'

'Well, I actually don't see a lot of him nowadays. Do you have any idea what he does for a living?'

'Yes, I do.'

'Then you know where to go to find him.'

'I'm not sure that he wants to see me. I'm actually trying to contact one of his people. The Countess von Widerstand.'

Belinda gave a twisted smile. 'You're out of date, Mr Andrews. The countess is dead.'

'No!'

'If you know about the countess, and you know what Clive's job is, then you must know that she was working for British Intelligence in Berlin. She had an Austrian father, you see.'

'And an Irish mother,' Andrews said thoughtfully. 'And you reckon she was killed when the city fell to the Russians.'

'She hasn't been heard of since. It's a logical conclusion.'

'Clive's conclusion, right?'

'He should know. Anyway, it's official.'

'Sure.' He sipped his drink, obviously choosing his words. 'Would you be interested if I told you that far from being dead, the countess is very much alive, and in Clive's care? I presume she's at a secret location, where I am quite sure he visits her, from time to time?'

Belinda got up. 'I don't know what you're trying to do, Mr
... Andrews, is it? But I think you had better leave.'

Andrews finished his drink. 'I'm sorry, ma'am. I thought you
might be interested.'

'I have never been interested in lies.'

Andrews remained seated. 'We, that is the American author-
ities in Germany, have in our custody a man named Stefan Edert.
He claims to have been the Countess von Widerstand's personal
trainer for four years. Whether that is true or not, we do not
know. But he sure seems to have known her pretty well. As for
instance, did you know that she has a blue sort of stain on her
right rib cage? He reckoned it was an old bullet wound. Right
rib cage. You with me? It's not a part of the body that women
generally expose, except maybe in a two-piece bathing suit, and
as far as we know the countess did not go in for public swimming, although she may have done with a close friend. You still
with me?'

Belinda had gone to the sideboard. Now she poured herself
another drink, and said, almost absently, 'She sustained that
wound in saving my life, six years ago.'

'Well, now, seems like you knew her as well as I did once.
Six years ago . . . that would have been when she was in England
as wife to that fellow Bordman, spying for the Reich. Before
Clive got to her.'

'After,' Belinda said. 'She had already become a double agent.
She and I were having a private talk, when this woman, her Nazi
controller, came in and was going to shoot me. So Anna tackled
her.'

'You mean she shot her first? She's supposed to be the fastest
thing with a gun since Annie Oakley.'

'Anna did not shoot her,' Belinda said. 'Because at that moment
she was unarmed. She broke her neck.'

'Jesus!'

'But to do that she had to take a bullet. She very nearly died
from the wound.'

'That must've made quite a bond. I guess you were pretty cut
up when you heard she was dead. So now you should be happy
to know that she's actually alive.'

'I do not know that, Mr Andrews.'

'That's a fact. So let me fill you in. This guy Edert was picked
up in Magdeburg last April. So we picked up tens of thousands
of erstwhile Nazis. We locked them up to await sorting. We were
trying to separate the bad Nazis from the acceptable Nazis. Well,

eventually we decided that he was a bad one. So he then decided to see if he could buy us off. He swears, under oath, that he helped the countess and her parents out of Berlin in March last year, and drove them to the Swiss border. I guess you know that the countess, for all her talents, never learned to drive.'

'Yes,' Belinda said. Could what he was saying possibly be true? Anna, alive? Oh, if only it could be true. But this man worked for the Americans. And she knew, because Clive had told her, that the Americans had condemned Anna to imprisonment, if not death.

'So this guy does know what he's talking about. He left them at the border. He was prepared to help her escape, he says, but he personally was not prepared to abandon the Reich while there was any hope. Seems he still believed Hitler's twaddle about secret weapons that would bring Germany victory. So we know that Anna, with her parents, got to Switzerland . . . and then disappeared. There is absolutely no trace of any of them. But then we have the British hand-out that without a shadow of a doubt, the infamous Countess von Widerstand died in the ruins of Berlin, fighting the Russians.'

Belinda regarded him for several seconds, then said, 'Would you like another drink?'

'Thank you.' Andrews got up and joined her at the sideboard.

She poured. 'And you're prepared to believe this itinerant Nazi before the British Government.'

'Wouldn't you? They're looking after their own. Fair enough. But this guy has a lot of pertinent facts, wouldn't you say?'

'And you would like to find Anna for yourself.'

'You bet. We used to know each other pretty well, once.'

'I see. A case of mad, passionate, undying love. Now tell me who you really are.'

'I did. Joseph—'

'Let me put it another way. Who are you working for?'

'Uncle Sam.'

'Who intends to put Anna on trial as a war criminal.'

'Now, what makes you think that?'

'Mr Andrews, I may be a little woman, but I am not a little woman as perceived by the male sex. It may interest you to know that I have also worked for MI6, and I'm fully clued up about what has been happening these past few years.'

'Holy shit! I beg your pardon.'

'Feel free. So now perhaps we can stop assing about. I think what you have had to say is very interesting. I would love to believe it; Anna was a very dear friend of mine, who twice saved my life. And if Clive did manage to get her out of Germany I would be delighted. But I do not know for certain he did that, although if he did and has got her securely hidden away, it can only be to keep her out of the hands of you people. So I'm sure you'll understand, Mr Andrews, that even if I knew where she was, the last thing I would do is tell you.'

Andrews sipped his drink. 'And you don't find it odd that you see so little of him, nowadays? Maybe you don't know as much about the way he works as you think. Miss Hoskin, Anna is Clive's mistress, and has been his mistress for seven years.'

Belinda put down her glass. 'Mr Andrews, just now I suggested that you should leave. Now I am telling you to get out. Now! Or I shall call the police. Better yet, I'll call Clive. His lot don't have to follow police rules and procedures.'

Andrews considered for a few moments, then finished his own drink and put down his glass. 'OK. I apologize. That was uncalled for. What I would like to do is convince you that Anna means as much to me as she does to either you or to Clive.'

Belinda went to the telephone.

'You could at least hear what I have to say.'

'I thought I had done that.'

'Listen, I guess you know that Anna was once in the hands of the NKVD?'

'I do know that.' Her hand still rested on the receiver.

'Well, when Clive comes on the phone, ask him who got her out.'

Belinda frowned. 'You did that?'

'I hate to blow my own trumpet, but I'm the guy, yes.'

'But yet you want to have her tried as a war criminal?'

'I have never wanted to do that. But things, situations, can change pretty rapidly in time of war, and, like Clive, or you, I guess, I obey the orders given me from above. My employers got the idea that Anna was betraying the Allies, and wanted her taken out. You have to understand that we were fighting a war for survival.'

Belinda blew a raspberry.

'OK, so I guess you were too. Even more so. But when one is in that kind of situation, one is inclined to make instant judgements.'

'You said, 'taken out'. Isn't that a phrase used in gangster movies to mean killing someone?'

'Well . . .' Andrews flushed.

'You unutterable bastard.'

'I told you, it wasn't my decision. And I hated it. And it didn't work out. Anna, as I guess you know, is just about the most dangerous woman in the world when she wants to be. I guess our man forgot that.'

'So what happened?'

'He took a bullet between the eyes.'

Belinda stared at him, then released the receiver, and resumed her seat on the settee, her knees pressed together.

Andrews sat beside her. 'He was one of our best guys, and I liked him. And you know what, I have an idea Anna did too. But as I guess you also know, she's a girl who does what has to be done, without fear or favour. And with due regret for poor Johannsson, I'm just happy that she did.'

'But you're here to finish the job.'

'I told you, times change. It was the Soviets who convinced Washington that she was a traitor to the Allies. Well, at that time, mistakenly, our top people thought the Soviets were the goods. Since then . . . I guess you heard that speech Churchill made at Fulton, a couple of weeks ago?'

'An Iron Curtain has descended on Eastern Europe.'

'Correct. President Truman was seated right next to the old man when he said those words, and totally endorsed them.'

'So now you're going to fight the Russians, is that it?'

'We don't aim to fight anybody right this minute. But we reckon that to maintain the status quo we need to use every resource we have. So . . . we want Anna back.'

'Do you think she'll want to come back? To you?'

'We reckon we can make it worth her while. We also reckon she needs us more than we need her. We happen to know that she is still top of the Soviet Most Wanted list. And they have very long memories. Clive may have got her tucked away some place he regards as safe, but they will find her eventually. Whereas, if she comes back under our umbrella, well, let's say we reckon we can do a better job of taking care of her than the Brits. Certainly with this left-wing government you have right now. With respect.'

Belinda got up and poured them each another drink, keeping her back turned to him as she did so. Could she believe him? Dare she? But if she did dare, could it be possible that she and Anna could get together again? Anna had indeed saved her life, twice. The first time had been when they had been rivals for Clive's attentions, as she had supposed; she had not then realized that she was already redundant. Thus she had engineered a confrontation, which had been interrupted by that dreadful woman Hannah Gehrig, hence the near catastrophic result to Anna.

They had not met again until four years later, when due to a crucial breakdown in their communications system, she had agreed to be recruited as a courier for MI6, using her Italian background as a cover to get into Germany, her brief to reopen contact with the countess. Instead she had betrayed herself to the Gestapo, and had been on the verge of undergoing an interrogation which she knew would have ruined her for life, when Anna, in her role as a senior officer in the SD, had arrived to take control.

As they had been under surveillance, Anna had 'tortured' her herself, but had managed to convey to her that if she would put up with it for a short while, she could get her out. This she had done, but before turning her loose to leave the country, had taken her to her apartment for the night. It was a night Belinda knew she would never forget. Anna might be every man's dream of a bed-mate, but what the poor sods were unable to grasp, caught up in their male chauvinist hubris, was that she was a law unto herself. Her passions, no less than her enormous skills, were hers and hers alone, to be used as she saw fit, and to her own satisfaction. And that night, more than two years ago now, her desires had taken her in a direction Belinda had never experienced, had never wanted to experience, until then. She understood that Anna had merely been turned on by what she had had to do for the sake of the Gestapo, that there had been no love, perhaps not even any affection, in what she had done to her. But that was irrelevant. She had fallen hook, line and sinker, perhaps accentuated by the knowledge that they might never meet again. And even after three years, she could remember every moment of it; when Clive had told her that Anna was dead, she had wept. The bastard!

But if she wasn't dead . . . she turned and handed Andrews his glass. He brushed it against hers, knowing, without understanding, both from her delay and her expressions, that he had won the day. 'So will you help me? Help us? Help Anna?'

'It might be possible. But if I help you, it will be on one condition.'

'Name it.'

'When you get to her, before you take her wherever you feel is necessary, I want to see her. To make sure she's all right,' she added, somewhat lamely.

Andrews studied her for several seconds. Then he said, 'You have it. How soon can you get the information?'

'Come and see me again tomorrow,' Belinda said.

The Quarry

'Welcome home, Mr Bartley.' Amy Barstow rose enthusiastically from behind her desk. Amy Barstow did everything enthusiastically, where her boss was concerned. He was her ideal man, six feet two inches tall, built like a rugby player, his face suitably rugged, his dark hair just starting to streak with grey, although he was only forty-three. When that was matched to his invariable good humour . . . well, almost invariable. She knew, of course, that he could never be more than a dream, for her; she was too aware of her own shortcomings, her inability to resist food that had caused her weight to spiral, and her resulting lack of glamour. Whereas he . . . she had never felt particularly hostile towards Clive's long-term girlfriend, the Anglo-Italian fashion editor. But towards his most recent acquisition, over whom he fussed like a mother hen, a task she was required to fulfil whenever he was unavailable, as over the past week . . .

What made it the more difficult to accept was the fact that it was impossible to blame any man for going overboard when he became involved with the so-called Countess von Widerstand. Although she could think of a few who would have had a nervous breakdown at the thought of getting too close to her, and her record indicated that quite a few who had taken the risk had not lived long enough to regret it. Stunningly beautiful she might be, and apparently irresistibly seductive as well, but she had also been SS trained as a killer, and as Amy had to keep a file on her, she knew she had used those lethal skills on an obscene number of occasions, and she was pretty sure there were more than she had recorded. But since the end of the war looking after her had become a full time job of work.

'Good to be back,' Clive said. 'Calls?'

'They're on your desk.'

'Ah . . .?'

'Nothing from Scotland, sir.' Amy could not prevent a note of satisfaction creeping into her voice. 'I made the transfer into the countess's account as you required. I suppose she's busy spending it.'

'Amy,' Clive said severely. 'You simply have to remember that her name is no longer the Countess von Widerstand. Or Anna Fehrbach. It is Anna Fitzjohn.'

'Yes, sir. I think you should remind Miss Hoskin of that.'

Clive had reached the doorway of his office. Now he checked, and turned. 'Say again?'

'Miss Hoskin has apparently mislaid the countess's . . . Miss Fitzjohn's address. So she telephoned and asked me for it. She wants to send her a card for her birthday. Odd, that. Her birthday isn't until May.'

Clive slowly returned into the outer office and stood before her desk. 'Are you saying that Belinda asked you for Anna's address? And you gave it to her?'

Amy frowned. 'But she already knew it, didn't she? I mean, they're old friends, aren't they? She'd just mislaid it.'

'Amy,' Clive said. 'Nobody knows that address, save you, me, and Mr Baxter. Nobody knows that Anna is alive, save for a very select group of people. Belinda is not one of them.'

'But—'

'When did she call?'

'Well . . . yesterday morning.'

'Holy Jesus Christ!'

'But, sir, Belinda, well, she's one of us. Isn't she?'

'She was one of us, on a temporary basis. That ended with Germany's surrender.'

'But she's Anna's friend . . .'

'Get her on the phone. Now.'

'Yes, sir.' Amy, mystified and not a little miffed at her boss's apparent overreaction to what she considered perfectly correct behaviour, picked up her telephone.

Clive went into his office and sat at his desk. There were, as Amy had indicated, several items that had cropped up during his brief absence in North Africa, but none of them were sufficiently important to interrupt the waves of alarm that were lapping at his mind. From that moment in the spring of 1939 when, in a mood of angry defiance of her SD employers for their savage mistreatment of her all because of a minor breach of security, Anna had agreed to work for MI6, he had sworn that come what may, the moment she was able to leave Germany, he would take care of her and guarantee her future, no matter what.

That promise had certainly been principally motivated by the fact that she had been lying naked in his arms at the time, and he had just scaled the heights of Mount Everest in sexual satisfaction, but his physical attraction to her had, over the years of watching her at work, albeit mostly from a distance, grown into something far deeper. He was still not sure that love, in the accepted, romantic, sense, had as yet truly entered the equation. It was difficult to envisage Anna in a moonlight and roses scenario. She had told him that Hitler, who had been a romantic, even if a demonic one, had compared her with the pre-Greek, Pelasgian Goddess of Creation, Eurynome, who had wandered the heavens, destroying and begetting as the mood took her. Well, he thought, Anna had never done any begetting, so far. It was another impossible concept, Anna sitting with a babe at her breast. But she was only just coming up to twenty-six. She had a lot of living in front of her, and it was his business to see that she did it, even if he had no idea what he was actually going to do with her.

Could Belinda pose a threat to her safety? In herself, no, he was certain. But Belinda, like everyone else, had accepted the official handout that Anna had died in the ruins of Berlin. Until, apparently, yesterday. What, or more pertinently, who, had brought that about? And there was no way of immediately warning Anna that there might be a looming problem; Billy Baxter had felt it a good idea at the time to select a house that was both isolated and lacking a telephone in which to install her, just to make sure she could be kept under total control; her only means of contacting the outside world was by using the phone in the neighbouring village. Now that idea looked likely to rebound with a vengeance.

His telephone jangled. 'Why, Clive,' Belinda said. 'I thought I'd have heard from you sooner.'

'I have been away. Now tell me just what is going on.'

'What is going on,' Belinda said, 'is that I have found out that for the past year you have been lying to me, to the nation, to the world. That is despicable.'

'It's called politics, darling. You do realize that if you make any use of your knowledge you are going to be charged with a breach of the Official Secrets Act. You could spend quite a long time in prison.'

Belinda blew one of her raspberries.

'But it may be possible,' Clive said, 'not to pursue the matter if you tell me just who has convinced you that Anna is alive.'

'Your old friend Joe Andrews. He's very keen on getting together with Anna. Again.'

Clive stared at the phone in consternation. 'You stupid, stupid bitch.'

'Well, really!'

'Don't you realize that Andrews is committed to having her executed?'

'No, no,' Belinda said. 'You're quite wrong. That approach has been abandoned. Now they want her back.'

Again Clive stared at the phone for several seconds. Then he slammed the receiver down and ran from his office.

'You're going out, Mr Bartley?' Amy asked. 'Mr Baxter said you should go up as soon as you arrived.'

'I'm on my way. But I anticipate being back down in five minutes. And cancel all my appointments for the next week.'

'Your trouble,' said Baxter, 'is too many women, at least at the same time.'

Billy Baxter was a small man whose trademark was untidiness. His thinning, greying hair always looked as if he had just finished scratching it, very probably because he usually had just finished scratching it. His sweater was invariably speckled with tobacco from the pipe he used as an emotional back-up. It was impossible to conceive of a less likely spymaster. But he had now completed nine on the whole successful years in the most demanding of jobs, that of attempting to control the MI6 agents in Germany. Clive, who had served him throughout those nine years, knew that he had genuinely grieved whenever one of his people went down, but he had never let that interfere with the assignment of the most difficult and dangerous tasks to the man, or woman, he had determined was most capable of handling it.

Of all his agents, the Countess von Widerstand had been the most difficult to control. He had begun by distrusting her, at least partly because she was a beautiful woman – a class that he profoundly distrusted by instinct – and because he knew that she had come to him via a sizzling love affair with the man now standing before his desk. But over the years he had realized her value, and if he still distrusted her actual objectives in life he had been increasingly concerned as his superiors, on both sides of the Atlantic – who saw her only as a destructive force that could be used to their advantage – had committed her to more

and more virtual suicide missions. Through all of which she had
sailed unharmed, thanks to her unique combination of irresistible
charisma and unhesitating deadliness.

Thus he had taken the responsibility for getting her out of the
maelstrom that had been the collapsing Third Reich and placing
her in a safe place until his superiors could determine what to
do with her. No one had yet reached a decision about that, and
suddenly the necessity for a decision had been dumped into his
lap. He started to fill his pipe, a certain sign that he was not as
calm as he pretended to be.

'Only one,' Clive said. 'And I am very inclined to break her
neck.'

'I don't think that would accomplish much,' Baxter pointed
out. 'Apart from getting yourself hanged, of course. The damage
is done. And you are being a little hysterical. Can't you accept
the possibility that Andrews could have told Belinda the truth?'

'Billy, Anna killed one of their people.'

Baxter struck a match. 'Who had drugged her and raped her
and thoroughly deserved to die.'

'That does not alter the fact that he was their agent, or that
he had been sent specifically to take her out, to satisfy the
Russians.'

'Granted. But it seems to have escaped your attention that
the Yanks are no longer bending over backwards to satisfy the
Russians, about anything.' He puffed with some contentment.

'I have to get up there, Billy.'

'Why? Because you think Andrews is still thinking of killing
her? After what happened to Johannsson he had better be travelling with a division of marines.'

'I never did appreciate your sense of humour. The fact is –' he
chose his words with care – 'Anna is becoming restless. She's
been up there for a year now, with just four visits to her parents
allowed in all that time. She feels, firstly, that she may as well be
in a prison, and secondly, that we have forgotten all about her.'

'Silly girl. Not that she isn't a problem. Now the war is over,
the overwhelming urge in this country is to stop killing people.
And as that is Anna's outstanding talent, well . . . OK, she's
bored. What does she do with her time? I suppose she could be
writing her memoirs, except that we'd have to clap a D-notice
on it.'

'I can tell you what she's doing right now.'

'I'm interested.'

'Well . . .' Clive looked embarrassed, 'She's learning to drive.'

'Say again? I thought—'

'That Anna can do anything. But even Anna can only do what she's been taught to do. When the SS trained her, they never thought to teach her to drive. Back in 1938 they never thought it would be necessary, certainly in a male-oriented society like Nazi Germany. The lack of that skill has proved both embarrassing and dangerous, from time to time. Right now one of her greatest ambitions is to correct that lack.'

'You gave her permission to take lessons?'

'Yes, I did. For God's sake, Billy, she has to do something with her time.'

'Hm. Well, when she gets her licence, you had better make sure she doesn't have access to a car.'

'Billy,' Clive said, with great patience, 'you are forgetting the point. Belinda gave Andrews that address probably yesterday morning. He could be already up there. And Anna knows who he is and who he works for. And that they sent Johannsson to do her. So maybe he wants to be friends. But you know Anna. As he is not travelling with a division of marines, what do you think will be her reaction when she opens her front door and finds Andrews standing there?'

'She's not armed, is she?'

'Well—'

'I never authorized that.'

'Anna feels unhappy without a weapon handy. And anyway, she doesn't need a weapon. I saw her break that woman Elsa Mayer's neck with a single chop. And we don't want to forget that Andrews is also a trained operative, even if he may be a little rusty. Right this minute, one of them could be dead, and I would lay odds that it'll be Andrews. I have to get up there, Billy. This could take some sorting out.'

'And if Andrews is the one standing?'

'I'll cross that bridge when I come to it.'

Baxter pointed with his pipe. 'This is an order. You are expressly forbidden to take executive action. No matter what he might have done, Andrews is still an American agent and we are still dependent upon American aid and support. If there is a worst case scenario, call in the local bobby and let Washington sort it out.'

'Just like that.'

Baxter sighed. 'Believe me, Clive, if anything has happened to Anna I will shed as big a tear as you. Call me as soon as you find out the situation.'

'I need the use of a plane.'

Baxter raised his eyebrows.

'It would take me at least another twenty-four hours to get up there by car,' Clive pointed out.

Baxter looked out of the window. 'It'll be dark in an hour. You can't get up there until tomorrow morning, anyway. And where do you propose to put this plane down?'

'There has to be an airfield somewhere around there.'

Another sigh, and he started to knock out his pipe. 'Try not to crash this one.'

'I think,' McLachlan the instructor said as the car came to a stop before the front door of the isolated house, 'that you could take your test tomorrow, Miss Fitzjohn. After only four lessons. That is remarkable.'

He spoke with genuine regret. In all his years he had never known quite as much pleasure as over the past couple of weeks. It was not simply the ease with which the young woman seated beside him had assimilated everything he had told her, the consummate concentration she had revealed when driving, the calm, but instant reaction she had displayed when avoiding the cat that had run across the road in front of them – the last time that had happened his then pupil had uttered a piercing scream, released the wheel, and clapped both hands to her eyes – it was the woman herself.

Even the fact that she was, by his standards, too tall – five foot eleven to his five seven – merely enhanced her attractiveness. The prosaic beige calf-length skirt and matching jumper equally revealed that she had superb legs and a bust to dream about. Her soft golden hair, so long that she had to scoop it up whenever she got behind the wheel to avoid sitting on it, made a nonsense of the age she had entered on her application form; if one could overlook her figure, surely she was fifteen instead of twenty-five. This impression was accentuated by her face, her slightly aquiline but utterly beautiful features, which he had never seen other than totally relaxed, dominated by the huge, innocent blue eyes.

Her jewellery, the gold bar earrings, the huge ruby solitaire on the forefinger of her right hand that he had seen when she had taken off her gloves to sign her application, the gold Junghans watch on her left wrist – how on earth had she come into possession of a German watch? – indicated that she was extremely wealthy, while the absence of any ring on the third finger of her left hand established that she was unattached. In addition, she had the aura of being a writer, who had apparently chosen to live in this remote part of the Highlands in an equally remote but large and clearly expensive house while she worked on her novel . . . had he not had a wife waiting at home with his tea, McLachlan knew he would have found it difficult to resist the temptation to make an advance.

Now she said, 'How very nice of you to say that, Mr McLachlan.' Her voice, low and caressing with a delightful Irish lilt, perfectly matched the rest of her. 'When can it be arranged?'

'I will see to it, and let you know.'

'Thank you.'

He got out of the car and came round it to open her door for her. He would have had to do this anyway, as she was in the driver's seat, but this enabled him to have a last look at the silk-encased calves and knees as she also got out. 'You'll be buying a motor car, then?' he ventured.

Anna straightened her skirt and indicated the small Austin in the open garage beside the house. 'I already have a motor car, Mr McLachlan. But at present only Mrs Bridie is able to drive it. Thank you again.'

She turned away and went to the front door. McLachlan watched her open it and disappear, and then drove away.

'How did it go?' Bridget Bridie was a large woman, the same height as Anna but at least twice her weight.

'He says I'm ready to take my test.'

'That was quick. I'll make a cup of tea.'

Her idea of a celebration, Anna thought, remembering the days when Birgit, her German maid, had invariably welcomed her with a glass of champagne. She wondered where the poor, silly woman was now, when she could have been here, with her, in total safety . . . and total boredom!

She went upstairs to her bedroom. It was a comfortable room, spacious and light, its two large windows overlooking the moors and even the distant roofs of the village. The situation was bleak; not all that far from the sea it was constantly swept by a breeze that even in the spring could be chilly. But the house itself was warm. The bed was comfortable, the appointments adequate, and if there was no en-suite bathroom, such luxuries being apparently unknown in old Scottish houses, there were only two of them to share the one available, and Mrs Bridie never got in the way.

Although they had now lived together for just on a year, Anna had still not discovered what Mrs Bridie thought of it all, whether indeed she considered herself a housekeeper or a gaoler; she never attempted to interfere in Anna's habits of exercising every morning and taking long runs across the moor by herself, although she did insist, whenever her charge wished to go into the village, on accompanying her.

Anna took off her gloves, kicked off her shoes and lay on her back on the bed, staring at the ceiling. Without Clive's regular visits she thought she might have gone mad. And the visits, however regular, were still only once a month: he was a busy man. Apart from that, she had only left this house for four trips of more than a couple of hours, to see her parents in their new home, in the south.

In the beginning she had sought nothing more. The feeling of utter safety, utter relaxation, the absence of bomb damage or indeed bombs, that was part of the ambience both of the house and Mrs Bridie, after seven years of living on a knife edge, of constantly risking her own life, and constantly robbing other people of theirs, had seeped over her like a hot bath. The memories had all been nightmares.

But they were also the entire substance of her adult life. They could not simply be tied up in a neat parcel and stowed in the attic to amuse future generations. She had, aged seventeen, been locked up in a Gestapo cell, waiting to be raped or tortured, just as she had, aged eighteen, been strapped naked to a table, again in a Gestapo cell, to have electrodes attached to her genitals and inflict unbelievable pain and unforgettable humiliation.

As a result of that unreasonable punishment for a minor offence, she had found herself in the arms of Clive Bartley and her life had taken on a new dimension. That had eventually brought her to this salvation, but the six years between had heightened the precariousness of her existence. She had been forced to shoot and slaughter her way across Europe, not to mention Russia and America, just to survive. Those years were there; they could never be eradicated.

But there were other factors constantly lapping at her subconscious, growing in intensity throughout the long winter months. When they had first got together, and he had persuaded her that her future, and the future of her family, had lain with the British rather than the Germans, Clive had sworn to look after her for the rest of her life. Well, so far at least, he had fulfilled that promise. But over the past couple of years, although they had in the beginning only been able to meet perhaps twice a year – whenever she had been sent on a mission to a neutral country by Himmler – he had increasingly suggested that he would like to share that future with her. That idea had appealed to her also. If, as an agent under his control, he had been forced to commit her to some of the most dangerous episodes of her life, he remained the only man she had ever known who she had been able to trust absolutely; there had been two others she had considered trustworthy, the American Joe Andrews and the Swiss Henri Laurent, and both had let her down with consequences that, but for Clive, could have been catastrophic.

Yet over the past year, when she had been entirely his to do with as he wished, the question of a permanent relationship, whether in or out of matrimony, had not been allowed to arise. Anna knew that the little Italian woman Belinda Hoskin had been his mistress for several years, without marriage, so perhaps he was not the marrying kind. But she would willingly have settled for being his mistress, if that could mean moving in with him. It was impossible to believe that he might prefer the domestic pleasures of Belinda to what she could offer. But then, Belinda did not have fifty-three corpses hanging round her neck and cluttering her CV. Perhaps even Clive found that too much to handle. And he did not know the whole truth of it, the deep inner secrets that haunted her, the fact, for instance, that one of the men she had been forced to execute by her Nazi masters had been the librarian at the British Embassy in Berlin, and Clive's personal friend, Gottfried Friedmann. Could they ever have a true relationship with that between them, however ignorant of it he might be?

The other constantly recurring and increasing nag at her mind was that she was, to all intents and purposes, destitute. She had never had to consider money very seriously in the past. Her father, as a newspaper editor in Vienna and before his arrest by the Nazis, had been comfortably off if by no means wealthy; certainly neither she nor her sister had lacked for any creature comfort. As an employee of the Reich, and even more so as a senior officer in the SD, money had simply been added to her bank account as and when the accountants thought necessary; if she had never received a fixed salary, there had never been any limit on her spending. Even her jewellery, which she prized, had never actually been hers; her SD masters had provided it to enhance her image as a wealthy socialite. That the SD had vanished into history, while she was still around, with the jewellery, was a source of intense satisfaction. But she was not about to sell any of it.

The British had never offered her any pay at all; they had relied on what had been, to them, the most important aspects of her character and her situation: her total commitment to getting her parents out of Germany, and her hatred for the regime that was blackmailing her into working for them. She had never resented this. The Americans, with their tendency to consider every aspect of life in terms of dollars and cents, had insisted upon offering her a salary, but she had never seen anything of it. It had, so they said, been deposited in an account, to be collected at the end of the war . . . supposing she was still alive. And as they had suddenly determined that she should not survive the war, she had to presume that money had been put to other use.

So now she was entirely dependent on the support of the British Government, who claimed not to know that she still existed. In fact, she was dependent upon Mrs Bridie, who controlled the accounts. Anna had no idea how much per month was being allowed for their subsistence, but none of it was hers to spend. Not that it mattered a great deal as there was not a lot for her to spend money on. Great Britain might have come out on the winning side of the war, but she might as well have lost it. The country was just about bankrupt, and almost everything was rationed, while the village, situated a mile from this house was entirely lacking in anything remotely resembling a boutique.

When Clive had first brought her to England he had given her an allowance to buy some clothes, but even in London the coupon-controlled choice had been extremely limited. When she thought of the wardrobe she had possessed when she had lived there as the Honourable Mrs. Ballantine Bordman, or even more the sumptuous gowns she had had to abandon in Berlin, not to mention her sable coat and hat, she could feel the beginning of an ulcer.

In fact, her situation was really rather amusing, because she was, or she intended to be, a millionairess. Only she knew the location, or indeed the existence, of the ten tons of gold she had had her two escorts drop into the bottom of the Horsel River; both of them were now dead. Just as she was the only person still alive who knew the whereabouts of the Nazi gold reserves, a hundred tons, which she had concealed on orders from Himmler; the last mission on which he had ever sent her. The men who had assisted her were now also all dead, again as ordered by Himmler; as they had all been members of the SS they did not lie heavy on her conscience. And that knowledge was the ace up her sleeve, her passport to a sunlit future. But getting hold of the ten per cent she had siphoned off for her own use had to come first, or it might not come at all; she did not even trust the British that far.

Now that her parents were at last safe, the recovery of that bullion had become her principal objective. She dreamed about it, had bought several large scale maps of the area around Eisenach, had committed every road, every hill, every stream, almost every building, to her photographic memory. While the gold had just about doubled in value. When she had 'deducted' it from the reserves she had been ordered by Himmler to conceal forever, she had estimated it to be worth five million dollars. Her recent studies of *The Times*, which Mrs Bridie purchased whenever she went to the village, indicated that the current value was nearer ten!

But she knew that she would have to hurry slowly. She could not possibly recover those ingots from the soft mud at the bottom of the river without help, and until she was sure where that help could come from, it would be dangerous in the extreme to let anyone know that she was in possession of such a secret. A year ago it had seemed perfectly simple: she would wait until things in Germany had settled down, then she would confide in Clive, hopefully by then her husband. and together they would organize the recovery. But now she was no longer sure of even Clive's commitment to her. And in any event, it seemed that the province of Erfurt was now under Soviet control; becoming again involved with the Reds was not something she dared risk without considerable support.

'Tea up,' Mrs Bridie called.

'Am I allowed to use the car, when I get my licence?' Anna asked.

'Why should you wish to use the car? Where do you wish to go?'

'I just want to drive. See the country.'

'We can go for a drive whenever you wish,' Mrs Bridie pointed out.

But I don't want to have you along, Anna thought.

'I know,' Mrs Bridie said brightly. 'Tomorrow we'll go into the village, to the library, get some new books.'

'Um,' Anna commented.

'You do like Graham Greene, don't you?'

'He's very good. But too . . . he makes me uneasy.'

'I don't like to see you so restless,' Mrs Bridie remarked. 'But if you want to go gallivanting on your own, well, we'll have to ask Mr Bartley, now, won't we?'

Anna finished her tea, got up from the kitchen table, strolled to the window and looked out at the moor.

'And as he was here a fortnight ago,' Mrs Bridie said, 'I shouldn't think we'll see him again until next month.'

'We can telephone when we go to the village,' Anna pointed out.

'I'm sure it really isn't that urgent, Anna.'

Anna felt like stamping her foot. Instead she continued to gaze at the moor, and felt a slight quickening of her heartbeat as she saw something moving. A car, on the distant road. And coming this way, which was sufficiently rare. 'There's someone coming. It must be Mr Bartley.' Then she bit her lip. Clive was very much a creature of habit in his domestic life; if he was appearing two weeks early it could only be because of some problem. Or some catastrophe, involving her parents.

'Let me see.' Mrs Bridie stood beside her. 'There's only sausages for dinner,' she complained.

'I'll just make sure who it is.' Anna went upstairs to her room, where she kept a pair of binoculars, not that there was usually anything to look at, save birds. She stood at the window and levelled the glasses, adjusted the focus, and frowned, while her heartbeat slowed, and then quickened again.

The car had disappeared behind a slight dip in the road, but now it had come into sight again, perhaps a quarter of a mile away. There was only the driver in it, but he . . . it was not a face she would ever forget.

Now she was ice cold. Handling situations like this was what she had been trained to do. She went to the wardrobe, opened one of the drawers at the side of the hanging cupboard, and took out the Luger nine-millimetre pistol. Clive had wanted her to give this up, once she was installed in the 'safety' of Great Britain. She had refused; not all of her enemies had disappeared with the ending of the war.

She checked the magazine to make sure that it was fully loaded, then thrust the gun into the waistband of her skirt and went down the stairs. Mrs Bridie was still standing at the window beside the front door. 'It's not Mr Bartley,' she said. 'I don't think I've ever seen this gentleman before.'

'I'm sure you have not,' Anna agreed. 'I'd like you to go to your room, Bridget, and stay there until I tell you to come out.'

'What?' Mrs Bridie turned, looked at the gun. 'What is happening? You're not meaning to use that thing? This is England. Well, Scotland. You can't go around shooting people. It's against the law.'

'Surely I am entitled to defend myself,' Anna said. 'Even in England. Or Scotland.'

'Defend yourself? From what?'

'Bridget,' Anna said, patiently. 'The man in that car is an old acquaintance of mine, and he has come here to kill me.'

'Here? In Scotland? I don't believe it. Anyway, I am responsible, both for your well-being and to see that you do not do anything that is against the law. So . . .'

'Bridget!' Anna allowed a trace of steel to enter her voice. 'If you do not go upstairs to your room, and stay there until I tell you to come out, I am going to hit you, very hard. Please believe me.'

Mrs Bridie stared at her. She might be twice Anna's size, but she had watched her charge working out, and she knew that slender body was as hard-muscled as any athlete's in the world, just as she had been warned of this young woman's lethal skills.

The doorbell jangled.

'Upstairs,' Anna said. 'And stay there.'

Mrs Bridie went to the stairs. 'I will have to make a full report of this to Mr Bartley.'

'I think you should,' Anna agreed. 'If only to find out how this man discovered where I am. Up.'

The bell jangled again. Mrs Bridie went up the stairs. Anna drew the pistol, rested it against her right shoulder, muzzle pointing upwards, and with her left hand slipped the bolt and pulled the door inwards, going with it so that she was not immediately visible.

The man ducked his head beneath the somewhat low lintel and stepped inside, looking left and right. 'Anybody home?'

'I'm right behind you, Joe,' Anna said.

Andrews remained absolutely still; he understood his danger. 'May I turn round?'

Anna closed the door and pushed the bolt home. 'If you put your hands on your head, and move very slowly.'

Andrews obeyed. 'Seeing you again is like . . . hell, I'm lost for words.'

'Or did you mean the first one?' He was wearing a double-breasted blue suit and she immediately identified the slightly full left shoulder. 'Take off your jacket. Slowly.'

'I came here to talk to you.'

'That's what Johannsson said. The jacket.'

Andrews unbuttoned the jacket and slipped it from his shoulders, exposing the holstered pistol under his left arm. 'Will you let me explain about that?'

'A death-bed confession? You can try. Use your thumb and forefinger to draw that weapon and lay it on the table. And Joe, you've known me a long time, so please don't be stupid.'

He extracted the pistol from its holster and put it down. 'I assume you wouldn't shoot an unarmed man.'

'I have shot quite a few unarmed men,' she said. 'I'm in neither the honourable behaviour business nor the romantic movie business. My brief is to stay alive.'

'I'm here to make sure you can do that.'

'I don't think even you can convince me of that, Joe.'

He licked his lips. 'I don't suppose you'd have anything to drink?'

'There's Scotch on the sideboard. Help yourself.'

She sat down on the far side of the room and crossed her knees, the pistol still pointed at him. He might presently be separated from his gun by several feet, but she knew that he was a highly trained operative with a long and successful career in the American Secret Service. That she was humouring him at all was because she could not forget that once he had saved her life.

He poured, and looked over his shoulder. 'For you?'

'Thank you, no. I have just had a cup of tea.'

Andrews sat down, facing her. 'You have become very English.'

'I think that is the general idea. Tell me how you managed to find me?'

'Belinda gave me the address.'

'Belinda?' Anna frowned. Clive had assured her that her hideaway would be known to no one but himself, his secretary, and Billy Baxter.

'Disturbing, isn't it? She didn't have it herself, but she obtained it from that secretary Clive has. Amy something or other.'

'Barstow,' Anna said absently.

'You got it.'

'I didn't know you knew Belinda.'

'I didn't, down to a couple of days ago. But we keep tabs on things, and we knew she was Clive's long-standing lady-love. So when we needed to find you again, it seemed a good place to start.'

'You are saying that Belinda wormed it out of Amy at your request? Why should she co-operate with you?'

'I persuaded her that telling me where you could be found was in your best interests. She is very fond of you, you know.'

Belinda, Anna thought, making a mental note. 'And she also told you that I was alive?'

'Oh, we knew that.'

'Tell me how.'

'We have in our custody a man named Stefan Edert. Ring a bell.'

'Stefan,' Anna muttered. 'What a fool I was not to execute him. And now you have come to complete the job you gave to Johannsson. If you can. The long arm of the OSS.'

'The OSS no longer exists. We are now the CIA.'

'How you people love initials. What does that stand for? Criminals In America?'

'It stands for the Central Intelligence Agency.'

'I see. Under Donovan.'

'No. Wild Bill has moved on to bigger, and hopefully better things. My boss is a man named Dulles.'

'Of whom I have never heard.'

Andrews drank, reflectively. 'I have an idea that you will. He has certainly heard of you.'

'But the overall pattern is the same.' She stood up. 'Finish your drink, and then you and I will take a little walk on the moor, and then I can come back and have my bath.'

If he realized how close he was to dying he didn't show it. But then, she remembered, Joe Andrews had never been easily scared. 'You were going to let me explain.'

'Was I? I must be getting old. My memory seems to be fading.'

'Anna . . .' he leaned forward. 'Please believe me. It was all a dreadful mistake.'

He paused, but her eyes were still ice-cold.

'The Soviets were out to get you. Well, I guess you know that. Apart from the attempt on Stalin, there were those six NKVD people you took out in Washington in 1941. They were suspicious from the start at the way you managed to get away with that without being arrested. They had no idea that you were working for us . . . well, you weren't at that time, but they knew you couldn't have done it without some kind of government collusion. Then that incident in Warsaw, where again you did for six of their people . . . Well, in 1941 we were helping them out with Lend Lease but we hadn't yet got into the war. They had to temporise. But in 1944 we were all in it together, and they were doing more to win the war than anyone else. And the old suspicion lingered. So they told the State Department they wanted our help in nailing you, or they were going to make that 1941 business public and blow a big hole in our credibility. And, well, FDR's advisers panicked. It was, after all, an election year and the Soviets were regarded pretty much as heroes at that time.'

'And elections are the most important things in your lives.'

'Look, the decision was taken at the very top. The President gave the Russian ambassador his word that as we had let you go in 1941, we would sort it out.'

'You are saying that President Roosevelt personally ordered my execution?'

'No, he did not. He knew you worked for us, and the orders were for you to be taken out of circulation. But it was felt, lower down, that if we merely retired you and you started to talk it could be disastrous. Believe me, I was aghast. So was Wild Bill. And so, believe it or not, was Johannsson.'

'But you all obeyed your orders, one after the other.'

'Haven't you, always obeyed your orders, whether given you by Heydrich, or Himmler, or MI6? Or, indeed, us?' He gave a wry smile. 'And Johannsson seems to have disobeyed his. I specifically warned him that if he let your femininity get between himself and the completion of his mission, he was a dead man.'

Anna's nostrils flared. 'You know what he did?'

'We have the Swedish report on the case. Naturally they don't know exactly what happened, but they do know that he had a sexual discharge shortly before he died, that he had also received, shortly before death, a couple of savage, karate type blows, one to the kidneys and the other to the side of the head. And of course, he was killed with a single shot to the head, from a Luger nine-millimetre automatic pistol. From our standpoint, that made identification of his killer positive. Would that be the same gun that you are pointing at me?'

'No. And the blow on the head was where I kicked him. And you don't know the truth any more than the Swedish police.' She sat down again, but the gun still pointed. 'Do you really suppose we had mutual sex? He drugged me, because I trusted him and so accepted a drink from him. I think drugging me was part of his plan to kill me by shooting me full of insulin, so that until and unless there was a post-mortem it would appear that I had died a natural death. But apparently when he saw me lying there he couldn't stop himself taking advantage of the situation. Only he took so long over enjoying himself that I woke up.'

'The bastard! I would say he got what was coming to him. Anna, we can't turn back the clock. But we can make it up to you.'

'How?'

'You know the Russians will get to you eventually . . .'

'Your buddies.'

'Not any longer. Belatedly, perhaps, we've woken up to the facts, that Stalinist Russia is not all that different to Hitler's Germany. Anna, if you come back to us, we can protect you in a way the Brits cannot. We'll put you back on our payroll, unfreeze all that back pay we have for you. There's something like twenty thousand dollars in that account.'

Twenty thousand dollars, Anna thought. And I have more than ten million waiting for me at the bottom of the Horsel!

Andrews misinterpreted her expression. 'And of course, there'd be more every month. Take home pay, Anna, tax free. We'll look after all your expenses. And you'll get out of this dump. The world will be your oyster.'

'Going where you send me.'

'Well—'

'Killing people you want killed.'

'Well—'

'Can you really draw a line between this CIA of yours and the SD? Or the NKVD, for that matter?'

'Anna, the world has moved on from the innocent days of the twenties and perhaps even the thirties. The war we just finished has changed all that. From here on it's a business of survival of the fittest. And it's the duty of every government to make sure it is their people who do the surviving, no matter what it takes.'

'And if I don't go along with you, and instead take you out on that moor and put a bullet through your lousy brain, your people would hunt me down.'

He grimaced. 'I'm afraid they probably would. You can't fight us and the Soviet Union, Anna. Not even with Clive behind you. And you can't be certain MI6 would be behind you, can you? If the chips really went down'

Bastard, she thought. But he was stating the simple truth. And right then she didn't know if Clive was ever going to be behind her, at least in the way she wanted. And the only way she was ever going to get at that bullion was to be able to move freely. And obtain outside help. From this lot? But if they had genuinely woken up to the Soviet threat . . .

Again he misinterpreted her expression. 'I'd also like to remind you that once I saved your life.'

'Why else do you suppose you're still sitting there? And I did pay you back.'

'I know you did. And I will never forget that day.'

She smiled, her eyes suddenly soft. 'Do you know, neither will I. So I guess I'm a fool after all. But not quite such a fool. You have God alone knows how many agents at your disposal. If you want me back, it has to be for a specific purpose. You'll have to tell me what that is.'

'We want you to go after Martin Bormann.'

Incident in Scotland

'**Y**ou need to rephrase that,' Anna suggested. 'Martin Bormann is dead.'

'You saw him die?'

'Of course I did not. I left Berlin in March. That was a month before the Russians captured the city.'

'Right. So let's add up. We know that Hitler, Goebbels and Himmler committed suicide.'

'You have proof of that? I thought Hitler's body was all but unidentifiable?'

'Apparently it was. But the Reds, who of course are the only people who actually saw it, and who now have it, are pretty sure that it's him. The other twenty-odd leading Nazis are on trial in Nuremberg. With two exceptions. You, and Bormann.'

'I was never a Nazi. You know why I worked for them.'

'I hope you don't ever have to make that point to the Reds. The point I am trying to make is that it was disseminated, and believed, that you were dead. But here we are, a year later, in possession of information, thanks to your friend Edert, that you are alive. No secret endures forever. Bormann had to have had people as close to him as Edert apparently was to you, if only to help him get out of Berlin, again as Edert did for you. But we have found no one, and no one has come forward, to confirm or deny his death. We know he was in the Bunker with the top brass until virtually the very end. But when the Reds finally broke in, he was gone.' He snapped his fingers. 'Just like that.'

Anna considered. 'If he managed to get out, surely he would have wanted to join his family. I assume you know where they are?'

'We do. He sent his wife and children to Bolzano, at the beginning of '45. I guess he could see the writing on the wall as well as anyone.'

'And they're still there?'

'Yes. But Frau Bormann denies any knowledge of her husband.'

'And you believe her?'

'No. But he certainly isn't around. And we've had her under constant surveillance, including a phone tap, and neither of them has made any attempt to contact the other. She seems to be pretty well-heeled at the moment, so we're wondering if she hasn't decided to let him sink or swim on his own.'

'Or she knows that he's dead.'

'How can she know that? She left Berlin two months before you did.'

Anna got up, took the bottle from the sideboard with her left hand, and replenished his glass, then poured one for herself. Her brain was racing. It had never occurred to her that Bormann might have survived. But if he had . . . Hitler's closest associate! The man who, it was said, not only knew all of the Fuehrer's decisions before they were made, but was thought to inspire most of them. And the order to dispose of the bullion, if issued by Himmler, had come from Hitler, personally. And Bormann? That would make him the only one, apart from herself, who knew where the bullion was hidden. But she had to be certain what these people really wanted. 'Does it matter whether he is alive or dead? One survivor out of the whole crew?'

'He isn't, you know. There is quite a list of them still knocking about. Not the very top, maybe, but important people. Important believers in the Nazi myth, the certainty that they can, and will, rise again.'

'So where are all these people?'

'We reckon most have got to South America. Places like Brazil, Argentina, Uruguay. Those governments are Fascist, no matter how they deny it. This fellow Peron, well . . . They also operate on a cash and carry basis. You have the cash, they'll carry you. Your old boss Himmler wasn't the only lad smuggling funds out of Germany, you know. Right now all these fugitives are lying low, waiting for the dust to settle. But they're there. They are a poisonous growth, Anna, dormant at the moment, only waiting for the right man to come along and re-activate them.'

'And you reckon Bormann is that man?'

'He was Hitler's closest associate, wasn't he? You knew him pretty well. Do you agree with that estimate?'

'I agree with the estimate, but I did not know Bormann very well,' Anna corrected. 'In fact, I did not know him at all. I only met him twice in my life, and we didn't like each other.'

'Oh!' He was clearly disappointed. 'You mean he doesn't go for women? But he was married, and had a clutch of kids.'

'That is not conclusive, Joe. But I have no reason to suppose he was homosexual. He never tried to touch me because he regarded me as Hitler's personal possession. I disliked him because he did not seem to have any redeeming, much less attractive, features. He disliked me because he felt I might have too much influence on Hitler; he regarded that as his prerogative.'

'Exactly my point, that he has always been so self-effacing he would be a difficult man to point out in a crowd, but that, as Hitler's closest associate he would be considered by many people to be the Fuehrer's natural successor. Now, you see, you knew him, however casually. You can identify him. And that is a difficult thing to do. He was always in the background, just a shadow at the Fuehrer's shoulder. Oh, there are a couple of photographs with him in them, but again, he is always in the background, and his features are so unremarkable, so commonplace, he could walk down any street in the world and not be recognized. Except by you.'

Anna smiled. 'So you want me to walk down every street in the world on the off chance of running into him, and recognizing him.'

'We're not quite that simple. As I said, we are pretty sure that he has gone, or shortly will go, to South America. We want you to follow fashion, as a Nazi fugitive. You will have all the money you need, and you will take up residence in either Rio or Buenos Aires, wherever you think would be more productive. You will live a normal, social life, but you will put discreet adverts in the newspapers indicating that the Countess von Widerstand would love to hear from her old comrades in arms.'

'Are you serious?'

'We understand it'll be a bit risky, exposing yourself like that. But our people will be keeping an eye on you, ready to take care of any problems.'

'You have no idea how reassuring that is. And suppose I find it necessary to take care of these problems myself?'

'We'll sort that out, too.'

'Even if I'm in an Argentinian gaol, hanging by my thumbs?'

'Yes.'

'You are making an awful lot of promises I hope you can keep.'

'Then you will come back and work for us?'

The temptation was impossible to resist. And it was a way, perhaps the only way, to achieve her ultimate objective and at the same time make sure no one revealed her secret first. 'If I do,' she said. 'I will require a quid pro quo.'

He frowned. 'You will have to explain that.'

'There is something I have to do. It can wait awhile, and I really would like to be free of this dump. So I will act as your bait to bring Bormann out of his closet, and if he does I will deliver him to you.' Supposing he survives our meeting, she thought. 'However, whether I succeed or not, when you take delivery or decide that it's not going to happen and call it a day, I want a promise of carte blanche and, if necessary, assistance to complete my own personal mission.'

Now he was looking apprehensive. 'If you'll tell me who the target is.'

'The target is not a human being.'

His frown deepened. 'Then . . .'

'Nor am I aiming to blow anybody, or any thing, up. I am not going to tell you what it is, Joe, but I can tell you that I will be able to make it worth your while, and by you I mean your government.'

He stared at her for several seconds, then snapped his fingers. 'The Nazi gold reserves.'

Damn, she thought. He was smarter than she had supposed. 'How do you figure that?'

'We know they are not in Berlin, where we also know they once were. So they have to have been taken somewhere else. Believe me, a lot of midnight oil has been burned on this one. And you know where they are. Christ almighty! Of course, who else would have been put in charge of that? But you mean you are prepared to sit on that kind of knowledge . . . how much?'

'A hundred tons of pure gold, in ingots.'

'Holy shit! And what kind of percentage would you be looking for?'

'I already have my ten per cent put aside. But I will need help in getting it. I will have to trust you, Joe. Again. But so help me God, if you renege on me, again, I will kill you.'

He gazed at her for several seconds. Then he nodded. 'I guess you would. I won't let you down again, Anna. I did not sleep a wink during those months I thought you were dead. Now, I swear—'

Anna held up her hand. 'No oaths, please. I have never heard one that was worth a shit when the chips were down. Just remember that we're partners for our mutual benefit.' She transferred the pistol to her left hand and held out her right. After a moment he took it, giving the fingers a gentle squeeze; she had to wonder if, for that moment, he had contemplated taking her on? But again, she reflected, he knew her too well, knew that she could shoot almost as well with her left hand as with her right, and knew too that she was capable of taking even him with her bare hands.

'And afterwards?' he asked, retaining her hand.

'We can discuss that afterwards.'

'No, we can't. If we help you get your money, you'll still be working for us. You must understand that.'

Anna gazed at him for several seconds. When I have ten million dollars in the bank, she thought, I am going to make the rules. But as she couldn't get ten million dollars in the bank without his help . . . she squeezed his hand in turn. 'It's a deal. Providing I get some time off to spend some of my money.'

'I think that can be arranged.'

'Well then,' she said, when his grip relaxed, 'all we have to do is get hold of Clive, put him in the picture, and get MI6's OK.'

'No way.'

Anna withdrew her hand, slowly. 'What did you say?'

'My people won't work with the British Secret Service right this minute.'

'Explain.'

'We don't go too much for their security. As you can imagine, the Reds are working round the clock trying to get the dope on the atomic bomb. We reckon they're just about there. And you know why? Because a couple of your high-ranking scientists, men with top level security clearance from MI5, have been leaking to Moscow. Now, they may be common or garden traitors looking for loot, or they may be misguided idealists who believe the Communist way is better than ours, but either way they've done the West immeasurable harm, and brought the prospect of an atomic war that much closer. We're unhappy about that.'

'I can't just walk away, Joe. He'd go spare. And besides . . .'

'You still have a lot going for him.'

'Shouldn't I? He's the only man who has never let me down.'

'Touché. But you don't reckon he's keeping you here while his government decides what to do with you? And if, at the end of the day, they decide you're too hot to handle, do you really suppose he will go against that ruling? Clive? With his record of devoted service to King and Country?'

Anna bit her lip. He was a bastard who was interested only in paddling his own canoe. But wasn't he simply putting into words the suspicions that had been slowly filling her own mind over the winter? 'I'll have to write him a letter.'

'Saying what?'

'That something has come up to which I have to attend. I'm assuming you people can get me out of the country?'

'You will be out of the country twelve hours after you leave here.'

'Well, then . . .' A last hesitation. But did she really have any choice? 'I'll just pack, collect my jewellery and do that note. What about my passport? It's a British one.'

'Bring it along, for the time being. We'll probably supply you with a fresh one, but until then, it might be useful.'

'What nationality will the new one be?'

'I'll have to take advice on that. I suppose, if you're going to surface as the Countess von Widerstand, or Anna Fehrbach, it'll have to be German. You have to be absolutely genuine.'

She considered for a moment, then nodded. 'I'll be ten minutes.'

'Good girl.' Then he frowned, and turned his head. 'What's that noise?'

'Another car. Oh, my God! Do you think it's Clive?'

'You expecting him?'

'No, I'm not. But nobody else knows I'm here.'

Andrews moved to the window, parted the curtain. 'It's a big car . . . and there are four men getting out. And I would say they're Russians.'

Anna stood beside him. studied the four burly men wearing lounge suits and slouch hats. 'Yes,' she said. 'Definitely Russians.'

'How in the name of God did they know where to come?'

'They didn't know where to come, you silly man. They followed you.'

'Holy Jesus Christ! I'd better talk to them.'

'What were you planning to say?'

'Well, I mean, the war is over . . .'

'Not to them, it isn't, at least where I'm concerned. They didn't follow you the length of Britain for a chat. They've come for me, and I'll bet there's a body bag in the boot of the car.'

'But they're carrying tommy guns! What are we going to do?'

'I'm afraid we are going to have to discourage them.'

Andrews gulped. 'Long odds. Shouldn't we at least make sure it's you they want?'

'Joe,' Anna said patiently. 'You're getting old. And two of them are going round the back. Now listen carefully. You get your gun, then sit tight here. Get on the floor behind that table, do not move or think of opening the door. And do not reply to any questions, comments or demands. Nothing upsets the opposition quite so much as being greeted with absolute silence. So keep still until someone actually enters the room. Then open up.'

'But—'

'When we don't let them in, they are going to shoot their way in. That'll be our chance, if we don't get hit before then. If they knock the windows out first, still only fire if someone tries to climb through.'

'You mean . . . Good God! You're going to try to take them out?'

'We are going to take them out, Joe. Just do as I say.'

She went to the kitchen, checked that this door also was locked. Through the window she could see the two men cautiously approaching; they had to suppose the inmates had observed their arrival.

She went up the stairs, paused at the housekeeper's door. 'Mrs Bridie, there is going to be some noise. I think you want to lie on the floor, under the bed, and stay there for at least half an hour after the shooting stops. Unless the house is on fire, of course.'

'Shooting? Fire? My God, Anna . . .'

'Do not open this door, under any circumstances short of fire. Just do as I say.'

She went to her bedroom. The adrenaline was pumping through her arteries, reminding her of how much she had been missing the constant, but to her stimulating, pressures of her adult life. And of all the many unpleasant people with whom she had come into contact, she hated the Russians, or at least those represented by the NKVD and its MGB successors, most.

For all her bold words to Andrews, she didn't know who would

win the coming battle; if she had in her time faced greater opposition than four to two, the tommy guns loaded the odds even
more in favour of the opposition. As she had told Andrews their
only chance was to wait for the opposition to make a mistake –
a strategy she had practised throughout the years with unfailing
success – but whatever was going to happen she intended to go
out in a blaze of glory. She brushed her hair – leaving it loose
and thus at its most eye-catchingly spectacular but securing it
on the nape of her neck with a tortoiseshell clip to prevent any
risk of it getting in her eyes – pocketed the spare magazine for
her Luger, and reached the stairs as there came a rap on the front
door.

She looked into the lounge. Andrews was kneeling on the
floor behind the table, his pistol in his hand. He looked at her
and she blew him a kiss, then returned to the kitchen. The two
men were not visible, but she suspected that they had gone to
ground behind a line of rhododendron bushes.

She knelt behind the stove, which was a solid iron range, and
listened to another bang on the front door. There were a couple
of moments' silence, then a voice called, 'Countess! We know
you are in there, with Mr Andrews. Open the door and come
out with your hands in the air, and you will not be hurt. If you
do not do this, we are going to come in, and there will be much
damage.'

As instructed, Joe did not reply. Another couple of moments
passed, then suddenly the tommy guns opened up. The chatter
was enormous; glass shattered and there were the thumps of the
bullets smashing into the woodwork of both the door and the
walls. The men at the back opened fire as well, and showers of
glass shards scattered across the kitchen; one lodged in Anna's
hair and she pulled it out.

The firing stopped, but the reverberations continued for some
minutes. 'Anna,' Andrews said.

'Sssh! Wait. Just remember, when they enter the house, you
shoot to kill. You will only have a few seconds.'

She could almost hear him gulp again. As she had suggested
when taking command of the situation, he might have been an
experienced field agent in his time, but that had been some years
ago; he was now nearing fifty. And even in his heyday, she
doubted that he had ever encountered a partner, and certainly
not a woman, capable of waiting with such deadly patience for
events to develop to her best advantage.

She listened to a conversation in Russian; she had learned the language during the year she had spent in Moscow. 'There is no sound, Comrade. They must be dead.'

'Vassily!' someone shouted. 'How is it at the back?'

'All quiet.'

'Can you force an entry?'

'I think so.'

'Then do it. The front door looks very solid.'

She could have been giving the orders, Anna thought, if they intended to attack in separated groups rather than all together. There was another prolonged burst of firing, and the back door, already splintered in several places, began to crack. At the same time a man appeared at the shattered window and sprayed the kitchen with bullets, but as he could not see her he was firing blind.

Anna used the noise to cock her pistol and make sure there was a cartridge in the breech. The firing stopped, and there were several heavy crashes as shoulders were hurled against the door. Anna began taking long, deep breaths. Her heartbeat had actually slowed, but her mind was coiled like a spring, waiting to be released.

There was a final crack, and the door swung in, sagging on its hinges. The first man stumbled through the opening, his tommy gun trailing from one hand; the second man was immediately behind him. Anna stood up, levelled her pistol, and shot him; as because of the way he was bent over she was unable to aim for her favourite target, the head, she aimed at the side of his body and then immediately turned her sights on the second man, who was staring at her in consternation while he brought up his weapon. He presented a prefect target; she shot him in the centre of his forehead.

The second man was groaning and clutching his ribs, blood seeping through his hands and frothing from his sagging lips. He was clearly dying, so Anna let him be and picked up the two tommy guns. Both men had satchels on their shoulders, and as she had anticipated, there was a spare magazine in each. She reloaded both guns, slinging one and tucking her pistol into her waistband.

'Vassily?' called the voice from the front of the house. 'Are you inside, Vassily? Come and open this door.'

'Anna,' Andrews whispered. 'Anna?'

'Sssh, and stay down,' Anna said.

She went out of the back door, inhaling the fresh evening air; it was just on dusk. Keeping against the wall, she moved round the house.

'Vassily!' The voice from the front was becoming a wail. 'Andreev, go and see what has happened.'

'Those were pistol shots, Comrade,' Andreev pointed out.

'So they fired a couple of shots.'

'But after the tommies stopped. They are not dead. She is not dead.'

'Are you afraid of a woman?'

'They said she was a killer.'

'A woman?' the commander sneered. 'I have given you an order.'

Anna listened to footsteps crunching on the gravel. But he was going the other way. She waited for a few seconds, then stepped round the corner. As she had expected, the commander was standing by the car, where he was out of any direct line of fire from the house. She didn't want to explode the car, which was parked next to Andrews', so she slung the second tommy gun as well, drew her pistol, and left the shelter of the house. 'Captain,' she called.

He turned, sharply, raising his gun, and she shot him though the head.

'Comrade Captain!' Andreev shouted. He had heard the shot.

Anna tucked away her pistol, its barrel warm against her stomach, and unslung one of the tommy guns. Then she stepped behind the car, beside the commander's body.

Andreev ran round the corner. 'Comrade Captain, they are both dead. And that shot . . .' He checked as he saw Anna. He carried his gun in both hands, but it was held across his body. His face contorted, and he started to turn the gun towards his enemy, but he was already dead.

Fifty-seven, Anna thought. And I had supposed I was finished with killing. She swallowed back a sudden desire to weep and went to the front door. 'You can open this now, Joe.'

It took him a few moments to respond, then the bolt was drawn and the bullet-scored door swung in. 'Anna . . .'

'You said you have some way of getting us out of England, quickly?'

'It is arranged, yes.' He looked past her at the two dead bodies. 'The other two . . .'

'Are in the kitchen.'

'How . . . I mean . . . well . . .'

'I have done nothing but kill for the past eight years, so I suppose I'm getting good at it. But as the war is officially over, I guess I'm in line for a hanging. So can we get the hell out of here?'

'Their guns . . .'

'Leave them. Put one beside each body, so the police can have no doubt what they were intending. I'm just going to pack my things, and I'll be right with you.'

Andrews replaced his unfired gun in his shoulder holster, and used his handkerchief to wipe sweat from his forehead; Anna had not been sweating at all.

'Well?' Baxter inquired. He had already filled his pipe.

Clive had just arrived back in the office, and slumped into the chair before the desk. 'I don't think the Wick police have ever seen anything like this before. As for Mrs Bridie . . . she may have to be retired.'

'But she knows what happened?'

'No, she does not, precisely. A man came to see Anna in the middle of yesterday afternoon. She can't remember his name, but I think we can assume it was Andrews. Before Anna let him in, she sent Mrs Bridie to her room, and told her to stay there, no matter what, until she called her.'

'She sent Mrs Bridie to her room? And Mrs Bridie went?'

'I know,' Clive said. 'She was in charge, and she thinks she's tough. But you've never seen Anna in her avenging angel mode; neither had Mrs Bridie. Anyway, she locked herself in, as instructed. And then Anna and Andrews seem to have talked for an hour or so.'

'Talked. I thought you said if he found her he would kill her?'

'I actually said, if he found her, she would kill him.'

'But neither of those things happened, so far as we know. So who killed the four Russians?'

'Who do you think?'

'I never thought Andrews was that good.'

'He wasn't. Those deaths bear Anna's imprints. Two of them were clean pistol shots to the head. The third chap had been hit in the left side; the bullet penetrated his lung and he must have died pretty quickly. The police say that all the bullets were nine millimetre, almost certainly fired from a Luger automatic. American operatives do not use Lugers.'

'What about the fourth man?'

'He was cut to pieces by a burst from a tommy gun. The tommy guns apparently belonged to the Russians; that is, there were four guns and four Russians. I suppose it is possible that Andrews got hold of one of the guns, but I still think it was Anna. That body was found, together with one of his colleagues, outside the house. The other two were inside.'

'Are you saying that the tommy guns were still there?'

'Another of Anna's trademarks; she never takes the other fellow's weapon, unless she really needs it. Anyway, forensics will establish the fingerprints. But of course, they don't have copies of Anna's prints. Or Andrews'.'

'So what did she do when the shooting stopped?'

'I would say she left with Andrews in the car in which he arrived, and which he almost certainly had hired, probably in London. Unfortunately Mrs Bridie didn't make a note of the number. I think she was too shocked.'

'But she was there when all this was going on.'

'Hiding under her bed, as instructed by Anna. Anna told her not to come out for half an hour after the shooting stopped. This she did. But she did hear the sound of a car engine about fifteen minutes before the half-hour was up. When she came out, both Andrews and Anna had disappeared. And it seems certain Anna doesn't intend to come back. She took with her all of her clothes and all of her jewellery.'

'Damn, damn, damn. She's for the high jump, Clive. Maybe we all are. The Russians are going to scream blue murder.'

'Billy, those thugs were armed with tommy guns. The house is all shot up. They started it. Anyway, there's no need for us to be involved. I told the police I was a friend of Mrs Bridie, paying a visit. She had driven into the village last night and called the police, and they were still there in force. To them I was just an irrelevance. They sent me off with a warning to keep my mouth shut.'

'After giving you the facts of the case?'

'Well, like I said, they were pretty shaken; the bodies were still lying about the place, and I suppose they felt I might be able to throw some light on what had happened. When they accepted that I knew nothing about it, as I said, they told me to clear off. As for Anna, all anyone up there knows is that she was a novelist trying to finish a book.'

'Clive, you are being naive. This is going to be the scandal of the century. With you and me and the department in the middle. One year ago we announced to the world that the Countess von Widerstand was dead. Now we have to hold up our hands and admit we were lying. I always knew that this goddamn thing was going to turn out badly.'

'But if we just keep our mouth shut . . . no one up there knew who Anna was.'

'And Andrews? If he knew to go looking for her, it's because he's found out that that she's alive. That means the State Department knows she's alive.'

'Surely we can do a deal with them?'

'And the Russians? Do you suppose they were there on spec? They were following Andrews. Because they felt pretty sure he would lead them to Anna.'

'How could they possibly have known that?'

'Doesn't matter. They did. And now four of their people are down. On top of all the others. So where is she?'

Clive shrugged, the movement redolent of misery. 'With Andrews, I suppose.'

'Then where is he, God damn. it? You been on to their Embassy?'

'The US Embassy knows nothing about the whereabouts of anyone named Joseph Andrews. The suggestion is that they have never heard of him.'

'They're lying.'

'Well, of course they are, Billy. They're protecting their own.'

'He has to be somewhere. She has to be somewhere.'

'They're long gone. It was dark when they left the house. I imagine we'll find Andrews' hire car in Rosyth.'

'Why Rosyth?'

'Rosyth is only about a hundred and eighty miles from Wick, say a six-hour drive. And an American destroyer, on a courtesy visit to Scotland and moored in Rosyth Naval Base, was unexpectedly recalled to the States, and sailed this morning.'

'That's a long shot.'

'It's logical. Andrews obviously had this laid on before he went near her. And when I got back just now this was waiting on my desk, mailed last night from Wick.'

Baxter took the sheet of paper. *My darling Clive, circumstances have taken over, and I have to disappear for a while. I will contact you as soon as it is safe to do so. Please don't go mad trying to find me. Anna. PS: I do love you.* 'She really is a loose cannon.'

Clive looked at his watch. 'Three o'clock. That destroyer only sailed at eight. We could still stop her.'

'Are you proposing that we attempt to get the Navy to stop an American warship on the high seas? What are you trying to do, start an international crisis? She's gone, Clive. We've lost her. To the bloody Yanks.'

'What I would like to know,' Clive said, 'is what Andrews told her to get her to trust him. To go away with him, for God's sake. Billy, I have got to get to the States.'

'I said, if Washington has got her, she's out of our reach.'

'Billy, no matter what she may have been led to believe, they are going to do her. Or at least send her to join the others in Nuremberg.'

Baxter shook his head. 'They won't do that. Anna on trial? All that beauty, spilling the beans on everything that has happened to her over the past eight years, all that she has been required to do, by Washington, by us, by Himmler? There wouldn't be a dry eye in the house, and she'd stand a good chance of being acquitted and becoming the heroine of the hour. While all of us, including the Yanks, would be depicted as utter rats.'

'So why have they taken her off, then?'

'She went, Clive. She went. Do you suppose that after doing for four Russians she'd hesitate at doing for Andrews if she didn't like the line he was shooting her? It must have been something pretty compelling. And she must have received assurances that they didn't want her blood. You just have to put her out of your mind, at least until she crops up again. She will. We have more important matters to consider. Like how we treat this balls-up. How are the press handling it?'

'They're not, at this moment. Because they don't know anything more than "Mysterious killing in lonely house", type thing.'

'But that can't last more than another twenty-four hours. Before then, we, you, have to put together a full report, on Anna's reasons for being there, mainly that it involved hiding our top agent from the Russians, and that there was a slip-up . . .'

'Belinda,' Clive growled. 'I'm going . . .'

'To stay away from her. If anything is to be done about Belinda, the decision will have to come from the top. They may well decide to let that one lie. She also could do a fair amount of singing if pushed.'

'If this were Nazi Germany, or the Soviet Union, for that matter . . .'

'It would be a case of a bullet in the back of the head as she came home from work one night. Unfortunately, as some would have it, we spent six rather expensive years making sure that this country did not become like Nazi Germany or the Soviet Union. You go and write up a complete report on Anna and why we handled her the way we did, bearing in mind that it is extremely likely to wind up on the Prime Minister's desk. All I can say is thank God it isn't Winston, right this minute.'

Clive stood up. 'And the Fehrbachs?'

'Shit! I'd forgotten them. You'd better go to see them and

explain what has happened. Reassure them that we are doing all we can to get Anna back in one piece, and that what has happened will not in any way affect their position or their safety. Providing they will promise not to talk to the press.'

'There is no reason why they should have to. No one outside of this office knows that there is any connection between them and Anna.'

'Clive, down to a couple of days ago no one outside of this office knew where Anna was. Just get on with it.'

Clive went down to his own office, where Amy hovered. 'Mr Bartley, I am most terribly sorry.'

He sat behind his desk. 'You should be.'

'Is there anything I can do? I mean, well . . .'

'You mean if I told you to drop your knickers and bend over this desk for a sound spanking on your bare bottom you'd do it?'

'Well . . .' She licked her lips, and he suddenly realized that she would indeed do it.

He sighed. 'Sadly, Amy, I have been commanded by the boss to put temptation behind me and get on with the job. Bring your book in and we'll start with that.'

Beria pushed the sheet of paper across his desk. Kamarov picked it up, read it, and sat down uninvited. 'This is incredible. When is it supposed to have happened?'

'It did happen, Comrade. That arrived this morning, from the London Embassy.'

'Does the Premier know?'

'He will have received a copy.'

Kamarov gulped. 'I hope—'

'That he will not hold you responsible? At this moment, I do not think he will.'

'At this moment, sir?'

'At this moment, Comrade Kamarov, we are not in possession of the facts. The British have not yet released them. They will have to, in time, of course; we shall see to that. But right now, all we know is that, on your recommendation, which had sound reasoning behind it, a tail was put on Andrews, and when he left London to drive up to Scotland a back-up squad was requested. This was supplied by our local MGB office, sadly without reference to us. I understand this; they were told that the matter was urgent. But I want you to get on the telephone to London, and find out what instructions were given. Obviously they knew that we wanted Andrews to lead them to the countess, and we must assume that he did that. Then they seem to have determined that the opportunity to seize her was too good to be missed. They had no idea what they were dealing with.'

'Well, sir, a woman—'

'The Countess von Widerstand is not a woman, Comrade. She is the embodiment of the Goddess of Destruction. Do you know how many of our people she has now destroyed? Twenty-one!'

Kamarov stared at him in disbelief.

'Three of them were killed by proxy, as it were, in Germany last year,' Beria went on. 'But she was still responsible. And she had the support of Andrews, who is a trained American operative.'

'Still, two people, against four of our best, armed with tommy guns . . .' Kamarov looked at the paper again. 'This just says that four of our people were killed. There is no reference to any other casualties. The countess and Andrews could both also be dead.'

'That would be most unfortunate.'

'Sir?'

'We want that woman alive, Kamarov. She has secrets that we need to know. And now—'

'There is still the sister,' Kamarov said eagerly. 'The original plan.'

'Yes,' Beria said thoughtfully. 'That might still work. Where is she now?'

'She is undergoing the rehabilitation you require.'

'And what state is she in?'

'I understand that it is proving a little difficult. You understand, well, eighteen months of constant mistreatment, of beatings and starvation . . .'

'I do understand,' Beria said. 'I sent her there in the first place. But I also instructed that there were to be no permanent injuries.'

'I do not think there are any scars. A least on her body.'

'But?'

'Well, who can say what goes on in someone's mind? I understand from the camp commandant that this woman is given to unpredictable, violent outbursts and can be quite dangerous. We should not ever forget that, like her sister, she was trained by the SS to work in the SD. That means, to be lethal. And it is safe to assume that she hates us.'

'Her feelings towards us are immaterial. The important thing is that she accepts her rehabilitation.'

'Well, yes. I would suppose it will be impossible to resist, as it means being able to get out of that hell and resume her life. But you do understand, sir, that she may well go straight to a newspaper and sell her story of Soviet injustice and brutality.'

'So many people are peddling stories of Soviet injustice and brutality I don't think one more is going to make much difference. Certainly when it is learned that she is the sister and the one-time assistant of the infamous murderess Anna Fehrbach. It will be interesting to see what she does first. Who she sees first.'

'What,' asked Joseph Andrews, 'do you think of life on the ocean wave?'

Anna had been given an oilskin to wear on deck, and this she hugged closer about herself as she leaned against the rail. The destroyer had rounded the Shetlands during the first night and on the third day of the voyage was well out into the North Atlantic; although the sun was actually shining and they were standing on the bridge wing, on the lee side of the ship and therefore reasonably sheltered, the April wind, out of the north, was still cold; her hair was flowing away from her head. 'I've tried it before.'

'On a liner. But a destroyer?'

'That too.'

'You're not serious.'

'In my short life I have, whether I wanted to or not, experienced most things. A large number of them unpleasant.'

'You know how much I'd like to change that.'

She had been looking at the whitecaps racing by; the destroyer was travelling very fast, rolling in the cross swell. Now she turned her head to look at him, and he suddenly felt chilled inside as well as out.

'I know,' he said. 'I've said that before.'

'Before you decided to kill me.'

'I thought I'd explained that.'

'You were obeying orders. I last travelled by destroyer three days after my meeting with Johannsson. I was on my way back from Stockholm to Rostock on a Finnish ferry, and we were torpedoed by a Russian sub.'

'Shit! But you survived. As always.'

'There was a German destroyer close by, and he picked us up.'

'That must have been quite an experience.'

'More than you think. The destroyer, for various reasons, couldn't get to Rostock, so he dropped us off in Konigsberg.'

'Konigsberg? But . . .?'

'That's right. Six hundred kilometres east of where I wanted to be, and surrounded by Russians.'

'And you survived even that? How did you get out?'

'Himmler had me flown out, in a 262. You ever flown in a fighter jet?'

'No, I haven't. But wait a moment—'

'Oh, yes,' she agreed. 'It was a single-seater. So I sat in the pilot's lap for just about an hour. You could say that we got to know each other quite well.'

'You are incredible. Are you ever going to write your memoirs?'

'Are you ever going to let me? Actually, we got to know each other better yet. He had been my sister's boyfriend.'

'I never knew you had a sister. Is she anything like you?'

'As regards looks, yes. Otherwise, no.'

He considered for a few moments. 'You said, had been your sister's boyfriend.'

'Yes. He's dead.' Poor Rudent, she thought. He had hoped for so much, from her, and from the future, as he had been one of the men who had helped her conceal those ten tons of bullion . . . and she had allowed him to live. 'He was killed by the Russians when we were escaping Berlin. He was my driver, you see. Damnation!'

'It wasn't your fault, was it?'

'No. I was remembering. Because you, and our Red friends, turned up, I haven't taken my driving test. I was supposed to do that in a couple of days' time.'

'You mean you are only now getting around to learning to drive?' He remembered that in Washington, five years ago, as he had told Belinda, she had been embarrassed by the lack of that simple skill.

'I've been a little pushed for time, from time to time.'

'I imagine you have been. So where is you sister now?'

'I suspect she's dead.'

'What?'

'She was captured by the Russians. They thought she was me. So they took her off, and, well, they wouldn't have had any reason to hang on to her once they realized their mistake. Will I have the opportunity to get my licence when we reach the States?'

He wondered if she was as cold-blooded as she pretended. No doubt the life she had been forced to live for seven years – eight

if this last year was included – had inured her to sudden death
. . . even perhaps her own. Or, more sympathetically, she had
found it necessary to develop that apparently impervious outer
skin in order to survive, certainly mentally. But either way, she
remained the most entrancing creature he had ever known.

He had first seen her, from a distance, at the Cheltenham
Race Meeting in England, in the spring of 1939. Then the beautiful the Honourable Mrs Ballantine Bordman had been the
current toast of English society, although so far as anyone, himself
included, knew she had been a German heiress, and also the
object of interest as no one could understand why someone so
glamorously attractive and so apparently wealthy should have
tied herself to a fat slob like Ballantine Bordman who was obviously as thick as two short planks. No one in those so-innocent
pre-war days had imagined that it could be possible she was a
German spy. That had again included himself. As for the fact
that only a fortnight before he had seen her she had been strapped
naked to a table being tortured by her employers, or that as a
result of that mistreatment she had allowed herself to be turned
by his old acquaintance and sometime colleague Clive Bartley
. . . back in 1939 beautiful, elegant, cultured ladies did not have
skeletons like that in their closets.

By the time he had next seen her, and actually met her, at a
reception at the German Embassy in Moscow at Christmas 1940,
the scandal had long broken. But still he had only known the
official story, that just hours before she was to be arrested by
the Special Branch she had managed to escape England, no one
quite knew how, and regain the Fatherland. And there she was,
as coldly beautiful as ever.

As he was in the business himself, even if disguised as an
official at the American Embassy, he had immediately been alert
to the fact that someone with the Countess von Widerstand's
talents and track record would surely not be employed as a simple
secretary in a foreign embassy. Partly because of that, and partly
because he had been unable to resist the temptation, he had dated
her and found that she actually had a warm and most delightful
personality.

But he had still considered her only as a spy, a gatherer of
information for the Reich. He had had not the slightest suspicion that her true profession was far more sinister, or that she
was actually a double agent. He had only discovered that when
she had virtually been condemned to death by Heydrich – who
had given her the task of eliminating Premier Stalin on the eve

of the German invasion, no matter what the cost to herself – and, in the absence of any other means, had turned to him to get a message to his old acquaintance Clive Bartley about what was going to happen. Even then he had not really understood what was going on, but Clive had also enlisted his help, following her arrest before she could complete her mission, to get her out of the Lubianka, if that could be possible. Well, he had done it, by means of pulling a gigantic bluff, and seen her in action for the first time when the guards in the Women's Section had refused to obey immediately Beria's directive. He had never seen anything like it in his life before, and while she was as compulsively attractive as ever he had been happy to hand her over to her British controller, assuming that he would never see her again.

But only a few months later she had turned up in Washington, more glamorous than ever. And this time seeking him out. If her brief had officially been for the Germans, as he had known she was actually MI6, they had been able to meet as friends, when he had discovered that she was prepared to repay him, in her own fashion, for having saved her life.

As he had told her, that had been the outstanding afternoon of his life, accentuated soon afterwards by a course of events that had left her working for the American Secret Service as well as the British, with him as her US controller. Even if he had never got her back to bed that had remained a dream until it had all gone sour, and his superiors, at that time anxious not to antagonize the Russians, had determined that she had to be eliminated. He had been appalled, had protested, and been overruled.

Once again he had assumed he would not see her again, and here he was, standing beside her on an American ship, having again watched her in action, even more devastatingly than on that day in Moscow. And more desirable than ever. But, after all that had happened, and her continued suspicion of him as a true friend, he did not know how far he dared attempt to restore their earlier relationship.

Neither of them had said much on the drive down to Rosyth; there had been too much on their minds. And once on board the ship, she had been the toast of the officers. They knew nothing of her, of course; even the captain had only been told that it was his business to transport the Countess von Widerstand to America as rapidly and as secretly as possible. But he, and his men, had been delighted at the prospect of sharing several days with so gorgeous a woman.

In those circumstances, he had thought it best to keep a low profile. Anna had been allotted a single cabin of her own, and he suspected that the Navy would not be happy to see him emerging from it. But as he had spent this morning on the radio to Washington they had a great deal to discuss, and at last he had managed to get her alone; the ship was very crowded. So he said, 'I don't think there is going to be time for that. Anna, we have to talk.'

'Damnation,' she said again. 'So near and yet so far. Ah, well, maybe there'll be another time. So talk.'

He drew a deep breath. 'You understand that at this moment you are officially dead.'

'Unfortunately, there seem to be too many people around who do not understand that.'

'The Russians can have nothing more than suspicions. And we aren't going to say anything.'

'That is very reassuring. It also means that you can dispose of me whenever you think fit.'

'That is not going to happen, Anna. You are too valuable. The point is, we can have no known relationship with a wanted Nazi war criminal, alive or dead. Therefore you will not clear immigration or customs when we reach Norfolk. You will be smuggled ashore, and placed in a secure and secret location while you are fitted out with a new wardrobe and equipped with every-thing that is necessary for your assignment.'

'I have been hibernating in a so-called secret location for the past year.'

'It was criminal of Bartley to leave you on your own up there. We're not going to make that mistake.'

'And you can, if necessary, operate outside the law in your own country. MI6 doesn't have that facility, at least in times of peace.'

'If you mean that we are allowed to protect our own, that's quite true. But it won't come to that, ever. You'll be staying with my mother.'

'Your . . .?' Anna remembered the utterly charming woman with whom she had spent a week in 1941, hiding from the possible repercussions of her shoot-out with the Russians in Washington. Never had she felt so secure, and so restful. Of course, it had helped that Clive had been able to share three of those days with her. That had been before it had all gone wrong, at least on the American side. But now . . . 'Will she want to receive me?'

'She knows nothing more than she did the last time you met,

that you are the Countess von Widerstand and that you are very important to us. So you have nothing to worry about.'

'I'm not complaining. And the sound of a new wardrobe sounds good. Do I get a fur?'

'Do you want a fur? Do you need a fur, to go to South America?'

'The Nazis gave me a fur, and I was seldom seen without it, except maybe in high summer. It can get chilly in the bottom half of South America, and if I do happen to be looked up by any of my old friends, they'll expect one.'

He sighed. 'OK, one mink coat.'

'A sable,' Anna said.

'What?'

'I always wore a sable. It shows off my hair.'

'Jesus! All right, one sable.'

'With a matching hat.'

'And a matching Rolls-Royce?'

'I haven't had a Rolls,' Anna said, ignoring the sarcasm, 'since leaving Bally; the Germans went in for Mercs. Anyway, it wouldn't do me much good, would it, if I'm not being allowed to take a driving test.'

He could never be sure when she was taking the mickey. He knew that she possessed a wicked Irish sense of humour, which presumably had been as necessary as a thick skin for someone in her profession, if she intended to remain sane. 'Maybe, when you come back, we can sort something out.'

'I'm glad you put it that way. I've always preferred the word 'when' to 'if'.'

'That's what I want to talk about. What happens after you get to South America.'

'Where I suddenly come alive again.'

'Well, not too obviously. But we must expect that both the Russians and the Brits will pick up on the reappearance of the Countess von Widerstand.'

'That prospect makes me very happy.'

'We intend to look after you.'

'How?'

'How would you like to have a lover?'

Anna stuck out her tongue.

'I'm serious. Someone like the Countess von Widerstand would have a lover. Don't you think?'

'And you are elected?'

'Would that be so very repugnant to you?'

'Joe, I don't want to be rude, but when I am in bed with a man, I like it to be just him and me, with nothing on our minds but sex.'

'I remember,' he said fervently.

'And believe it or not, despite my reputation, I have never tried three in a bed. And Lars Johannsson was rather a large man.'

'So I have to carry that millstone round my neck for the rest of my life.'

'We shall have to see how this turns out. But right now, it's there.'

'I'll accept that. Actually, my new boss feels that I may be a bit past field work.'

'I'd agree with him.'

'Because I didn't fire a shot? You told me not to fire until they actually got into the house. I had no idea you were going to take over on that scale.'

'Taking over on that scale, as you put it, is the only way to survive that kind of situation. So if you're not actually lining up for the job, who is?'

'A guy called Jerry Smitten.'

'You have got to be pulling my leg.'

'Jerry is one of our very best men. I'm not going to claim that he's in your league, but I can assure you that he's in a higher league than any heavy likely to be thrown at you by either the MGB or MI6. And that includes Clive.'

'Sounds like fun. What exactly is our relationship?'

'Jerry has already been posted to Rio.'

'Isn't that a little bit obvious?'

'Oh, he's not one of us, officially. He's with a real estate agency which we happen to control. You and he are going to meet, accidentally – it's all arranged – and he will be, smitten.'

'You are making my day. I hope he is reasonably attractive.'

'The girls in the office say that he's a knock-out.'

'Which undoubtedly means that he's an arrogant bastard. Why Rio? I thought the choice of location was to be mine?'

'The department has opted for Rio. Their information is that you are more likely to make contact there.'

'I see. How much will this Smitten character know about me?'

'He's been given the file to read.'

'I see. And how will I actually know him, supposing I don't swoon at the sight of him?'

'The word is Georgia girl.'

'Georgia girl. Sounds like a movie.' She looked past him 'Good morning, Commander Norstrum.'

'And to you, Countess. I reckon Mr Andrews has had you long enough. And it's time for lunch.'

Sisters

'Countess!' Eleanor Andrews held Anna's hands.

'Anna, please.'

'And I'm Eleanor, remember?' Like her son, she was tall, and somewhat angular, with a long face and pointed features. Anna supposed that she had never been beautiful, or even pretty, but she exuded a warmth that was irresistible. 'How good to see you again. How long has it been?'

'Getting on for five years,' Anna said.

'My! And do you know, you have not changed a bit.'

'You always were a flatterer,' Anna said.

'I always tell the truth, you mean. Now, I have put you in the same room you had the last time you were here. I hope that will be all right?'

'That will be perfect.'

Eleanor escorted her up the stairs. 'Whatever happened to that pretty little maid of yours?'

'I'm afraid she has moved on.' Presumably to Hell.

'Oh, well,' Eleanor said sympathetically. 'Nothing lasts forever. Here we are.'

Anna followed her into the room, went to the window to look out. 'This place always makes me think of Heaven.'

The apartment in Berlin she had been given by the SD and which had eventually been bombed to rubble by the RAF, had been the last word in luxury, but had merely looked out on to the street and the buildings opposite. This place . . . she understood that the estate had shrunk considerably from the old Andrews' holding, which before the Civil War had been surrounded for miles in every direction by cotton fields, but it still overlooked gardens, lawns and little woods, even if the roar of a freeway could be heard in the distance. No bomb had ever been dropped here, and while she supposed there might once have been the tramp of Union soldiers on the drive, that was over eighty years ago. The air was clean.

'Well,' Eleanor said. 'You just make yourself at home and relax. I think Joseph would like a word.'

She left the room and was replaced by her son, who carried a small parcel. 'Happy?'

'I think I have been happier here than anywhere else in the world.'

'Well, then, when this is done . . .'

Anna shook her head. 'No, Joe. I have never been in the business of looking too far ahead; at least emotionally: it has always been too painful. Besides . . .' She gave one of her roguish smiles. 'Would you have me stand up the Smitten?'

He sighed. 'OK, business.' From his pocket he took a passport.

Anna opened it, slowly. 'I already have a passport, remember?'

'A British passport, in the name of Anna Fitzjohn.'

'Which you felt should be replaced with a German one in my real name. This is not a German passport.'

'Our superiors feel that you should have an American passport. If you get into trouble, we will find it easier to get you out, if you are an American citizen.'

'I see.' She turned a page. 'Oh, for God's sake. You can't be serious.'

'Don't you like it? A photographer will be in today.'

'Anna O'Flaherty? What refugee from the Keystone Cops dreamed that up?'

'It's a good old Irish name.'

'And how do I stop myself from laughing every time I'm so addressed. Oh, all right. What next?'

'The dressmakers will be in tomorrow morning. They work for us, and while they don't know who you are or what you're doing, they know that you require certain specialties.'

'Do I?'

'That howitzer of yours . . .'

'I'm not giving up my Luger, Joe. Clive wanted me to do that when he installed me in that 'safe' house. If I'd gone along with that idea, we'd both be dead.'

'Point accepted. All we want you to do is modify your approach. You carry the Luger in that shoulder bag that you're never without, right? It's too big and heavy to be carried anywhere else, save in a holster, and you have to agree that ladies simply don't walk down the street, at least in this country in peace time, with a pistol holster on their belts. Now, normally, there wouldn't be a problem, at least in this climate. All women carry bags. That yours is slightly larger than the average is your choice. But in Brazil, not only do people wear far less clothing but they don't as a rule carry shoulder bags, except perhaps when shopping. There is also the point that these guys we are hoping are going to come out of the woodwork are people who know you and your methods, and will be keeping an eye out for that famous bag.'

'I presume you are going to tell me what this is all about, some time before Christmas.'

'We think you'd be better off with this.'

He held out the parcel. Anna took it, carefully unwrapped the paper, regarded the box inside with disfavour, as she had a pretty good idea what it contained. She released the catch and flipped up the lid, contemplated the little pistol, complete with its holster and attached to a thin leather belt, embedded in the setting with even more disfavour. 'This is a Walther Polizei Pistole Kriminal.'

'A PPK. Ten out of ten.'

'It is intended for policemen on the beat.'

'Again correct. Have you ever used one?'

'The first two men I killed were with a Walther.' The memory of that poor, agonized man running across the target range in front of her, knowing he was about to die just so that she could prove to her trainers that she could kill, would be with her to her grave, she knew. Just as the memory of poor Gottfried Friedmann sitting on her settee, with her arm round his shoulders, unaware that her pistol was within an inch of his ear and that he had been condemned to death by Heydrich for discovering too much about her was a recurring nightmare. 'But the circumstances were unusual. It is not really lethal.'

'Of course it is lethal. You have just said you have killed with one.'

'At twenty-five yards, or very close up. I could hardly miss.'

'But you never miss. And how often have you had to shoot a man at more than twenty-five yards?'

'Well . . .' Anna took out one of the two magazines. 'Seven point six five. That is barely a quarter of an inch. You would have to hit the target dead centre to kill.'

'Don't you always hit, dead centre?'

She was not to be mollified by flattery. She took the holster out of the box, drew the pistol and palmed it. 'They call this the ladies' gun.'

'That is because it will fit into a lady's hand, as you are demonstrating, and better yet, into a small evening handbag.'

She took out the silencer. 'Brauch.'

'They are the best. You'll see that it fits into that little pocket in the belt.'

'Very neat. But is it necessary? This little thing doesn't make a lot of noise.'

'Enough. With that silencer, there is no noise at all.'

'A silencer,' Anna pointed out, 'reduces muzzle velocity.'

'It will still kill at twenty-five yards.'

'If I'm to use a silencer in any event, there is a nine millimetre version which is far more efficient.'

'That makes it too big and too heavy.'

'Too big and too heavy for what?'

'The dressmakers coming in tomorrow are going to fit you out with special clothes.'

'Oh, yes?'

'Your dresses, like most dresses nowadays, with have a zip up the back. But there will also be a zip on the side. This will enable you to get your hand inside the dress very quickly and unobtrusively.'

'What for? Am I supposed to play with myself in public?'

'I'm trying to concentrate. All the dresses will be made with a full skirt. I understand it is the latest fashion.'

'I'm listening.'

'This enables them to conceal any small protuberance on your stomach. They used to do this in the old days to conceal women's pregnancies virtually up to the moment of delivery. So you will be wearing, under you skirt, this belt with the holster attached. It will fit neatly into your groin, easily accessible through the side vent in the dress, but not easy to discern. Even the normal body search, as you know, is a matter of sliding the hands from the armpits down to the thighs. Not into your knickers. You with me?'

'When I stop laughing. You've obviously never been searched by Albrecht.'

'Who is Albrecht?'

'I have an idea it could be was. He was Himmler's butler, who was required to search everyone visiting the Reichsfuehrer at his apartment. He believed in getting to know his subjects very closely, especially if they were good-looking women.'

'Please, Anna. We're trying to protect you in every way we can.'

'But apart from ruining my love life, you are not offering me a bullet proof bra.'

'Well, we could do that, I suppose.'

'Forget it,' Anna said. 'I don't wear the things.'

'There is someone to see you, Herr Laurent,' said the male secretary.

'Is there an appointment?'

'No, sir.'

'Well, then, tell him to make an appointment and I may be able to see him in a day or two.'

'The young lady seems to think that you know her, sir.'

Henri Laurent leaned back in his chair. His youthful appearance, the sleek black hair brushed straight back from his forehead, the athletic body encased like a glove in the immaculate dark blue three-piece suit, the handsome features, the powerful dark eyes, always surprised clients meeting him for the first time, as they invariably expected so well-known an investment banker to be middle-aged and overweight.

The more perceptive might have discerned that he understood the effect his appearance usually had on other people. And especially those of the opposite sex, providing they were the least attractive. 'Did you say young woman?' he asked.

'Oh, indeed, sir.'

'And is she, ah . . .?'

'She is most handsome, sir.'

'I assume she has a name?'

'Fehrbach, sir.'

'What?' Laurent sat bolt upright. 'Fehrbach? You are sure?'

'That is the name she gave, sir.'

Laurent stared at the young man, but without seeing him. He was looking at quite another face, which returned to haunt his dreams often enough. If Anna Fehrbach, Countess von Widerstand, was the most beautiful woman he had ever known, much less who had shared his bed, she was also the woman he least wanted to see again. He could not doubt that by now she knew that he had intended to hand her over to the Swiss police to avoid any risk of being implicated in the deaths of the two Gestapo agents she had shot in Geneva in 1943 on her way to see him on behalf of Himmler; his reputation as a banker did not leave him room for a relationship with a wanted international serial killer to become public.

He had been 'dissuaded' from that course by that British

bastard Clive Bartley, who had simply pointed out that if he did not comply with British requirements to get Anna out of the country, they would publish details of the vast amount of money, stolen from the victims of the Nazi regime, that he had laundered for Himmler. But Bartley had also assured him that he would never be troubled by Anna again. And in any event, would Anna dare come back, even looking for vengeance? If the Swiss police were not aware that the Countess von Widerstand was actually a pseudonym for an Austro-Irish woman named Anna Fehrbach, the countess herself was still wanted for murder.

The secretary was waiting, clearly surprised by his boss's reaction. Laurent pulled himself together. 'I think I should see the young lady now, Rudolf. But I would like you to be present.'

'Of course, sir.' Rudolf opened the door. 'Will you come in, please.'

Laurent rose, and gazed at the woman in the doorway. It was . . . the long yellow hair, the same classical features, the tall, inviting body . . . but something had happened to it. The flawless face had become coarsened, the silk-like golden hair seemed to have thickened, the body to have lost its ever-present sensuality .. and the eyes, if large and blue, were curiously lifeless, like those of a shark. Which was not to say that this was not a most attractive woman, but to compare her with the Anna he remembered was to compare a cart horse with a thoroughbred.

'Anna?' he asked. 'It cannot be.'

'Anna is my sister, sir. I am Katherine Fehrbach.' She spoke perfect German.

'Your . . . good God!' He sank into his chair, and as an afterthought gestured her to one. 'And she sent you . . .?'

'No, sir. I have not seen Anna since September 1944. I am trying to find her.'

Laurent gazed at her while he took stock of the situation. Then he remembered that they had company. 'Thank you, Rudolf,' he said. 'That will be all.'

Rudolf looked more mystified than ever, but he left the office, closing the door behind him.

'In 1944,' Laurent said, 'Anna was serving the Reich. And you . . .?'

'I was her private secretary.'

'My God! She never mentioned that she had a sister. But you left Germany in September of that year? Where did you go?'

'I went to Russia, Herr Laurent.'

'In 1944 Germany and Russia were at war. You mean you defected? To Russia?'

'No, sir. I was abducted from Warsaw by a Russian undercover squad.'

'Warsaw! My God! The incident publicized by Goebbels! When Anna shot six Russians dead.'

'Yes, sir. But she could not stop the rest getting away, with me.'

'And you have spent eighteen months—'

'In Gulag Number Forty-One, Herr Laurent. Do you know what a gulag is?'

'Well . . . I have heard—'

'It is a prison camp. Where one has no rights at all, and no duties, save those of submission.'

Laurent licked his lips as he found himself imagining what this handsome and voluptuous young woman would have undergone. For eighteen months? 'But they let you go, eventually. Did they say why?'

Katherine shrugged. 'They told me the War was over, and they had no more reason for holding me. They kidnapped me in mistake for Anna, you see. But now they say they are no longer interested in her, either.'

If you believe that, Laurent thought, then you really are a dumb blonde. Or your brain has been addled by mistreatment. 'So they repatriated you . . . to Austria, or to Germany?'

'To Switzerland.'

'I'm afraid I don't understand. Are you Swiss?'

'I don't understand either, sir. As to whether I am Swiss . . . I have a Swiss passport which is apparently genuine. I don't know why they gave me that. I don't know why they gave me good clothes to wear, put me in a clinic for a month to regain my health. They said they were trying to atone for the dreadful mistake they had made.'

'And you believed them?'

Katherine's lips twitched. 'No, sir. But—'

'You are here, out of Russia, and that is all that matters. I quite understand that.' And, he thought, you don't have a clue as to what is happening. You do not understand that they are using you as a bait, either to draw Anna out of hiding, or to lead them to her. And in the first instance, you have led them to me. God Almighty! The last thing he wanted was to become involved with the MGB. But . . . 'How did you know that I was acquainted with your sister?'

'Anna told me of you. Every time she came to Switzerland, it was to visit you. For Herr Himmler.'

'Did you tell anyone in the gulags this? Anyone in Russia?'

Now her lips twisted, violently. 'I did not tell them anything, sir. No matter how often they asked. But now . . . I hoped you would be able to tell me how to locate Anna. She is my only living relative. She will be able to look after me.'

'Of course.' How the hell was he going to handle this? But if the MGB really were on her trail, and had pointed her in the right direction, if he played his cards right he would not only make sure that they passed him by, but it might also assist them in catching up with Anna. Did he really want to send all of that beauty, with whom he had shared so many unforgettable hours, to perdition, whether in the form of a hangman's noose or a living hell in a gulag? But of all his nightmares, the worst was having Anna one day walk through that door: he knew her too well, that she never forgot or forgave an injury, much less a betrayal.

And there was this young woman to be enjoyed, first. She might not be in Anna's class, but she was an acceptable substitute. And having sex with someone who had been in the hands of the MGB for eighteen months should be a most interesting experience. But there was a caveat, which needed to be explored. 'You say you were your sister's secretary?'

'Yes, I was.'

'That would have been while she was working for Herr Himmler.'

'Well, of course. That is how I know of you.'

'Oh, quite. So I may assume that you know about the SD?'

'I was a member of the SD,' Katherine said, proudly.

'Good Lord!'

'Is there something wrong with that?'

'Ah . . . when the Soviets released you, did they give you any, well, information, on the state of the world today?'

'I know that Germany lost the war, Herr Laurent.'

'And therefore you know that Herr Himmler is dead. So are Hitler, and Goebbels. And the entire remaining Nazi hierarchy are presently on trial in Nuremberg, for crimes against humanity.'

Katherine's eyes became animated, but cold. 'You're lying.'

'I assure you I'm not.'

'But that is impossible. The Fuehrer was a head of state, conducting a war against the state's enemies. How can he be accused of crimes against humanity? Was Bonaparte accused of crimes against humanity?'

'I'm afraid that times have changed since Bonaparte's day. Nor, to be fair, were his crimes, caused purely by going to war, comparable with the excesses of the Nazi regime. I hope you agree.'

Katherine's eyes were blazing. 'You are insulting the greatest man who ever lived.'

'Ah. Would I be right in assuming that you were a Nazi?'

'Of course I was a Nazi. I am a Nazi. I shall be a Nazi until the day I die.'

'Well, if I were you, I wouldn't boast of it. They are not very popular right this moment.'

She might not have heard him. 'Are you saying that Anna is under arrest?'

'It's a long story.' He was thinking very hard. Was any advantage to be gained by telling her the truth about her sister? She obviously had no idea that Anna had been an English spy. Her reaction to learning that, if she was as fanatical a Nazi supporter as she appeared, might be amusing. But did he want to be the one to tell her the truth? Certainly not if he intended to enjoy her, or to send her after her sister. And if she did manage to find Anna, and discovered that she had devoted her adult life to bringing the Nazis down . . . the Russians might be redundant. He would have to feel his way. 'Did you know that your parents are alive?' he asked.

Katherine's head jerked. 'Where are they?'

'Anna got them out.'

'Anna? But then—'

'I don't know precisely where they are at the moment. But I think I can tell you where they went. Unfortunately . . .' he looked at his watch. 'It is rather a long story and I have an appointment in five minutes.'

'Oh!' Her face fell.

'But why don't you have lunch with me, and I will tell you the whole story. Would you like that?'

'Oh, please.'

'Well, then, return here at twelve thirty, and we will . . . have a long chat.'

'Ahem!' Amy Barstow said.

Clive looked up. His normal good humour had been totally absent over the past few weeks, even if the events in Scotland had so far been hushed up as an unexplained catastrophe. 'Yes?'

'You won't believe this, ' Amy said. 'But there is a Miss Fehrbach to see you.'

'What?' Clive rose to his feet as if she had just fired a shot.

'It's not the one you want,' Amy said, apologetically. 'This one's name seems to be Katherine. But there is definitely a resemblance.'

Clive tried to think. When first outlining her situation, back in 1939, Anna had mentioned that she had a sister, also apparently incarcerated with her parents. But that was seven years ago, and she had not mentioned her since. Not even throughout the last year, when there had been few of the distractions that had surrounded their always brief wartime meetings. Nor, he realized, had she brought her sister out with her; he had been so caught up in getting Anna to safety it had not occurred to him to ask after her.

'Do you think she'll know where Anna is?' Amy ventured.

'I don't see how she possibly can. But I'd better see her.'

'Would you like me to stay?'

'I don't think that will be necessary.'

'As you wish, sir.' Amy opened the door. 'Mr Bartley can see you now, Miss Fehrbach.'

Clive stood up, and did a double take. 'Miss Fehrbach! Anna's sister! You are almost the spitting image.'

'Thank you, Mr Bartley. That is a compliment.' She spoke English with the same delightful trace of an Irish brogue as Anna.

'Do sit down.' He indicated the chair before his desk, and sat himself. Amy rather ostentatiously closed the door. 'I'm afraid I'm a little confused,' Clive admitted. 'I mean, I knew that Anna had a sister. But, well . . .'

'We were separated, towards the end of the war.'

And not at the beginning, he wondered? 'And now . . .'

'I would like to be with her again. Herr Laurent said you might know where she is.'

'Herr Laurent,' Clive said thoughtfully; he, of course, had known all along that Anna was alive and in British hands. But that was a secret he had been bound to keep, if he wanted to keep himself out of trouble. Now . . . an act of charity to an unfortunate young woman? That bastard? 'You have come from Switzerland?'

'I am Swiss, sir. Now.'

'I see. What were you before?'

'Austrian, sir. Well, I suppose, German, after the Anschluss.'

'Of course. And now you are trying to find Anna. That is very natural. When last did you see her?'

'About two years ago.'

'In Switzerland?'

'In Austria. Before I fled the country.'

'You met her in Vienna?'

'Yes. That was where we lived.'

Clive knew that Anna had not been in Vienna, probably since the entire family had been arrested in 1938, but certainly since she had started working for him the following year. And this girl obviously had no idea how involved he was with Anna, or vice versa. Yet Laurent had sent her to him. Was he trying to get his own back for the way he had been blackmailed at the end of the war? 'May I ask why you fled Vienna for Switzerland, in 1944?'

'It was dreadful there. Nazis everywhere, strutting about the place. Not enough to eat . . . I only stayed because I hoped that Anna might come home. But when she did, and I found out what she was doing—'

'What was she doing?'

'Well, killing people for the Reich . . .' She frowned. 'Herr Laurent said you knew all about her.'

'He did, did he? She is supposed to have done these things because the Nazis held her parents hostage for her loyalty. Do you know about this?'

'Isn't that what she would claim?'

'True. And of course, you were never a Nazi yourself?'

'God forbid.'

'Of course. You'll forgive me, Miss Fehrbach, if I just attempt to get my facts straight. You fled Vienna two years ago, for Switzerland. You had no trouble doing this?'

Katherine shrugged. 'It was difficult.'

'But you made it. What did you do when you got to Switzerland?'

'They sent me to a camp. I only got out a few months ago.'

'And were immediately granted Swiss nationality. What a pity all the peoples in Europe are not so civilized.'

Katherine made a moue. 'I had a friend.'

'Of course. I assume you have a passport?'

Katherine opened her handbag and handed over the document.

Clive thumbed through it. It certainly looked genuine, even if the information it contained was clearly false; the birthplace was given as Geneva. He handed it back. 'Would this friend who helped you be Herr Laurent?'

'No, no. I met him at a party.'

'And . . .?'

'Well, he came up to me and said, just as you did: You are

the spitting image of someone I know. So we got talking, and when he found out who I was, he told me that you might be able to tell me how to find Anna.'

'Why did you want to find her, if you had been disgusted when you discovered what she did for the Nazis?'

'Anna is the only living relative I have left in the world.'

'You have your parents.'

'Oh. Yes. I'd forgotten that. We were never close.'

Clive regarded her for several seconds, then he said, 'I think I can arrange for you to see them.'

'And Anna?'

'I'm afraid that would be difficult, right now. As Herr Laurent seems to have told you, I located her in Switzerland at the end of the war and brought her to England because we wanted to question her about various matters to do with the Nazi regime. But she escaped our custody, and we do not know where she is.'

'You mean she is a wanted criminal?'

'She is wanted.' He was sticking carefully to the truth. 'What charges may be brought against her when we finally catch up with her is a matter for the Director of Public Prosecutions.'

'But your police are looking for her. Is that because she was a Nazi?'

'She is wanted for war crimes, as a Nazi, certainly.' Again, that was perfectly true . . . if not by the British.

'Oh, Lord! And if she is caught . . . will she be executed?'

'The precedent for dealing with those found guilty of war crimes will be set at Nuremberg. But I'm afraid it is a possibility. I am sorry not to have something more cheerful to offer you, Miss Fehrbach. But I can at least put you in touch with your parents. Would you like that?'

Katherine seemed to awaken from a trance. 'I do not wish to see my parents.'

Clive raised his eyebrows.

'They think I am, was, a traitor to the Reich,' she explained.

'I see. Well, then, you really have had a wasted trip. What will you do?'

'Can I stay in England?'

'For a while, as a visitor. But you will not be able to work, without a permit. How are you off for money?'

'I have money.'

'Ah! Well, then . . .?'

'I shall go back to Switzerland.'

'Probably a good idea.' Clive stood up, held out his hand. 'I'm sorry I wasn't able to be more helpful.'

Katherine squeezed his fingers. 'You had no help to give.'

The door closed behind her, and a few moments later Amy came in. 'Well?'

'There is something very peculiar going on,' Clive said.

'You mean she's not genuine?'

'Oh, she's genuine, all right. I mean, she really is Anna's sister. But that's about it. Just about everything else she said in this office was a lie.'

'You mean she's not really looking for Anna?'

'No. I think she is genuinely looking for Anna. But not as a long-lost sister. And she is being financed on her quest.'

'By whom?'

'I think that is something we need to find out. Get me Hawthorne, in Basle, will you?'

Anna always took off her sandals to walk on the beach; she liked to feel the sand crunching between her toes; nobody in Brazil wore stockings, anyway, at least during the day. Further following fashion she wore a pale blue sundress with a halter neck, which left her shoulders and arms exposed; she did not really want to accumulate either a suntan or freckles, but first thing in the morning there was only the breeze and the rippling surf to be enjoyed.

Her hotel overlooked the beach, so she came over here every morning after breakfast for a stroll. And this really was a beach; it extended for as far as the eye could see right up to the Sugar Loaf Mountain dominating the entrance to the harbour, and the fact that it was backed, almost the whole way, by high-rise buildings in no way detracted from its beauty; somehow that set the scene, a counter to the blue of the ocean that stretched endlessly eastward, and a portent of the crowds of sunworshippers who would soon be arriving to disport themselves and display themselves. Who would ever have thought that she, Anna Fehrbach, would be strolling along Copacabana!

She felt delightfully relaxed, even if she knew that the relaxation was temporary. But she had been told to do nothing until contacted by this Smitten character, and this had not happened yet. Thus for a week she had basked in luxury, and in the luxury of doing nothing more than eat, drink and walk in the sun, in utter anonymity. She was registered under her new name of Anna O'Flaherty, as indicated by her passport.

The blow took her entirely by surprise; she gave a startled exclamation, tripped, and crashed on to the sand before she could use her hands for a breakfall, so that she was winded. Her sun glasses flew to one side, her broad-brimmed straw hat to the other, her shoulder bag thumped into her stomach, and her shoes were knocked from her hand.

'*Madre de Dios!*' A man knelt beside her. 'Senorita?' A torrent of Portuguese flowed over her.

Anna pushed herself up, turned round and sat. 'What happened?'

'The lady is English,' said another voice, and she realized that she was surrounded by several young men, all wearing swimming trunks and all worth a second look, for varying reasons. They were from the group that had been playing volleyball a little further up the beach, as they had done every morning she had walked here. She had in fact stopped to watch them from time to time, because they were all so very masculinely well-endowed. And they had certainly been interested in the beautiful young woman with the flowing golden hair and the exceptionally long legs. Now they were peering at her, anxiously, as she pushed hair from her face, which was in any event covered in sand, as were her clothes, and discovered that her skirt had ridden up to her thighs and the legs they so admired were totally exposed. Hastily she pulled it down, less from modesty than from a fear they might discern the holster nestling against her knickers; she had taken up wearing the gun every day in order to get used to the feel of it. 'Actually,' she said, as she regained her breath. 'I am American. My shoes.'

One of the men held them out. Another picked up her glasses and a third retrieved her hat.

'We are most terribly sorry,' the English-speaking man explained. 'The ball, it bounced away, you see, and this fool went after it without looking where he was going. Apologize to the lady, Jerry.'

Anna turned her head to look at the man who had apparently charged into her shoulder. He was actually very good looking in a Hollywood fashion, although she could not go for his little moustache; men with little moustaches evoked too many memories. But his fair hair was attractive, as were his blue eyes, and he was certainly a hunk. And his name was Jerry!

'I am so terribly sorry,' he said.

'It was an accident,' Anna conceded, although it obviously had not been an accident. 'I don't think anything's broken.'

He held her hand to raise her to her feet, her skirt dropping into place. 'You're covered in sand. Shall I . . . um . . .'

'I think I can brush myself off, thank you.'

'You know, you remind me of someone I once knew. A Georgia girl.'

'That is the oldest approach in the world, Mr . . . ah?'

'Smitten, ma'am.'

'Smitten. Well, Mr Smitten . . .'

His companions were drifting back to their net, and one of them called something in Portuguese.

'These guys want to get on with their game. But say . . . you all right?'

'Yes, I am all right.' She waited; the ball had to remain in his court, for the time being.

'Well, um, any chance of seeing you again? I mean, I'd sure like to make it up to you.'

'Well . . . I'm in the Metropole. Just over there.'

'The Metropole. Right. And I guess you have a name?'

'O'Flaherty,' Anna said. 'Anna O'Flaherty.'

She sent her dress to the hotel laundry to have something done about the sand, and then had a shower and washed her hair. Then she bound it up in a towel and remained in her room for the rest of the morning, reading a novel, having opened the double French doors on to the balcony overlooking the beach, so that she could enjoy both the view and the fresh sea breeze; the room was air-conditioned but that was no substitute for fresh air. Her shoulder was actually quite sore, and she had barked her right knee. She was aware of tension, slowly building. Her holiday was over. And Jerry Smitten was promising. Apart from his looks, which she discounted – she had allowed herself to go for Henri Laurent's looks and that had been a mistake – he seemed to know his business. She had been in Rio a week, and on six days of that week she had walked on the beach, and watched the young men playing volleyball. As they had obviously been doing this for some time, he must have set it up, or at least joined the group, almost as soon as he arrived last month. But he had waited with consummate patience until there was no risk of anyone suspecting that it had been other than an accident. Now he had every reason to call her, to buy her that placatory drink.

So now she could prepare to go into action. Not that she expected immediate results. But the adrenaline was flowing.

The phone rang at noon. 'Senorita O'Flaherty?' Most of the

hotel staff spoke English, or at least American. 'I'm sorry to bother you, but there is a gentleman asking for you.'

'Has he a name?'

'Ah . . . Smitten.'

'Oh, yes. I met him this morning. I'll receive him up here.'

'Of course, senorita.'

She was still wearing her bathrobe, and decided against dressing; her looks and her sensuality had always been her most potent weapons in establishing her superiority – until and unless it became necessary to use force, but even then they had proved valuable assets.

Five minutes later there was a tap on the door. 'It's open,' she called.

He came in, and did a double take. She quite liked what she was looking at as well. He was wearing a lightweight lounge suit, with a quiet tie and carried a white panama hat, an outfit that enhanced the breadth of his shoulders. 'The girl said I should come right up,' he apologized.

'I have been trying to remove some of the sand.'

He closed the door. 'It had to be completely genuine.'

'It was. I must show you my bruises, some time. Would you like something to drink?'

'What have you got?'

'Nothing. But I can order something.'

'I kind of hoped we'd have lunch together.'

'I think that's a splendid idea. But they don't seem to eat around here until two, so there's time for a drink. Champagne?'

'In the morning?'

'You, Mr Smitten, have got to learn to live a little.' She picked up the phone. 'What have you got in the way of champagne? . . . Freixenet? I've never heard of it. . . . Ah, Spanish. Champagne cannot be made in Spain. . . . Because, my dear lady, it has to be made in Champagne. . . . You mean it is wine made by the same method. Very well. If that is all you have, send up a bottle. And two glasses. Thank you.'

She hung up and turned towards Smitten, who had been studying her while she spoke. But that might have been because the bathrobe, which only came down to her knees in any event, had fallen away from her thighs as well. 'I guess everything they say about you is true.'

Anna adjusted the robe and sat down, crossing her knees, thus again totally exposing her legs. 'I don't know what they say about me.'

'It's pretty unbelievable stuff, when you read it, kind of cold. But seeing you in the flesh . . .' He laid his hat on the table and sat opposite her. 'Say, did I do that?'

He was looking at her knee. 'Actually, the sand did that. But you were a contributory factor. You mean the fact that I have nice legs convinces you that everything they have written about me must be true?'

'Well . . . you really killed more than twenty people?'

'Is that what they put?'

'Yeah. You know how these guys like to go overboard.'

'Information always lags behind reality. Your people are a little out of date.'

'You mean you have done more than twenty stiffs?'

'Sadly, Mr Smitten, at the last count it was fifty-seven. May I call you Jerry?'

He stared at her with his mouth open, and there was a rap on the door. She got up and allowed the floor waiter into the room. He placed the tray containing the ice bucket on the table and she signed the chit. 'You want me open the bottle, senorita?'

'That would be very nice of you.'

The pop brought Smitten bolt upright in his chair.

'Thank you,' Anna said, and closed the door behind him. She poured, and handed Smitten his glass. 'Happy days.'

He gulped at the drink. 'You were putting me on, right?'

'Wrong.' Anna sat down, again crossed her knees, sipped. 'Does this bother you?'

'Bother me? Shit! I'm supposed to be your bodyguard.'

'You are to watch my back. I assure you that it's just as worthwhile as my front. Well, according to taste. Now tell me, didn't you serve in the war?'

'Well, of course I did. Subs. I got to be Lieutenant Commander.'

'Congratulations. Did you sink any enemy ships?'

'Sure. We got three merchantmen, and a destroyer. Those were confirmed.'

'So we could be talking of about six hundred people, I would say. Do you know how many survived?'

He shrugged. 'Not too many, I guess. We weren't hanging about to find out.'

'And my fifty-seven upsets you?'

'Hold on a minute. There were eighty of us.'

'That still works out at seven plus apiece. And if you were a lieutenant commander, you were the skipper. You gave the order to fire your torpedoes, each time.'

'Well . . . I never saw any of those guys face to face. But you . . .'

'So maybe you were lucky. Or maybe I was. I could at least keep track, and remember. Now tell me your set up. First, you had better top yourself up.'

He had drained his glass. He got up, and poured. There was a slight clink as the bottle touched the rim of the glass. 'We operate a real estate office. All legal and above board. I was sent from our New York head office to gain experience. This is good, because it will be obvious to anyone that you can't spend the rest of your life in an expensive hotel. So, as you're claiming to be American, you naturally go to an American outfit, and I show you round and so get to spend a lot of legitimate time in your company. So we get very fond of each other, and, well, one thing leads to another. Right?'

'It could happen. So now that we're set up, I'll insert that ad tomorrow.'

'You don't reckon we should leave it for a while? Like, get to know each other better?'

Anna finished her drink, got up, and topped them both up. 'I was told you are one of the best.'

'Yeah. Well . . .'

'I'm prepared to take that on trust.'

'I was thinking more of the personal side.' He could not stop himself glancing at the bed.

'And I am thinking more of that lunch you offered me. Our relationship has got to develop gradually, just in case anyone is keeping an eye on us. There's one thing, though: if you really want to get up close and personal, get rid of the moustache.'

'What?' His hand instinctively went up to his lip.

'It's up to you, of course. But I find moustaches very off-putting.'

'Hell! I wouldn't be me without it.'

'You were without it once, I'm sure.' She drained her glass and got up. 'I'm going to get dressed.'

'Oh!' He stood in turn. 'You mean you wish me to leave.'

'Why should you do that? You said you'd like to know me better. When I'm dressed, we'll eat.'

Criminal Matters

She had definitely unsettled him, the more so as he watched her strap on the Walther. But that had been deliberate, just to establish who was the senior partner, and to see how quickly, and how well, he recovered. Actually, he recovered very well, once they were away from her bedroom and in a seafood restaurant overlooking the beach, where he was apparently well known.

And he remained fascinated. 'I guess you've done this sort of thing often,' he ventured.

'Had lunch overlooking the sea? Not very often. Eating al fresco isn't all that popular in Europe, at least over the past few years. You need clear skies to enjoy it.'

'I reckon you know what I mean. Exposing yourself to extreme danger. Aren't you the least scared? Apprehensive? Well, tense?'

'I have nothing to be scared, apprehensive, or even tense, about, right this minute. I enjoy minutes like these.'

'But knowing what's going to happen . . .'

'I do not know what is going to happen. Whatever it is, I, and you, must be prepared to cope with it as it turns up. But I am exhilarated, at the possibility that something may turn up.'

'Exhilarated,' he commented. 'And the fact that you may be making contact with some of the most dangerous men in the world doesn't bother you.'

Anna munched a prawn. 'I have spent the last eight years, quite literally rubbing shoulders with the most dangerous people in the world. But in our line of work, one should always look at things from the other person's point of view. Don't you realize that if anyone of interest to us does read my ad, he is going to be thinking, if I follow this up, I am going to be making contact with the most dangerous woman in the world? That is what they call me, you know. And I believe they are right.'

He studied her for some seconds. Then he said, 'You are a very confident woman.'

'I'm alive,' Anna pointed out.

*   *   *

She was playing a mischievous but irresistible game with him, she knew. That was her Irish sense of humour bubbling up. Actually, she thought she was going to like him, providing he measured up, and providing she deflated his American ego. But perhaps she had already done that. She wondered if he would shave off his moustache.

He wanted to spend the afternoon with her, and then take her to dinner, but she declined, reminding him that their romance had to follow a slow and clearly genuine course, to make sure that any observer could have no doubt that it was genuine. 'Pick me up tomorrow morning,' she said. 'And show me some real estate.'

'And what are you going to do for the rest of the day?'

'Relax. And submit that ad.'

Which was not difficult to do; she had already composed it in her mind. 'The Countess von Widerstand is anxious to contact old friends. She is staying at the Metropole Hotel.' She had the reception clerk translate it into Portugese, and telephone it to Rio's leading newspaper. 'Are you really a countess?' the girl asked, impressed.

'That's what they say,' Anna replied, with utter truthfulness.

She could hardly expose herself more blatantly than that. But supposing things did develop, and along the lines she anticipated, she could not help but wonder what the interior of a Brazilian gaol was like. And then reflected that it could hardly compare with a Gestapo torture cell, and the Americans had promised to extricate her even from a murder charge. Supposing she could trust them. It was at least possible that they were using her to locate Bormann in the hope, or perhaps even the certainty, that as Bormann was unlikely to surrender himself to her, there would be a confrontation which should end in his death, as in fact she intended, after which she could be abandoned. But she was pinning her faith on the Nazi gold reserves.

She ate in the dining room and had a brandy in the bar afterwards. Wearing a low-cut black evening gown, which set off her golden hair, worn loose, to perfection, she was the object of attention, and as she was on her own, several men approached her, but she politely saw them off – they were all Brazilian. She found herself thinking about Clive, wondering what had been his reaction to her absconding, as he, and certainly Baxter, would see it. Her feelings towards him had not changed, even if she remained resentful at his apparent neglect, and suspicious of the reasons for it, stirred up as she had been by Andrews' suggestions. But she knew, were he to walk into the bar at that moment she would throw both arms round his neck. He would simply have to be made to understand that she could not live the rest of her life in limbo, as regards them as a pair. He was the one who had to make the decision, and it had to be made outside of the jurisdiction of his superiors.

Her thoughts had been heading in that direction throughout the past year. The appearance of Joe and then the Russians had simply crystallized them; MI6 could not even protect her! While Joe had promised her so much, once this assignment was completed. Of course he had promised her so much in the past, and like Clive had been unable to deliver. But this time, with so much profit in it for him and his government, she thought he would come good. Of course, once they got their hands on the gold they might try a nasty, but then, Himmler's orders to the men who had accompanied her on that last mission had also been to try a nasty, and return to Berlin without her . . . and they were all dead.

I am a monster, she thought. Or am I simply taking on the world, and so far, winning? Or at least, as she had pointed out to Jerry, staying alive. But when she was in possession of both her life and ten million dollars . . .

Belinda opened her door, gazed at the woman standing there. 'Anna?' she whispered. 'Oh, my God! Anna!' She threw both arms round her neck, hugged her, and then stepped back, frowning. 'You're not Anna!'

'No, I'm not. I'm Katherine.'

'Katherine?'

'Her sister.'

'Sister? I didn't know Anna had a sister.'

'Oh? I thought you knew her quite well.'

'Who told you that?'

'Herr Laurent. Do you think I could come in?'

Belinda looked past her into the corridor. 'Is Andrews with you?'

'Who?'

'Shit!'

'I beg your pardon.'

'Oh, come in.' Belinda stepped back and allowed her into the flat, then closed the door. Laurent, she thought. She had not seen the Swiss banker since the summer of 1944. He had entertained her to dinner, she recalled with some pleasure; such a handsome

and charming man. But he had done that because he had known
that at the time she was working as a courier for MI6, and was
on her way to Germany to meet Anna . . . a meeting that owing
to circumstances had not taken place. And this young woman
might, should, have news of her sister; it was now over a month
since she had given that bastard Andrews the address he wanted,
and he had still not brought Anna to see her. Although, from the
way Clive had behaved on the phone he might have put a damper
on that. She had actually toyed with the idea of going up to
Scotland herself, but had reflected that Clive might be prepared
to do something about that as well, and in any event, if Anna's
location was supposed to be such a deadly secret she had probably been moved somewhere else. But if this kid knew where
she now was . . . 'Sit down,' she invited. 'I was just pouring
myself a drink. Would you like one? Scotch?'

'Scotch what?'

Belinda raised her eyebrows. 'Scotch whisky. Have you never
heard of that?'

'I think so. Is it strong?'

'It can be. I can add water, if you wish.'

'Thank you.' Katherine sat on the settee, looking around her
with interest; Belinda's flat was both elegant and comfortable,
apart from the absence of any photographs.

Belinda fussed at the sideboard. 'I did know your sister quite
well, once. But one loses track of people, and with the end of the
war . . . were you involved in that? In the war, I mean. I suppose
you had to be. If you're Anna's sister, you must be Austrian.'

'Half Austrian.'

'Of course, you have an Irish mother. You can tell it from
your accent. Was it terrible, being in Austria, in the war?'

'I don't know. I was in Germany, with Anna. I was her secretary.'

'You . . . my God! Then you know . . .' Clive had never
mentioned her. Oh, he was another bastard. But then, he had
always kept secrets from her.

'Know what?'

'Well . . .' Belinda handed her a glass. 'That she was a double
agent.'

Katherine sipped, made a face, and put down the glass on the
table beside her chair. 'I don't understand you.'

Belinda frowned at her. 'But . . . Laurent . . . if he sent you to
me . . . you mean you didn't know that . . .' I seem to have put
my foot in it again, she thought.

'Mr Laurent said you were a friend of Anna's.'

'Because we both worked for British Intelligence. During the War.'

Katherine stared at her. 'Anna worked for the British?'

'Well, of course. That's why they, Clive, brought her to England. She's his mistress.'

Katherine continued to stare at her for several seconds, and Belinda started to feel uneasy; never had she seen such concentrated fury in anyone's eyes. 'Are you all right?' she asked.

'I am . . . surprised,' Katherine said. 'You say that Herr Laurent believed this?'

'Of course he did. Because it was true. I think she was his mistress, too. But if you worked with her . . . If you were her secretary . . .'

'Yes,' Katherine said. 'I cannot believe that you are telling me the truth, or that she would keep such a secret, could keep such a secret.'

'Oh, she's very good. That's why she was so successful. But I must say, I am also surprised, that she should have kept such a secret from her own sister. And that she didn't bring you out with her.'

'We got separated,' Katherine said.

'But you knew she was coming out.'

Again Katherine turned that devastating stare on her. 'I need to find her,' she said. 'Tell me where she is.'

'I wish I knew, believe me.'

'You are lying.'

'Well, really,' Belinda said.

'Everyone is lying to me,' Katherine said. 'But you . . . pretending that my sister was betraying the Reich . . .'

'I am not pretending anything. And you never even guessed,' Belinda said, thoughtfully. 'You poor kid.' Then she frowned again. 'But you . . . you mean that you were a Nazi?'

'Yes, I was a Nazi.' Katherine got up. 'I still am. Are you going to rush out and summon a policeman?'

'Well . . . No. As you're Anna's sister. But I think the best thing you can do is to leave England.'

Katherine stood above her. 'Because you, MI6, are keeping her hidden, awaiting trial. Perhaps you have already executed her. Confess it.'

'Oh, you are being ridiculous. You're demented. You need help.' Belinda attempted to get up herself.

*　　*　　*

'There's a Detective Chief Inspector Hartland to see you, sir,' Amy announced.

Clive looked up from his desk, frowning, his thoughts immediately drifting to Anna. Could the police possibly have a trace of her? He didn't know whether to be over the moon or aghast. 'You'd better show him in.'

He stood up as the policeman entered the office. They had met before, once or twice socially, more often on business, when Scotland Yard had been looking for a villain who had escaped overseas. Hartland was a self-effacing man, of medium height and medium build, with unremarkable features and thinning brown hair. His manner was invariably apologetic. Clive sometimes wondered if he was apologetic even when arresting someone; his brilliant record indicated that he did that quite often. 'Chief Inspector!' he said. 'What brings you to this den of iniquity?'

'I really am sorry to bother you, Mr Bartley.' He glanced at Amy, waiting in the doorway. 'A personal matter.'

'Thank you, Amy.' Amy made a face, but left the room and closed the door. 'Do sit down. How personal?'

Hartland lowered himself into the chair before the desk. 'I do not usually handle cases of this sort, as I'm sure you appreciate, Mr Bartley. But the circumstances, which could possibly affect MI6, well, my superiors felt it should be dealt with at the highest level.'

'I'm intrigued.'

Hartland took a notebook from his breast pocket, flipped over the pages. 'I understand that you are acquainted with a woman named Belinda Hoskin.'

Clive frowned. 'Yes. What's she done?'

'Acquainted?'

'As I am sure you have already discovered, Chief Inspector, we have been very good friends for a long time. Nine years to be precise.'

'May I ask when last you saw her?'

'Oh . . . must be about two months. We have rather drifted apart.'

Hartland produced a pencil and made a note. 'Your last contact with Miss Hoskin was two months ago?'

'No. I said that was the last time I had seen her. I spoke with her on the telephone about four weeks ago.'

Hartland waited, pencil poised.

Clive grinned at him. 'Sorry. It was a departmental matter.'

'Then may I ask you to account for your movements on the day before yesterday?'

'What the devil do you mean by that?'

'Mr Bartley, yesterday morning Miss Hoskin's body was discovered by her cleaning lady. This was at –' he looked at his notes – 'nine o'clock.'

Clive was staring at him with his mouth open.

'Apparently, Miss Hoskin had usually left for her office when the cleaner arrived; she had her own key. As you may imagine, the woman was in a state of shock. Still is. Our people were called, and our forensic team established that Miss Hoskin had been dead for rather more than fifteen hours. That is, she was killed some time before six o'clock on Wednesday evening. We have established that she left her office at half past four. They have told us that it usually took her about half an hour to get home. Therefore, she must have reached her flat about five, and as she was certainly dead by six, it would appear that her killer was either waiting for her, or arrived almost immediately, or most likely of all, followed her from the magazine office. But he was clearly known to her. There is no sign of a forced entry.'

'And you are thinking of me as a suspect?'

'Everyone who had anything to do with Miss Hoskin is at present a suspect, Mr Bartley. Our first task is to eliminate everyone who could not have committed the crime.' He again waited pencil poised.

Clive's brain was spinning. But he kept his voice under control. 'I understand, Mr Hartland. For the record, I did not leave this office until six fifteen on Wednesday afternoon. Miss Barstow will confirm that. She was here with me.'

Hartland made a note. 'But you do have a key to Miss Hoskin's apartment. In fact, you are the only person, apart from Miss Hoskin, of course, and the cleaning lady, who does have a key to that apartment.'

'What makes you so certain of that?'

'Miss Hoskin kept a diary.'

'Good God!'

'Actually, in going through her things, we discovered twelve diaries, covering the past twelve years. Before she met you. The diaries are fairly detailed.'

'Holy Jesus Christ! Look, Hartland, those diaries must be turned over to us.'

'I agree, there are some interesting references. Did she actually work for you?'

'Yes, she did. On a temporary basis, as a courier. That is classified information.'

'We'll have to take advice on that. But obviously it would be best for everyone if you were to co-operate.'

'I can assure you that the department had nothing to do with her death.'

'Directly. I accept that. But I am sure you can tell us where to look.'

'You think it's a hangover from her wartime activities? Why?'

'There are three reasons. One is that she does not appear to have had any domestic enemies, or indeed, relationships, except for you. Although there are some references to an Anna, sometimes referred to as Bordman, and others as Fehrbach. Would that be the German spy, known as the Countess von Widerstand? I remember the Bordman case quite well.'

What a shitting mess, Clive thought. But still he kept his voice even. 'Your assumption is correct, Chief Inspector. As I have said, Miss Hoskin did some work for us during the war, and I'm afraid she came into contact with the countess.'

'Who seems to have made quite an impression, going on the comments in the diaries. But of course, the countess cannot have had anything to do with Miss Hoskin's death, as she herself died in Berlin a year ago.'

Another interrogatory pause. But Clive had no intention of giving anything away, certainly until he had spoken with Baxter. 'That is our understanding, yes.'

'Still, it provides a possible link between Miss Hoskin's murder and her wartime activities. This is supported by my second reason for supposing there is, or could be, such a link. The killing was a highly professional job. More of an execution than either a crime of passion or a chance encounter with an intruder. As for instance, there are no fingerprints to be found, apart from those of Miss Hoskin and her cleaning lady. There were two glasses in the sink, and while one bears the prints of Miss Hoskin, the other had been wiped clean. That is our third reason. The fact that Miss Hoskin shared a drink with her killer, and thus that she was known to her.'

'Oh, shit!'

'Exactly. And then there is the method of execution.'

'How?' As if he could not guess.

Another look at his notes. 'Miss Hoskin was killed by a blow to the neck. What is often, loosely, referred to as a karate chop. This blow, as I am sure you know, is intended to inhibit the flow of blood through the carotid artery to the brain, thus inducing loss of consciousness, and in certain cases, death. But to be lethal it has to be delivered with extreme force and timing and in exactly the right place. That is, by someone who had been specifically trained to deliver it. However, when a post mortem was carried out on Miss Hoskin yesterday afternoon, it was discovered that not only was the artery severely damaged but that two bones in the neck beyond it had been fractured. Whoever hit Miss Hoskin with such consummate force and accuracy, had to have been trained, not merely to use unarmed combat, but specifically to kill. In other words, a professional assassin.'

'Shit,' Clive commented again 'Shit, shit, shit.'

'So tell me who it is. Or even who it could be.'

'I'll have to take advice, from upstairs.'

Hartland considered for a moment, then looked at his watch. 'Very good. But I'd like to hear from you by four o'clock this afternoon.'

'Good God!' Baxter said. 'You mean she's been here all this time? But why should she kill Belinda? Didn't you tell me that they were rather close friends?'

'Anna did not kill Belinda,' Clive said.

'Oh, come now. She could as well have signed her name. Didn't you see her kill that woman Mayers with a single blow to the neck? Didn't that poor fellow in Prague go the same way? And what about that woman Gehrig? She broke her neck while carrying a bullet in her gut.'

'Billy, Anna could do all of those things because she was trained to it at the SS school. But she wasn't their only pupil, you know.'

'Are you trying to tell me that there is another Anna roaming around? God help humanity!'

'I don't think there is anyone quite as good as Anna, but I imagine there is at least one left who has been trained to deliver that blow.'

'Another friend of yours, I suppose.'

'I wouldn't describe her as a friend. Anna's sister.'

'Anna's what? I never knew she had a sister.'

'Neither did I, until, believe it or not, Wednesday morning. She came to see me.'

Baxter reached for his pipe. 'You'll have to explain that, very carefully.' Clive did so, while Baxter scattered tobacco. 'But you say all of that was a pack of lies.'

'Yes. So obviously that I got on to Basle. Hawthorne has some information that for some reason never reached us before. Not even from Anna herself. Do you remember that shoot-out in Warsaw in 1944?'

'When the Reds tried to snatch Anna and six of them bought it? How could I forget?'

'But some of the Russians got away. Remember?'

'Well, I suppose not even Anna could do them all.'

'Yes. And Goebbels' official story was that the attempted kidnap had failed. But what no one ever told us, as I say, including Anna herself, is that the attempt did not entirely fail. They got away with someone they thought was Anna.'

Baxter's pipe slipped from his lips and had to be caught. 'This girl?'

'It had to be. Superficially, she looks very like her sister. That means that far from being in Vienna throughout the war, she was in Germany, and more, working for, and with Anna.'

'But not for us?'

'Obviously. That is why Anna never mentioned her. The point is that Anna was SD, and anyone working for her or with her would also have been SD, that is, SS trained, to kill, with a gun or with her hands. This girl did not have a gun.'

'Why didn't you report this, immediately?'

'I only heard from Basle this morning. And when I saw her on Wednesday, I wasn't sure it was important, in the context of finding Anna. I mean, this girl Katherine didn't know where she was, either. She wanted me to tell her that.'

'But you sent her to see Belinda.'

'Of course I did not, Billy. Everything she told me was such a pack of lies that I simply told her we had no idea where her sister was, or even if she was alive, and sent her off.'

'Then who sent her to Belinda? Who in the world apart from us knew that Belinda had ever had any dealings with Anna?'

Clive snapped his fingers. 'Laurent!'

'Jesus! I'd forgotten about him.'

'I think I need to have another chat with him.'

'Now, Clive, just remember that the war is over. Strong-arm tactics have got to be put on hold, at least for the time being.'

'But memories of what went on in the war are still very bright, especially with this trial going on in Nuremberg. Laurent still wouldn't want anyone to know that he laundered several million dollars of stolen money for Himmler.'

'Hm. I suppose you could be right. But what in the name of God made him point this homicidal sister at Belinda?'

'That,' Clive said, 'is what I propose to find out. I'll leave you to field Scotland Yard.'

Baxter started to refill his pipe.

Beria regarded his subordinate without enthusiasm. 'I would like you to explain to me exactly what happened this time.'

'Tserchenko is somewhat confused.'

'Tserchenko is always confused. So what does he say took place?'

Kamarov looked at the paper he was holding. 'As he reported earlier, the man Laurent sent Fehrbach to London. Tserchenko doesn't know what he said to her, but he obviously considered that was her best chance of picking up the countess's trail. Once in England, she went, undoubtedly on Laurent's recommendation, to MI6.'

'That is information? We knew all along that the British Secret Service was concealing the countess.'

'Yes. But this is the interesting bit. When she left MI6, she had some lunch, and then that evening visited a woman named –' he checked the report – 'Belinda Hoskin. Obviously she was sent there by the Secret Service.'

'That is a 'secret' service?' Beria asked contemptuously.

'They may have had a motive.'

'Ha! So what happened after that?'

'Tserchenko does not know. When Fehrbach left the apartment of this Hoskin, they lost her.'

'What?'

'I know. Sheer incompetence. However, we do know that she is back in Switzerland.'

'Having accomplished what?'

'We do not know.'

'Well, obviously, she did not find her sister. Do you think this woman Hoskin is worth investigating?'

'I think she might well have been,' Kamarov agreed, somewhat nervously. 'Unfortunately, she is dead.' Beria gazed at him, and Kamarov's anxiety increased. 'We don't know that Fehrbach killed her, although it seems likely. As to why . . . I suppose we could inform the British police where she is to be found.'

'Would that bring us any closer to finding the countess? The whole concept of using Fehrbach to find her sister has been a fiasco.' Kamarov prudently did not remind his boss that it had been his idea. 'Now you say that stupid girl is back in Switzerland, no doubt living off the money we gave her. Her funding will stop, now.'

'Of course, Comrade Commissar,' Kamarov agreed. 'Our people in Geneva wish to know if you require any action to be taken with respect of the man Laurent?'

'Who did you say he was?'

'A Swiss banker. He is the man to whom Fehrbach went immediately on being set free.'

'You mean she knew him already?'

'I do not know, sir. But he is certainly the man who directed her to England.'

'Hm. Perhaps he would be worth investigating.'

'Perhaps. But he, and the sister, are no longer relevant.'

'Explain?'

Kamarov took the newspaper cutting from his pocket. 'This arrived this morning from our embassy in Rio de Janeiro.'

Beria studied the clipping, which had an attached translation. He raised his head. 'Can this be genuine?'

'Well, Comrade Commissar, we know that the title Countess von Widerstand, Countess of Resistance, is entirely spurious, manufactured by the Nazis. Therefore this cannot possibly be someone genuinely possessing that name: there is no such family. And Brazil makes sense as a refuge for someone like the countess; they have no extradition treaty with any other country. In fact we know that there are several Nazi war criminals living there already. It would seem reasonable that, having got there, Fehrbach would seek such congenial company. Some of them may well be her friends.'

'That is good thinking,' Beria said.

'Thank you, sir. With your permission, I will despatch Tserchenko and a squad immediately, and I will instruct the embassy in Rio de Janeiro to keep her under surveillance until he gets there, just in case she decides to move on. But, in view of what happened in Scotland, to make no move against her until Tserchenko arrives to take command.'

'Excellent. There is just one adjustment you need to make.'

'Sir?'

'By all means use Tserchenko. He can identify her. But you will command the operation.'

'Me?'

'You, Comrade Kamarov. This woman cannot be allowed to escape us again.'

Kamarov considered. 'You do realize, Comrade Commissar, that this operation may take some time. Brazil is a long way away. We are talking about perhaps a month to get there, and if you want her taken alive, well, several days to set her kidnapping up, and then a month back. And a Russian ship will have to be laid on for the return journey, as she will not be travelling voluntarily.'

'You, and your squad, will go by heavy bomber. We will treat it as a courtesy visit to Brazil. I will arrange that now.'

'But . . . eight thousand miles . . .'

'You will fuel in Cairo, and then go on to Dakar in West Africa. You will fuel there, and then fly across the South Atlantic to Belem; Dakar is where Africa bulges farthest to the west, and Belem is where Brazil bulges farthest to the east. It is the shortest crossing, and it is the one used by the Americans during the war for moving their senior personnel to and fro. You will be there in two days. You will return by the same route, with the countess safely stowed away.'

'A heavy bomber,' Kamarov muttered. 'All of these arrangements. Is this woman really that important?'

'Yes,' Beria said.

'You'd better sit down,' Baxter recommended.

'I'm on my way to catch a plane for Geneva.'

'No you're not.'

Clive sank into the chair before the desk.

Baxter held out the clipping, which had a transcript attached. 'That came in from Rio, this morning.'

Clive looked at it. 'My God!'

'I think you need to take up smoking.' Baxter already was.

'But how the hell did she get there?'

'Courtesy of your friend Andrews, I would say. I'm sure you'll agree that this is more important, certainly to us, than chasing around after either Katherine Fehrbach or Laurent. Now that we know where Anna is, we can get her back.'

'How?'

'We shall extradite her, of course.'

'As it seems to have slipped your memory, Billy, let me remind you that we have no extradition treaty with Brazil.'

'Shit!'

'As for getting her back . . . for what purpose?'

'Eh? Because she's ours. Yours. Don't you want her back?'

'Yes, I do. But not to be handed over to the Russians, or to be put on trial for murder here. Whatever she did was in self-defence.'

'Only she can testify to that. And Andrews, of course. If she and he have made it up, he should be willing to give evidence on her behalf. Although how the hell he managed to persuade her both to forgive him, and run off with him, is still a mystery to me. Unless . . .' He paused, thoughtfully.

Clive laid the paper on the desk. 'Maybe the answer is right here. Just think, Billy. Firstly, she goes off with Andrews, a man who just over a year ago tried to have her killed. OK, she may have felt obliged to get out with whoever she could after dealing with those Russian heavies. So she makes her way, with or without his help, to Brazil, which she knows is a safe haven; we are pretty certain there are quite a few wanted Nazis there already. But having got there, she announces her presence, virtually to the world. It just doesn't make sense.'

'It would, to anyone not entirely besotted with the woman.'

'Would you like to explain that?'

Baxter's pipe had gone out. He knocked it out, scattering ash, and started to repack the bowl. 'Has it ever occurred to you that Anna may have been stringing you along? It could be for eight years? According to our man who got into the OSS set up in 1944, it certainly occurred to Wild Bill Donovan.'

'And you agreed that he was being ridiculous.'

'Maybe I did.' Baxter struck a match. 'I suppose I was under her spell then, as much as you. But maybe his unbiased interpretation of the facts was the more accurate. You have to admit that as you had been Bordman's minder in Berlin in 1938, when she first cropped up, Anna knew exactly what you were when she fell into your arms on that March day in 1939.'

'Now, look, Billy, we've been through all of this . . .'

Baxter held up his free hand. 'I know. She had just been brutally tortured by Heydrich and wanted out. May I ask you a question?'

'She had the marks of the whipping they gave her.'

'That wasn't the question. Would you agree that Anna is the most consummate professional spy, agent, assassin you have ever encountered? Or even heard of?'

'Well . . . yes, she is.'

'Right. And would you agree that if you had a mission for her to carry out, and it involved cutting off the last joint of her little finger, and you could convince her that it was important enough, she would self-mutilate without hesitation? Just as she would take a whipping if required to do so by her boss?'

Clive's face seemed to freeze.

'And while she has given us some very useful information, from time to time,' Baxter went on, 'can you be absolutely sure that it wasn't coming our way anyway? While the only big job we gave her, the assassination of Hitler, was a flop.'

'She was given duff material. By us.'

'Again we have only her word for that. That type of bomb worked in controlled tests, but not when it was in her hands. And the second bomb, the one used by Stauffenberg, certainly did go off, even if it did not produce the result we were hoping for. So she claims to have killed a lot of Germans; the only deaths we know of for certain, apart from a few dozen itinerant Russians, are three of our people and the crippling of a fourth, who later also died.'

'That was an accident, and you know it.'

'I do not know it, Clive, and neither do you. Again, we are accepting what she told us. As for the Reds, wouldn't she be even more likely to do that as a Nazi? Oh, and the list does include one American.'

'Look, the man was trying to kill her.'

'Has Andrews confirmed that?'

'I haven't seen Andrews since before that incident.'

'Right. So again, all we have is what Anna has told us.'

'Are you suggesting that Johannsson is actually alive? The Stockholm police . . .'

'Of course he's dead. But wouldn't he be even more likely to be dead if he found out that Anna was doing the dirty on her American employers, and made the mistake of confronting her with his knowledge?'

'And the two Gestapo agents she shot in Geneva? I saw their bodies.'

'That could have been something personal.'

Clive stood up. 'If that is your considered opinion, Mr Baxter, you must excuse me.'

'Where are you going?'

'To my office, where I shall write out my resignation. You will have it in half an hour.'

Baxter pointed with his pipe. 'Look, simmer down and sit down. I just want you to look at the situation from every possible point of view, because it may well involve our necks as well as anyone else's. And I am speaking literally.'

Clive sat down again.

'The business with the Russians,' Baxter said, 'has not yet come into the open. Seems that our employers are not yet certain how it should best be handled, and they have been able to point out to Moscow that the dead men were certainly part of a hit squad, which they would have to explain were it to become public knowledge. All the press knows so far is that a woman named Anna Fitzjohn was living in that house, and that she has disappeared. No one in their wildest flights of fancy has yet supposed that a single woman, who came across to those who met her as both very good-looking, very sweet, and rather inno-cent – Anna's trademarks – can possibly have destroyed four men who were all found with tommy guns lying beside them. So, total mystery. But the media, and the public, are going to want answers eventually. And Anna is the only one who can supply those answers. She has to come back, for all of our sakes.'

Clive tapped the paper. 'As I said just now, there is another, and even more plausible explanation for what she is doing in Brazil. The Yanks cannot possibly have gone to all this trouble to get her out of England in one piece just to pat her on the shoulder and say bye-bye and good luck. She's working for them. And she's working at what she does best. They've sent her after someone.'

'I don't give a damn what she's being employed to do, for the Yanks. She is still ours.' Again Baxter pointed with his pipe. 'I want her back, Clive. She's your baby, and your career. So go get her.'

'You mean—'

'Yes. Drop everything and get on a boat to Rio.'

'A boat,' Clive commented. 'You do realize that will mean an absence of at least two months.'

'Hm. Good point. We can't have that. You'll have to get on to our people there and let them handle it.'

'If we try that one, someone else is likely to be killed. And this won't be an accident.'

'Good point. All right. Use this Pan-American seaplane clipper thing. I believe it can get you to the States in a day or so.'

'That will still be several thousand miles from Brazil. And do I really want to set foot in the States? You wouldn't let me go last month, remember? They know who I am, and Andrews at least will know what I'm after. Listen, didn't our people, and the Americans fly to and fro across the Atlantic during the war?'

'I know Churchill did it once in a long-range flying-boat, but he had to fuel in the Azores. And even so he only just made it.'

'I'm not thinking of the North Atlantic, Billy. They used the route Dakar–Belem. That's the shortest distance, where the two bulges most closely approach each other. If I can get down to Dakar and then across, it'll only be a short hop to Rio. I could be there in two days.'

'You still have to come back, with parcel. You're talking about needing an RAF aircraft for at least a week, maybe longer. I'd have to get authorization from the very top.'

'Well, if it's that important, I suggest you get the authorization.'

Baxter regarded him for several seconds. Then he jabbed with his pipe. 'Don't come back without her, even if she has to be in a box. And Clive, if it does come down to a box, just make sure she's the one in it, and not you.'

'I hope I didn't hear that correctly,' Clive said.

Baxter flushed. 'I'm not suggesting that I want her dead. I'm just saying don't wind up dead yourself.'

'And equally, if I do persuade her to come back, I want a guarantee that she won't be charged with anything.'

'I'll work on it.'

'Not good enough, Billy. I want that guarantee, in writing. From the very top.'

'You think I have that kind of clout?'

'You, Billy? You're the most valuable man in the Service. Send that guarantee to me, care of the British Embassy, Rio.'

'I'll work on it. But . . . if I do get a guarantee, you had better not come back without her.'

'The view really is stupendous.' Anna stood on the veranda of the villa perched high on the hills overlooking the city, and beyond, the ocean. From her vantage point she could make out both the Sugar Loaf and the huge Christ Statue rising above the harbour.

'It is that.' Jerry Smitten stood behind her, and now, very cautiously, he put his arms round her waist to bring her back against him. 'The owner is away.'

Anna took off her straw hat and leaned her head against his shoulder. He had been growing on her over the past week, and not only because he had shaved off his moustache, although that had enhanced his good looks, and somehow also his virility. He was going to be very definitely an outlet for her frustrations. She was starting to suffer from impatience in her old age, she supposed; it was really absurd to hope for a reply to her ad in a week. But she had only put it in for a week, and today was the last day.

And in any event, she was supposed to have an affair with this character. 'Why is he selling?' she asked.

'His wife doesn't like heights.'

'Did he know this before or after he built the villa?'

'It was meant to be a surprise present for their twenty-fifth wedding anniversary. Twenty-five years. Say, how old are you, anyway? Or is that a question I shouldn't ask?'

'It is a question you shouldn't ask. However, as it appears to be relevant to the conversation, twenty-five years is a lifetime to me. Actually, I'm going to be twenty-six next month.'

'Wow!'

'I'm not sure how to take that.'

'You don't look a day over eighteen.'

'You say the sweetest things. Did you seriously think I was eighteen?'

'Well, heck, no. I mean, not after reading that CV, and then talking with you.'

'If I were eighteen, that would mean an average of three deaths a year from the day I was born. But you know, it still works out at better than two a year, from the day I was born.'

'You can joke about it?'

Anna freed herself and walked back into the huge lounge, kicking off her sandals as she did so. There were scatter rugs, but the mosaic floor was cool on her bare feet. 'If I couldn't joke about it, Jerry, I would have gone mad years ago. But I really am pleased at your observation.'

He had followed her. 'Which one?'

'About my age. One of the men who taught me everything I know once said to me that up to the age of twenty-five a woman should endeavour to look older than she actually is; after the age of twenty-five she should endeavour to look younger.'

'Profound. This was a Limey, right?'

'He was a colonel in the SD. Have you ever heard of them?'

'Some. Very hush-hush. Himmler's personal hit squad. Say . . . holy shit!'

Anna had opened a door at the far side of the lounge. 'This the master-bedroom?'

'No, this is for guests. The master is down that corridor. But you mean you worked for the SD?'

Anna went down the short hallway. 'You mean they didn't mention that in my CV?'

'It just said you worked in German Intelligence as a double agent for the Brits.'

'I suppose they didn't want to upset you. I was a senior officer in the SD, Himmler's PA' She opened the door. 'Now, this is what I call a bed.'

'It's outsize king-size. Never been used.'

'Let's try it.' She tossed her hat on to a chair and threw herself on the bed, on her back, and bounced, her skirt flying; she was wearing her sundress 'Good springs. One should never wear knickers in bed.' She raised her hips and slipped the flimsy silk down her thighs. She had never worn these before the past couple of weeks – in Europe she had always used cami-knickers – and had been introduced to them by the women who fitted her out in Norfolk. Now, in the Brazilian warmth, they were her only underwear.

The knickers reached her ankles, and she kicked them off. Jerry was staring at her.

'Do you always have that on?'

She unbuckled the belt and laid the little holster on the floor beside the bed. 'Required by our joint bosses.'

'I thought you had a gun in that shoulder bag.'

'I do. But they seem to think I need overprotection. Don't tell me you're not in the mood? Or are you having second thoughts about sharing your all with a mass murderess?'

He licked his lips. 'It's just that you're . . . well, kind of sudden.'

'I have always regarded that as an asset.' She released the belt for her dress, rose to her knees, lifted it over her shoulders, and threw it after the knickers, then fluffed out her hair. 'This is all there is.'

He sat on the bed beside her. 'You are just beautiful.'

She studied him, then rested her hand on his cheek. 'You really don't want to make the mistake of falling in love with me.'

'Why not?'

'Because, my profession is killing people. I am not ever going to be a success at nursing the baby and washing your under-wear. And I can't cook. Even if I could make a go of that, there are too many people out there who are determined that I should not.'

'You're saying that you are living on borrowed time.'

'That is exactly what I'm saying.'

'And you can say it so calmly?'

She shrugged. 'I've lived with that realization for eight years. Now, we're supposed to be lovers. Are we going to have sex, or have I entirely put you off?'

'You could never put me off, Anna.'

'Well, then . . .' She lay back, her head on the pillows.

He stood up, took off his jacket,

'My God,' Anna remarked. 'What is that?'

He removed the shoulder holster. 'A Colt forty-five. It will blow a man apart at a hundred yards, bring him down at a far greater range than that.'

'It must weigh a ton. I'm surprised you don't walk with a list.'

'It's to protect you.'

'I feel utterly reassured. Now come to bed.'

He laid down the holster and undressed. He certainly had a fine physique, but he had definitely lost his ardour.

'You'd better let me do some work on him,' she suggested.

'Just let me touch you.'

'Be my guest.'

He kissed her on the lips, very gently, then moved his head to kiss her throat, before tracing the gold chain down to the crucifix between her breasts. 'The CV didn't say you were a Roman Catholic, either.'

'It was a long time ago. But I like to be reminded. It keeps me human. I'll take it off, if you prefer.'

'Why? It's beautiful. Especially where it's situated right now.'

'It depends on how you like sex. If you want me on top, it could bang into your teeth.'

'Would you do that? Get on top, I mean.'

She wondered just how much of a sexual background he actually had. 'I will do anything you would like me to.'

'Holy cow! Where have you been all of my life?'

'Killing people,' she reminded him, wickedly.

'Oh. Yes.' He lowered his eyes to continue studying her; she thought he might be trying to commit her to memory. 'This is quite a birthmark. May I touch it?'

'Of course. But it is not a birthmark. It is a bullet wound.'

His finger had already stroked across the blue stain on her lower right ribs. Now his head jerked upwards. 'A what?'

'It is difficult to survive eight years in my profession without coming an occasional cropper. Have you never been hit?'

'No. But there? I mean—'

'It could have been fatal? As it was, it cost me three broken ribs and three months in hospital. And a husband.'

'I didn't know you were married.'

'I was, once.'

'And you mean he got shot too?'

'No, worse luck. He just didn't like the idea of me being shot.'

'And that was a reason for a break-up? That doesn't make sense.'

'It was the circumstances that upset him. Look, he's ancient history.'

'Oh. Right. I'm sorry. There's so much about you . . . does it hurt?'

'It happened seven years ago. Now we've talked enough about me.' She reached down to hold him. 'You're the one who needs help.'

Incident in Brazil

'Y ou know,' Anna remarked, as they drove back to the beach, 'I might just come back one day and buy that house.'

Jerry turned his head. 'We're talking half-a-million dollars.'

'Sounds reasonable.'

He concentrated on the road. 'You get paid that much for what you do?'

'Unfortunately, no. But it does have spin-offs.'

'I'm not with you.'

'I'll explain when I get around to buying it.'

He pulled into the forecourt of the Metropole. 'What now?'

'For me, lunch and then a siesta.'

'Oh! Ah . . . dinner?'

'That sounds nice. Call me. Not before six.'

'Six.'

She got out, blew him a kiss, and entered the cool air conditioning of the hotel lobby, collected her key from reception. As always after good sex, she felt delightfully relaxed. And it had been her first for over a month! It had begun slowly; Jerry had obviously been terrified of her – a situation she was quite used to in her partners, except for those who knew her very well, and that count was now down to one – and something of an innocent, but once he had realized that she would indeed do anything he wished he had become most enthusiastic, even if his desires had been limited by, she reckoned, a rather inhibited background.

Equally, however, as always after sex, good or bad, she was in a hurry to have a shower and a douche. She went to the lifts, stepped in, and took off her hat. She pressed her floor number, and the doors were just closing when they were parted again by a man, who joined her and allowed them to close behind him.

She had to assume that he was a tourist as he wore an open-necked and very floral shirt, a white fedora, two-tone brown shoes, and from his complexion was definitely not Brazilian. She put him down as in his early forties, and running to stomach. But she smiled at him politely. 'Mine is the seventh floor.' Her hand hovered over the panel. 'Which is yours?'

'I am content with your choice, Countess,' he said in German.

Anna's hand dropped from the panel to her shoulder bag, instinctively releasing the catch.

'You were expecting me?' the man asked, anxiously.

'I was expecting someone,' Anna acknowledged. 'Do I know you?'

'We have never met. But I have seen you, in Berlin.'

'Then I must have seen you.'

'But I am not so memorable, eh?'

You said it, not me, Anna reflected. 'You must forgive me, Herr—?'

'Schuler. Hans Schuler.' He held out his hand, and Anna released the bag to take it, watching his left hand as she did so. But the shake was legitimate. 'We could not believe our fortune, when we saw your advertisement in the newspaper.'

'We?'

'Well, one tends to stick with one's old associates, doesn't one? But to have someone of your distinction joining us . . . we thought you were dead.'

'It seemed a good way to be, at least in Europe.'

'And your real name is Anna Fehrbach, is it not?'

'Tell me how you knew that?'

'One of us is, was, an officer in the SD.'

'Tell me his name.'

'Gunther Gutemann.'

'Good God!'

'You know him? He said you did.'

'Yes,' Anna said, 'I knew him.' How very well had she known him! They had met in 1941, when he had been assigned to return her to the SS training camp for a refresher course after her escape from Russia. Then he had just been an appendage, but four years later, by which time she had become a senior officer in the SD and Himmler's personal assistant, she had selected him as her bodyguard for her ill-fated tour of the fighting fronts as 'Minister of Morale'.

Much to his delight, the intimacy engendered by that tour had led them to bed, but his ardour had cooled considerably after that famous incident in Warsaw. Up till then, he had known of her capabilities only by repute, but that night he had seen her in action for the first time, as she had gunned down six of the Russians who were part of the squad engaged in kidnapping Katherine under the impression it was her.

That exploit had not saved Katherine. Poor, poor Katherine! But Goebbels had seized the opportunity to publicise her exploit to the world. While Gutemann, standing beside her with a gun in his hand, had been so paralysed with awe as she had delivered six bullets each with deadly accuracy that he had not fired a shot . . . rather like Joe Andrews in Scotland, she thought.

After that episode, and their subsequent return to Berlin, they had drifted apart, and he had not been around when she had made her escape from the city. So equally, she had supposed him dead in the ruins, or a Russian prisoner.

'He is most eager to see you again,' Schuler said.

The lift stopped on the seventh floor and Anna stepped out. 'But he would not come himself.'

Schuler followed her. 'There are . . . reasons.'

'I see.' Anna unlocked the door of her room, waited for him to enter, then closed it again. 'So when do we meet?'

'I am to take you to him.'

'To Major Gutemann?'

'And others.'

'Who are?'

'You will probably know them when you see them.'

'I see. When is this meeting to take place?'

'You are invited to lunch, Countess.'

However eager she was to carry things forward, she had to remind them of her erstwhile seniority and her on-going arrogance. And she had no intention of entering the lion's den without a back-up. 'Then I must decline.'

'But Countess . . .'

'I have had a busy morning, and it is now my intention to have a bath and a quiet lunch, and then a siesta. But I am prepared to meet your associates for dinner, if that is convenient.'

'Dinner.' He looked quite crestfallen.

'It is only a few hours away. Is it that urgent?'

'Ah . . . I will have to find out.'

'Well,' she said. 'Do that and telephone me here.'

'Yes.' He continued to regard her, uncertainly, so that she had to wonder if he was considering attempting to force her to accompany him. She hoped not. For all her reservations she had no desire to lose contact with her target by laying out their messenger boy.

He clicked his heels. 'I will telephone you this afternoon.'

'Not before four.'

He opened his mouth, and she smiled at him. 'I shall be asleep, until then.' She opened the door, and after another hesitation, he clicked his heels again and left.

'Katherine?' Laurent peered at the young woman, not at all sure that he wanted to see her again. She had proved a most interesting but also alarming companion in bed, entirely lacking Anna's silky sensuality; Katherine had been hungrily demanding, more concerned, he felt, with satisfying her own needs than in anything he might want or do. He put that down to her years in a gulag, where she had clearly been raped time and again, and at least as often by women as by men.

But she had also conveyed a sense of uneasiness. If the very idea of Anna made him uneasy, it was because of a knowledge of who she was, and of what she was capable. But Anna had never been fanatical about anything. Ever since he had first met her he had been struck by her clear-headed single-mindedness. She always knew what she intended to achieve, and she always went straight for it. The only sideways glances she ever permitted herself were in order to protect her flanks, as it were. This girl's fanaticism was perhaps even more frightening, certainly when combined with her violently passionate nature. And by telling her how she could find her sister, who she would soon discover had been a traitor to her beloved Reich, he had supposed that he could eliminate them both, at least from his life. Now . . . 'Did you not find Anna?'

'No, I did not.' Katherine sat before his desk, uninvited.

'Did you go to the man Bartley?'

'He agreed that he had arrested her and taken her to England, but that she had escaped from his custody and disappeared.'

Laurent stroked his chin. 'That is what he said?'

'Isn't it true?'

He supposed it could be. In which case the bastard had got

what he deserved: he had considered Anna to be his mistress. But if she was no longer controlled by the British, but was roaming the world . . . , looking for vengeance? 'I suppose it must be, if he said so.'

'So I went to see the woman Hoskin.'

'And?' Almost he held his breath.

'She told me nothing but a pack of lies. I did not like her.'

'What lies?'

'She said that Anna had been working for the Allies throughout the War, that she had been a traitor to the Reich.' Those sinister eyes shrouded him. 'She said you knew this.'

Again it was time for another very quick decision. But quick decisions were not really his forte. He needed to temporise while he thought about it. 'I only knew Anna as an agent for Herr Himmler. You say you saw Bartley. Surely he would have known if she was a double agent.'

'As I said, he told me she was wanted for war crimes.'

'In which case she would hardly have been working for him. That woman was stringing you along.'

'That's what I thought. She made me so angry!'

'What did you do?'

'Oh . . .' Katherine made a vague gesture with her hands. 'I left her. I had to get away.'

'And so you came back here. So what are you planning to do now?'

'I have no more money.'

'I thought you were quite well off?'

'My income has ceased.'

So the Russians had written her off. Than was actually a relief; if they were no longer interested in her, they would no longer be interested in him. 'That is a shame.'

'So, I was wondering . . .' Katherine's tongue came out and circled her lips.

My God! he thought. She would like me to take her on. My own tame tigress? I would have to be crazy. But then he frowned. My own tame tigress. My own ultimate protection against Anna? At least until Anna was finally located, and dealt with, presumably by whoever got to her first.

'Well,' he said. 'I think perhaps we could come to some arrangement.'

Anna's heartbeat had quickened. If she had been growing a little impatient at not having her advert answered sooner, she had not anticipated suddenly finding herself in the midst of what sounded like a mini-colony of Nazis. Was it possible that Bormann might actually be present, and her assignment about to end so quickly?

But as she had told Joe, she had always made it a rule not to anticipate beyond making sure that she was ready for any eventuality. She had her shower and douche, and called the number Jerry had given her.

'Gold Coast Realty.' The woman's accent was reassuringly nasal, although it then went into Portuguese.

Anna waited until the spiel was finished. 'All I want to do is speak with Jerry.'

'Oh! Say, you're English.'

'Irish,' Anna corrected.

'Ah! Right.'

'Jerry,' Anna reminded her.

'Oh, yeah. He's gone to lunch.'

'He was going to call me this afternoon, but something has come up, and I need to see him sooner than that. So the moment he comes in, will you tell him that she needs him to contact her, immediately.'

'He has a client this afternoon. I don't think he'll be free much before four.'

'I thought all Brazilians took a siesta.'

'This guy is from Chicago. All hustle and bustle.'

'All right,' Anna agreed. 'After four o'clock will be all right. But no later than five.'

'I'll tell him.' Now the woman's tone was doubtful; clearly she was wondering who this dame was, laying down the law. 'Anna, you said? I'll need your surname.'

'Anna will do.' She hung up, and then ordered lunch in her room, before sleeping soundly for an hour. She was tense, as in Scotland coiled like a spring waiting to be released, but at the same time quite relaxed, as she always was when about to go into action.

She awoke at half past three to the sound of heavy rain, had another shower – even with the air conditioning she was finding it very warm – and surveyed her wardrobe. It had not been suggested that she would be attending a formal occasion, but as it would be evening and might include a meal she chose a high-necked and entirely modest dark green evening gown, realizing as she did so that the one thing her American outfitters had neglected to include in her wardrobe was a raincoat.

She had not worn this gown before – there had been no

occasion for it – and obviously it would be incongruous to wear a shoulder bag with such elegance; in any event, as Joe had pointed out, the men she was going to meet, and certainly Gutemann, would know all about her, and what the bag contained. She put on her knickers, then strapped on the belt, having checked the Walther's magazine. For all her reputation, she had always relied on overkill as much as speed and accuracy – there was always a spare magazine in her shoulder bag – thus she placed the spare magazine for the little gun in her evening bag; with its limited range and stopping power she might well need the extra bullets. Then she put on the dress, settled it, and stood in front of the mirror. The zip on the side vent slipped down at a touch of her fingers, her hand was inside and then out again with the pistol, all in the one movement and in hardly more than a second. I am learning new tricks, she thought.

The telephone jangled. She sat at the table and picked it up. 'Countess? It is all arranged. I will call for you at six.'

'May I ask how many of us will be present?'

'There will be eight guests, Countess. Four men, including myself, and four women, including yourself.'

'That sounds delightful. And you say that the only one who will be known to me is Major Gutemann?' He would have to assume that she knew Bormann.

'I believe so, Countess. But you are known to all of them, at least by repute.'

'How nice. I will be in the lobby at six, Herr Schuler.'

So, she thought, if Bormann is around, he is taking no chances; there was still a lot of work to be done. She brushed her hair, applied make-up, and then sat down, keeping absolutely still. She was composing herself, as she liked to do whenever she had some idea of what was coming, framing and hardening her mind to combat and overcome whatever might be soon to happen.

The situation was complicated by the fact that if Bormann was not present, if this was a trap, she could not just shoot her way out of it. She had to learn his whereabouts no matter what she had to undergo first. And of course, there was always the farcical possibility that he was not in South America at all!

While the presence of Gutemann could be either a safeguard or an additional complication. Having watched her at work, he knew everything of which she was capable. But only with the Luger she had always carried in the past. Tonight she would be unarmed, so far as he would be able to see. Would that lessen, or even remove, his fear of her, perhaps encourage him to get amorous all over again? She remembered that he had been quite good in bed.

The tap on the door ended her reverie with a start. She looked at her watch: five fifteen. She knew who it should be, but old habits died hard, and the possible opposition now knew where she could be found. She got up, drew the Luger from the shoulder bag, screwed her silencer into place, and stood against the wall where the door would open to cover her, the gun held against her shoulder. With her left hand she released the latch. 'It's open.'

The door swung in, temporarily concealing her. 'Anna?'

Anna pushed the door shut, and he turned to face her. 'God Almighty! Do you always greet people like that?'

'I'm alive,' she reminded him.

'But . . . that dress, and the gun. Wow!'

Anna unscrewed the silencer and restored the pistol to the bag. 'You're late. And you're dripping.'

'It's raining out there.'

'I had noticed. Does it ever stop?'

'It should ease off by dusk. I'm sorry I took so long getting to you. This guy took up more time than I had figured, and I got your message late. Something up?'

'I hope so. Sit down.'

He did so, and she also sat, and related the lunchtime events.

'Holy shit!' he commented when she finished. 'And you're going along with this?'

'That's why I'm here, isn't it?'

'Yeah. But . . . shouldn't I come with you?'

'I don't think they're expecting you. But I want you to be around.'

'You got it. Where?'

'I have no idea. You done any surveillance work?'

'It's part of the training.'

'Right. This character Schuler is coming to pick me up at six.' She looked at her watch. 'That is half an hour from now. So you go on down and get into your car and wait, and then follow us. Under no circumstances must Schuler realize he's being followed. Can you manage that?'

'Sure I can. What happens when we get there? Wherever.'

'You take up a position where you can keep an eye on things. I imagine the meeting will take place in a house; I've been invited to dinner.'

'At six o'clock? These people eat late.'

'I'm being collected at six o'clock,' Anna explained

patiently. 'It may be a long drive. And I imagine our discussion will take place before we eat, and may be a lengthy one. That's not relevant. What is relevant is that you identify the location and the house so that we can find it again. But you are not to reveal yourself unless there is a considerable disturbance, or shots are fired. I assume you have that howitzer with you?'

He tapped his shoulder. 'And when I come in, belatedly, I find you lying dead.'

'I am not anticipating that. But you must be where you can hear what's going on. I'm only carrying my little toy, and it doesn't make a lot of noise. But if I do have to use it, I may need a back-up.'

'You'll have it.'

'Right. But just remember one thing. I am not going there to cause trouble. I am going to a reunion of old comrades. I don't think our target is going to be there. I have to work it so that I either get to see him at some later date, or at least find out where he is. If we have to start shooting, we have failed, completely, in our mission. You got that?'

'Yeah. But hell, the thought of you, looking like ten million dollars, just walking into the midst of those thugs . . .'

'Jerry,' she said, 'as I told you, as far as those thugs are concerned, the biggest thug of all is me. Now move it.'

He squeezed her hand, and left. She allowed him ten minutes to get clear, put on her jewellery, inspected herself in the mirror a last time, and considered her sable. But it was a warm evening, and just in case the rain hadn't entirely stopped, she didn't want it to get wet. She pulled on her gloves, tucked her handbag under her arm, and took the elevator down, went into the lobby, handed over her key, and sat in one of the comfortable cane armchairs, trying to control the adrenaline flow: it was too early for that. But what she had not told Jerry was that if, by any chance, Bormann was present, she intended to complete her side of the operation there and then.

At six o'clock sharp, with Prussian punctuality, Schuler entered the lobby, wearing a white dinner jacket. 'Countess!' He bent over her glove. 'You look positively radiant.'

'You say the sweetest things,' Anna replied, 'I hope you have an umbrella.'

'Oh, the rain has stopped. It is a fine evening.'

She could see that his clothes were perfectly dry, and accompanied him outside to, predictably, a large black Mercedes; the rain might have stopped but she had to hold her skirt up as the ground was very wet. 'This is a very expensive car,' she remarked, as she sat beside him. 'Is it yours?'

'Unfortunately, no. It belongs to a friend.'

'He must be a wealthy friend.'

'He is a financier, yes.'

'A Brazilian?'

'Yes. He is a sympathizer.'

'Do I meet him tonight?'

'No. He likes to keep in the background. But I know that he will wish to meet you. You will not object to this?'

'I would not object to anything, from a . . . sympathizer.'

'That will make him very happy.'

They were in the suburbs. 'Is it a long drive?' Anna asked.

'The villa is in the hills. It will take us about an hour to get there. Would you like something to drink? There is a flask of schnapps in the glove compartment.'

'All the comforts of home,' Anna agreed. 'But I think I can wait.'

Soon even the suburbs were behind them, and they were following an empty road, winding slowly upwards. What a hoot it would be, Anna thought, if they were actually going to the villa she had visited that morning; Jerry had not seemed to know very much about his client, apart from the fact that he was wealthy. But that had been further south.

It was quite dark by now, and Schuler switched on his head-lights, at the same time looking in his rear-view mirror. 'Hm,' he commented.

Damnation, Anna thought. 'What is the matter?'

'We are being followed,' he said.

Oh, that stupid boy! Anna thought. He had said he knew how to carry out surveillance, and now he had obviously closed up too far. 'Isn't there usually traffic on this road?' she asked, innocently.

'It is a lonely road,' Schuler said. 'But now . . . this fellow is a madman.'

'What?' Anna twisted in her seat, and saw a pair of headlights glaring out of the gathering darkness.

'There was another car back there, some time ago,' Schuler explained. 'He was driving on his sidelights, and I lost him. But this idiot has virtually pushed him off the road, and, my God, he is going to do the same to us.'

They were entirely illuminated by the lights immediately behind them, and now there was a shattering sound. Anna had

not heard the shot above the roar of the engines, but the rear
window had disintegrated, showering glass everywhere.

'My God! They are shooting at us,' Schuler shouted. 'What
are we to do?'

He had clearly been a civilian during the war. 'Drive faster,'
Anna suggested, unwilling to reveal the fact that she was armed
unless it was absolutely necessary.

But it was too late. After the shot, Schuler had instinctively
slowed, and now the other car was alongside them. This shot
Anna heard, even as Schuler's brains scattered across her gown.
The car swerved violently, and was clearly about to leave the
road. Anna reached for the door handle, and as the vehicle
plunged down the embankment she opened it and fell out. The
ground was soft from the rain but the force of her landing
knocked all the breath from her body, and she was rolling
helplessly through some very rough and very wet bushes, and
thought how fortunate had been her decision not to wear her
sable. She held both arms across her face to protect herself,
but listened to the material of her gown ripping. Then she
came to a stop against a tree, again winded, feeling as if she
had just been subjected to a severe whipping in a swimming
pool.

The car was still careering down the slope, but now it hit the
bottom of the shallow ravine and burst into flames. The other
car had pulled to a halt at the side of the road, and men were
getting out. 'You fool,' someone said in Russian. 'We wanted
her alive.'

'She could still be alive,' another man protested.

'In that inferno? Well, get down there and see. What a fucking
mess.'

Anna agreed with him immediately, because, had she possessed
her Luger, she could have disposed of them all before they even
realized where she was. But they were at least fifty yards away,
and in the gloom and possessing only the pea-shooter pressing
into her groin, she could not be sure of any fatal shot; she had
to wait for them to come to her. And as her handbag was in the
blazing car she had only five cartridges available . . . to deal with
four men. But she still intended to kill them all: as they were
Russians, she could have no doubt that they were MGB.

One of the men scrambled down the slope, some twenty feet
from where she lay. She felt her arms and legs and ribs to make
sure she was not hurt – there were bruises and some cuts but
nothing sufficiently painful to suggest a fracture, although her

gown had virtually disintegrated. Needless to say the side zip had jammed, so she pulled up what was left of her skirt and drew the Walther, located the silencer and screwed it in – stealth had to be her principal asset at this stage – then carefully rose to her knees.

'It is not your fault, Comrade Kamarov,' said a third voice, and this one Anna recognized. Tserchenko!

'The commander always takes the blame,' Kamarov grumbled.

'Comrade Kamarov!' The first man had reached the burning wreck. 'I see only one body. It is the driver.'

'Thank God for that!' Kamarov said. 'She may still be alive. Tserchenko, get down there and find her.'

'Comrade Kamarov,' Tserchenko protested. 'If that woman is alive, we are all dead men.'

'You are being hysterical,' Kamarov snapped.

'What about that fellow?' asked a fourth voice. 'I think it is the car we passed a couple of miles back.'

'But he has stopped. Why has he stopped back there?'

'He must have seen the flames.'

'Well, you will have to take him out. Tserchenko, I told you to get down there and help Sarakov find the woman.'

Anna could only hope that Jerry was alert enough to keep under cover, and positive enough to return fire, accurately. Cautiously she stood up, against the tree.

There was a crackling noise as Tserchenko came down the slope, pushing his way through the bushes. 'Sarakov?' he shouted.

'I am here, Comrade Colonel. There is no sign of the woman.'

'She is there. Watching us. Preparing to kill us.'

In the dark she still could not be absolutely sure where they were. But at least they were making a lot of noise, rather, she thought, like frightened little boys whistling in the dark.

From above her there came a shout followed by an explosion; although the report had clearly come from a large calibre weapon she couldn't be sure whether it was the forty-five or whether the Russians were equally heavily armed. Then the man shouted, 'I have him, Comrade Commissar!'

Shit! she thought. That poor, innocent kid. But he need not be dead; she had to help him. There was a rustling sound quite close. 'Would you be Comrade Sarakov?' she asked, softly.

There was a gasp, and the man blundered through the last of the bushes. Anna had already levelled the little gun, held in both hands as her muscles were still jumping from her tumble. Now she picked out his head and squeezed the trigger. It made only the slightest pfft, and Sarakov also went down without a sound save for the rustling of the bushes through which he fell.

But Tserchenko had heard the rustle; he also was quite close by. 'Sarakov?' he called again. 'Sarakov! Where are you?'

'Over here,' Anna said.

There was a moment's silence, then several shots were fired. Anna had anticipated this response, and as she spoke she had dropped to her knees. The bullets whined above her head, several smashing into the tree. Then there was a click.

Anna stood up again, and moved forward. 'Good evening, Comrade Tserchenko.'

Tserchenko stared at her; he was only a few feet away, and if she was hardly more than a shadow in the gloom, her hair still shimmered. 'Oh, shit!' he said. 'Oh, shit! Comrade . . .'

'Time to go,' Anna said, and shot him between the eyes.

Tserchenko's gun was empty and she couldn't waste the time scrabbling in the mud and the bushes to find Sarakov's weapon with Jerry's life in the balance. She kicked off her shoes, gathered her hair and pushed it into the collar of her gown to reduce the possibility of it being seen in the dark, and climbed the slope back to the road, hampered by the shredded remnants of her long skirt, which, if torn in several places, kept trying to wrap itself round her legs when it was not snagging on bushes or branches, and by the fact that she was carrying her pistol – she was not going to risk holstering it at this moment, although she unscrewed and stowed the silencer as it was no longer necessary.

She reached the road on her hands and knees, just behind the Russian car. Fifty yards away Jerry's car was stopped against the side of the road. She could make out two men, one standing above a lump on the ground, the other kneeling beside it. Her brain began to seethe; however incompetent he might be, Jerry had been growing on her.

She hitched up her tattered skirt, tucking it into the holster belt to free her legs entirely, and crawled along the embankment, knees sinking into the rain-softened earth.

'He is armed,' said the kneeling man. 'But the gun has not been used.'

'He could still have something to do with the countess. Finish him off. From those shots Tserchenko must have found her. She had better be alive.'

Anna had dropped on to her stomach and wriggled along the muddy parapet; she was now within twenty yards of them. She extended her arms, the Walther again held in both hands. 'I'm alive,' she said.

Kamarov turned with a gasp, reaching for his pocket, and she shot him through the head. The other man also turned and started to rise. Anna's first bullet struck him in the abdomen and he dropped to his knees again, gasping in pain. Anna's second bullet was to the head.

She stood up, and walked to the men. Both were dead. But she was more interested in Jerry. The headlights were still on, and she knelt beside him. He had been struck in the body and was bleeding heavily. But his eyes were open. 'Anna,' he whispered. 'Anna! I guess I wasn't much good.'

'You distracted them,' she assured him, and rolled him on to his back; his revolver was still in its holster. 'How much pain?' she asked.

'I don't know. It's all around. God, Anna, I'm going.'

'Not right now.' She tore open his shirt to expose the wound, which was jagged and nasty and bleeding copiously, then slid her fingers round his back. There was no exit wound, so the bullet was still in there. But she reckoned it was too low to have hit a lung, and in any event there was no blood mixed with his gasping breaths. In fact, she thought he might have been hit roughly where Hannah Gehrig had hit her, seven years ago.

She had survived with only a scar. But she had had help readily at hand. Jerry was lying on a deserted road, as far as she knew several miles from the nearest habitation, and even if the wound was not fatal he would certainly bleed to death if something wasn't done, and very quickly.

She put up her hand to brush hair from her face, and stared at the mud. She looked down at herself; both she and the remnants of her gown were also covered in mud. Mud! Probably germ-filled mud, but it might work, until she could get help, which would certainly include antiseptic injections.

It was time to think with her usual clarity; there was a lot to be done to cover them both. Jerry seemed to have lost consciousness. She pulled off his jacket, removed his belt and holster and threw them down the slope into the shallow ravine, then took off his shirt. She crawled to the embankment and scooped up as much mud as she could carry, returned to him, and packed the wound; it certainly stopped the bleeding. Then she tore his shirt into strips and bound it round his body. There wasn't quite enough so she tore off what was left of her gown from the waist down, and used that as well.

As any help she could obtain would obviously concern the police, she took off her own gun belt and carefully cleaned it and the pistol – which was now empty in any event – to remove any fingerprints, then threw them down the embankment. Then, gritting her teeth and using all of her strength, she got Jerry into the back of his car, covered him with his jacket, and inserted herself behind the wheel. McLachlan had said that she was ready to take her test; she hoped he was right.

This car, a large American make, was totally unlike the vehicle in which she had learned. It had no gear stick but instead a lever on the steering column. It took her some seconds, accompanied by some terrible grating noises, to get the hang of it, and then it was necessary to make a five-point turn on the narrow road, and on one of them the wheels almost went over the edge. Swearing, she corrected the error and then was driving back towards the city. McLachlan had never allowed her to drive faster than thirty miles an hour. Now she found it simple to push the speed far past that, and race towards the distant lights. Before long she encountered a car coming towards her, and straight at her, it seemed. Its horn blared and she swerved violently to avoid it, her immediate reaction that she should try to stop it to obtain help disappearing in the effort, while before she could recover the other vehicle had vanished into the night.

'Idiot!' she muttered, but a few minutes later she heard the wail of a siren. She looked in her rear view mirror and saw two lights gaining on her very rapidly. Police! Just what she wanted. She slowed, and the two motorbikes drew abreast of her, waving and pointing. She obligingly pulled into the side of the road and braked, and their faces appeared at the windows on either side. The man nearest her spoke rapidly, and she shook her head. 'I am sorry,' she said. 'I do not speak Portuguese.'

The man on the other side of the car was shining his torch into the interior, lingering on the long, white, if mud-stained legs, and then on the bodice of her dress. 'I speak English,' he said. 'Do you realize, senorita, that you were breaking the speed limit, and driving on the wrong side of the road?'

'Was I? I did not know that.' That's why that car nearly hit me, she thought.

'Have you been drinking, senorita?'

'No, I have not been drinking. I have only ever driven in England before. I did not know it was different here.'

'Do you realize that you are covered in mud and blood?'

'It's not mine. The blood, I mean.'

He considered this for a few moments, then said, 'Let me see your driving licence.'

'Ah. I haven't got one.'

'What did you say, senorita?'

'I mean, I haven't got it with me.'

'I think you had better get out of the car, senorita.'

'Listen,' Anna said. 'There is a man in the back seat who is very badly injured. That's where I got the blood. I must get him to a hospital. That is why,' she added. 'I was driving so fast.'

The flashlight beam moved, reluctantly, to the back seat. 'That man is dead,' the policeman said.

'No, he is not dead. But he will be if he does not get help, quickly.'

'That is a wound. Did you wound this man, senorita?'

'Well, really,' Anna said. 'He is my boyfriend. Do I look the sort of woman who would go around wounding her boyfriend?'

The flashlight played on her face for several seconds, then the two policemen talked for a few moments, then the English-speaker said, 'Very good. We will take you to a hospital. But you drive carefully, eh?'

'It is remarkable,' the surgeon said, in English. 'All of that mud.' He surveyed Anna, and clearly considered adding, 'All of this mud.' In view of her tattered condition she had been given a hospital gown to wear while she waited to find out Jerry's condition, but she had also obtained the use of a mirror, briefly, and knew that there was mud on her face and embedded in her hair.

'It was the only way I could stop the bleeding,' she explained.

'And it did that. There will have been bacteria, of course . . .'

'Will he live?'

'Oh, yes. We have got the bullet out. There are some broken ribs, and he will be in hospital for some time, but we have given him a transfusion and an antibiotic injection and I do not think there will be any danger of infection.'

'Thank God for that. Then if you'll excuse me, I really would like to get back to my hotel and have a bath. I will call again tomorrow.'

'Ah . . .' the surgeon looked at the waiting nurse, who spoke in Portuguese. 'There is a police inspector downstairs waiting to interview you,' he translated.

'Oh, God,' Anna complained, and looked at her watch, having to clean mud from the dial. It had been seven thirty when she had reached the hospital, and although the emergency operation had been started immediately, it had still taken a long time. Now it was eleven fifteen. 'I made a statement. All I wish to do is get out of these torn and filthy clothes.'

'I understand,' the surgeon said. 'I am sure he will not detain you long. But you know what the police are like; they have to dot Is and cross Ts.'

Anna sighed, and allowed herself to be escorted down to a private room.

'I am Inspector Jaime d'Andrade,' said the little man with the big moustache. 'You appear to have had quite an experience, senorita.' He also spoke excellent English.

'Yes, we have.'

'The young man is going to be all right?'

'So the doctor says.'

'That must be very relieving to you. Just as I am sure it will be relieving to you to know that my men have been to the scene of the incident and have found evidence corroborating your story. But it is so unusual I would like to go through your statement again. Do please sit down.'

Anna sighed and sat opposite him across the table; he picked up the statement that the traffic policemen had required on reaching the hospital, and which had been carefully written down by the English-speaker. 'You and your boyfriend were taking a drive in the hills before going out to dinner.'

'That is correct.'

'And you were overtaken by two cars, driving very fast and very erratically.'

'Yes.'

'And soon after they passed you, they began shooting at each other. You could recognize this? That they were using guns, I mean.'

'I was in the British Army during the war,' Anna said, which was reasonably true, but she felt it prudent to add, 'In the ATS. The Auxiliary Territorial Service.'

'And they taught you to shoot?'

'Yes.'

'Not that you have ever had to use that skill, eh?'

'Of course not.'

'But you recognized the sound. Very good. You and your boyfriend were still driving behind them.'

'Well, we didn't know what was going on.'

'Of course. Then you say, one of the cars left the road and plunged down the embankment, and burst into flames.'

'Yes.'

'But the shooting went on.'

'The people must have got out of the car before it caught fire.'

'If the shooting went on, it would appear that one did, anyway. There is a body in the burned out car, and two others not far away. But the other two bodies were found some distance away from the car that remained on the road. Were these the men who shot your friend?"

'Yes. When we saw what was happening, we stopped, and my boyfriend got out. I begged him not to, but he felt he might be able to help. Then one of the men shot him.'

'But you got him into the car, turned it, and drove away. The men did not shoot you as well.'

'They may have fired at me. There was a lot going on.'

'But if they did fire at you, they missed, eh? I think you behaved most gallantly, Senorita O'Flaherty. And then some-body fired at them, as they no doubt deserved. But you must have stopped at some stage after escaping.'

'Yes. Mr Smitten was groaning terribly, so as soon as I felt we were safe I stopped to see if I could help him.'

'That is when you packed his wound with mud. And ripped your dress?' He looked down at the table, as if attempting to see through the wood to her legs. 'And got covered in mud yourself.'

'I could think of nothing else to use to stop the bleeding. And I tore my dress deliberately to use as a bandage.'

'And that was also when you lost your shoes?'

'Ah . . . yes. I didn't realize it at the time. I think they got stuck in the mud and came off. I was so distraught I never noticed it until I was back in the car. Then my only thought was to get Mr Smitten to hospital.'

'You are a woman of great courage and determination. But I see that you have scratches on your arms and legs. And some bruises. How did you get those?'

'As I explained, when I got out of the car my feet caught in the mud, so I tripped and rolled down the slope. I had to climb back up.'

'Of course. Your determination is exemplary. Well, that seems to cover everything. I'm afraid that we will have to retain your car for a few days, for forensic examination. Oh, and we will require your driving licence.'

'Ah!' Anna said. 'I do not have a driving licence.'

He raised his eyebrows; his moustache seemed to move upwards with them. 'You were driving an automobile.'

'Well, I had to, if I was going to get Jerry to a hospital. I have taken driving lessons, but I have not yet received my licence.'

'As I said, you are a courageous woman. I do not think there will be a prosecution. Now, one of my men will drive you to your hotel. I assume you are remaining in Brazil for a while?'

'I am on holiday. I am not going anywhere, certainly until Mr Smitten is recovered.'

'Of course.'

Anna stood up. 'May I ask, have you any idea who these men were, why they were shooting at each other?'

'Well, we have some ideas, but very little else. None of the victims appear to have been carrying any identification. At least the man in the car may have, but his body and his clothes were almost entirely consumed by the fire.'

'Ugh!'

'I am sorry, senorita. I did not mean to upset you.'

'I am only glad I did not see it.'

'Of course. But there are also some very confusing aspects to this case, which will take some unravelling. As for instance, five men are dead. One would suppose there would have been one survivor, at least.'

'Maybe the survivor got away,' Anna suggested.

'That is possible, certainly. But if he wanted to get away, why didn't he use the remaining car? The keys were in the ignition. And then, we have recovered six weapons. Four of them are large calibre automatic pistols. Our findings will have to be confirmed by the post-mortems, but by our initial forensic examination of the bodies, and the report of the surgeon who operated on your friend, both the man in the car and your friend were hit with shots from these guns. But there was also a very large calibre revolver lying in the bushes. This was not used at all. In fact, it was still in its holster when we found it. But the really puzzling thing is that the other four were each hit, and killed, by a small calibre bullet. That indicates the sixth weapon, a Walther PPK, which we also found in the ravine. You know of this gun?'

'I have never heard of it.'

'Well, it is a very small pistol, and fires a very small bullet. It is used mainly by women, for protection rather than as an intentionally lethal weapon. Why should men armed with much more effective weapons choose to use this small gun, if they intended to kill the opposition?'

'You say all these men were killed with this gun.'

'No, no. Four of them were. Three with a single shot, the other with two. Whoever fired that gun was a professional marksman, because, do you know, in the belt alongside the pistol itself there was a silencer. Not the sort of thing your average person carries, and indeed, the average person carrying such a gun, for self-protection, does not use a gun belt. But here is the most puzzling thing of all. There were fingerprints on all of the weapons, except for the heavy Colt, which as I said was never drawn from its holster, and the Walther. Whoever fired that gun took the trouble to wipe it clean of prints before throwing it away.'

'Well, then,' Anna said, 'that makes it plain. There had to have been a sixth man.'

'But you saw no such man.'

'I didn't see any of them, Inspector. It was dark, and as I said, they started shooting the moment we stopped and Mr Smitten got out. When he was hit my only concern was to get him back into the car and get away. Look, Inspector, I am very tired, I am filthy, and I have had no dinner. May I please be taken back to my hotel?'

'No dinner,' he said, and looked at his watch. 'My God! It is past midnight.'

'Yes,' Anna said grimly.

'Of course you must be taken home. Please forgive me for keeping you here so long. It is such a mystery, you see.'

'Good luck,' Anna commented.

The Gathering Clan

'Senorita O'Flaherty!' The somewhat sleepy reception clerk woke up with a start as he peered over the counter. Anna had left the bed-gown at the hospital, and he was looking at a mud-stained face, a mud-stained and bloodstained tattered dark green top, a mud-stained pair of white knickers, and two very long mud-coated legs, with mud-covered bare feet. 'What has happened?'

'There was an accident,' Anna explained.

'But you could be hurt. I will call the doctor.'

'I have just come from the hospital and I am perfectly all right. Now listen. I have had no dinner. Is room service still available?'

'Room service is available twenty-four hours of the day, senorita.'

'Remind me to recommend this hotel. Right. I want you to send me up a plate of ham sandwiches, a yoghurt, and a bottle of that rather nice Freixenet wine. Pronto.'

'Of course, senorita.' He took her key from the cubby-hole, and with it, two slips of paper. 'Ah—'

'Yes?'

'A gentleman called to see you.' He studied the first slip. 'At half past seven this evening.'

'What sort of gentleman? What did he look like?'

'I do not know, senorita. I was not on duty at that hour. This gentleman seems not to have asked for you by name, but by description, which the clerk recognized.'

That needed thinking about. 'And the other message?'

'There was a telephone call, at nine o'clock.'

'And I suppose you weren't on duty then, either.'

'Well, no, senorita. I came on duty at ten.'

'But the clerk on duty noted what this caller wanted?'

'It says, a gentleman asked for Miss O'Flaherty, and on being told that she had left the hotel, hung up.'

'Hm.' She would have liked to wait on a good night's sleep and get her thoughts in order, but in view of everything that had happened, and might still be happening, she didn't think she had the time. 'Is it possible to send a telegram at this hour?'

'Of course, senorita.' He pushed the block of forms across the desk.

Anna wrote quickly. Jerry down. Contact made and lost. Advice and assistance, please. A. She addressed it to Joe's Virginia home, the only address she had for him. She didn't suppose he'd be there, but she had no doubt that Eleanor would know how to contact him in a hurry.

The clerk studied it, then nodded. 'This will go immediately, senorita.'

'That's what I wanted you to say. It is of course confidential.'

'Of course, senorita. All telegrams are covered by the law of confidentiality.'

'Good man. Now I'm off for a bath. Send up that supper.'

She rode up in the lift. She was very tired, and her bruises and scratches ached, but there was a lot of thinking to be done. The evening had been a total catastrophe. As she had explained in her telegram, not only had she lost Jerry for the foreseeable future, but she had lost her contact with the Nazi colony. Whatever answers Joe provided, supposing he could provide any, there was going to be an inevitable time lag before the status quo could be restored. And meanwhile . . .

There was some faint hope that the telephone call might have come from the proposed dinner party, trying to discover why she and Schuler had not arrived. But would they pursue getting in touch with her once the news of the shoot-out on the road, which had to lead to the villa they were occupying, broke, as it would tomorrow? In fact, today.

The lift reached the seventh floor, and she went into her room, turned on the bath, and then took off her mud-coated gloves and jewellery, left her hair loose as it had to be washed, discarded what was left of her ruined clothing, dropping the rags on the floor, still deep in thought. And contemplating her bare feet, which were both muddy and bloody from the scratches they had suffered. Damnation! She thought. So many questions had been thrown at her so quickly, and she had been exhausted, both emotionally and physically . . . but misplacing the shoes had been a bad slip. And as the police were sure to find them, a couple of miles from where she had said she had lost them, she had to get her story straight before they came back to her.

The loss of Jerry was no less serious. If he had proved no great help when the bullets were flying, he was her only contact here in Rio. Joe had said that the entire real estate office was in the pay of this CIA, but she had no idea how much they knew of her business here in Brazil . . . and how much they were supposed to know. Not for the first time in her life she had been cut adrift from her support system; she had not enjoyed it on any of the previous occasions.

The bath was ready. She turned off the taps, and there was a knock on the door. She wrapped herself in a towel, tucking it in under her armpits, and allowed the waiter to wheel the trolley in, thus clearly making his day. 'You want me open the bottle?' he asked.

'Please.'

He did so. 'You want me to do anything else?'

'Not that I can think of at the moment.'

'I am Manuelo. I will come back for the trolley, eh?'

'When I am finished with the trolley,' Anna said, 'I will wheel it into the corridor. You can collect it any time you like, but I do not wish to be disturbed. Savvy?'

She had virtually to push him out of the door before she could get back to her bath. Getting clean also took some time. There was mud everywhere, her cuts were stinging, and when she was finally satisfied with her body, she discovered that there was even more mud than she had supposed in her hair. She wound up standing and using the shower, but even so she reckoned she needed a session with the hotel hairdresser when she woke up.

As for her caller, who did not seem to know her name . . . she wondered if he would return, and if he might open up an avenue towards Bormann, although why, if he was one of the men expecting her to dinner, he should have come to the hotel when she could be expected to arrive at any moment, she could not determine.

The sandwiches and wine made her feel better, and after wheeling the trolley into the hall and hanging out a Do Not Disturb notice she slept soundly, despite her various aches and pains, to be awakened by the buzzing of her telephone. Sleepily she stretched out her arm and lifted the receiver. 'Yes?'

'Senorita, are you all right?'

'Why should I not be all right?'

'Well, it is so late.'

'Eh?' She looked at her watch: ten o'clock. 'Good heavens! I was very tired. Did you have a reason for waking me up?'

'There is someone here to see you, senorita.'

'Who?'

'Excuse me. Miss O'Flaherty wishes to know your name senor.'

'O'Flaherty? Good God! Just tell her that I'm an old friend,' said a voice in the background.

Oh, my God! Anna thought. Clive!

He has come to arrest me, she thought. And take me back. But he cannot do that, here in Brazil, unless I wish to go. And meanwhile . . . it was such a treat to hear his voice. And to see him again . . . on her terms! 'Tell Mr Bartley to come up,' she said, and replaced the phone.

She got out of bed, gazed at herself in the mirror, and grimaced. She had protected her face well enough during her tumble down the side of the ravine, while the high-necked bodice of her gown had protected her breasts and upper back, but there were scratches on her thighs as well as her calves, and a spreading yellow bruise on her left hip. What a fuck-up. She washed her face, cleaned her teeth, and brushed her hair, finishing as there was a tap on the door. She put on her dressing gown, and considered. It was a long time, not, indeed, since Geneva in 1943, that Clive had actually seen her in action; it might be no bad idea to refresh his memory. She opened her shoulder bag, took out the Luger, and screwed in the silencer. There was another tap on the door. 'Anna?' he called.

She performed her usual exercise, standing behind the door and turning the key with her left hand. 'It's open.'

The door swung in, and he stepped through. Anna pushed it shut. 'Long time no see.'

He swung round to face her, and the levelled pistol. 'Anna!'

'Is that a greeting, or an explanation?'

'My dearest girl . . . you do cause us some problems. And what's this O'Flaherty nonsense?'

'I agree it's a hoot. My new employers chose it. And you are as usual adopting a one-sided view of life. You must be hot. Take off your jacket.'

'Anna . . .'

'I am outside of your jurisdiction, Clive, and at this moment you are in mine.' She allowed that familiar trace of steel to enter her voice. 'Take off the jacket.'

A last hesitation, then he obeyed.

'Good God!' she commented. 'Is that a Browning nine millimetre?'

'It is standard issue,' he pointed out.

'It would just about blow me into two pieces. Were you intending to use it?'

'Are you intending to use that?'

'If I have to. But as I think I am somewhat more accurate than you, I do not have actually to kill you. Take off the belt. Or would you like me to shoot it off?'

He removed the belt and laid it and the holster on the table. 'I thought we had something going.'

'We did. And I'd like to think that we may have again. But you are going to have to prove it. Why don't you sit down.'

He chose one of the two armchairs. Anna sat at the table. 'You're a long way from home. I assume you have a reason.'

'I'm here to collect you.'

'Suppose I don't want to be collected?'

'Look, you left us with quite a problem.'

'Again, that one-sided point of view. Try looking at it from the other side. You guaranteed my security, and placed me in an absolutely "safe" house while your superiors decided what to do with me. They appear to have conveniently filed me under F.'

'I came to see you every month.'

'Oh, big deal. Don't get me wrong. I enjoyed every minute of your visits. They were the highlights of my life. But they amounted to thirty-six days out of three hundred and sixty-five. I wasn't in a safe house, Clive, I was in a prison, with only that dimwit Bridget Bridie for company.'

'I know. I am so terribly sorry. Matters have been so fraught since the end of the War and the change of government . . .'

'My heart bleeds for you. But I was at least safe, wasn't I? Only I wasn't safe at all. First of all Joe shows up, courtesy of Belinda and that shit Edert. Then the Soviets. So they obviously followed Joe. But how did they know he'd be looking for me?'

'I don't know.' He frowned. 'You didn't do for Andrews as well, did you?'

'If I had done that, I wouldn't be here.'

'And you honestly think you can trust him? Trust the Americans? After they attempted to kill you? Anna, pragmatism is their middle name. They'll use you as long as they have a job for you, then they'll discard you like a dirty sock.'

'Not this time. Look, I haven't breakfasted. Would you like to join me?' She picked up the phone with her left hand. 'I'd like breakfast for two, please.' She hung up.

'Anna . . .' he almost wailed. 'You cannot take on the whole world. Listen, since the Russians have discovered that you're still alive, they're going to keep looking for you. I mean you've done twenty-one of their people . . .'

'Twenty-five.'

'What?'

'There was some trouble last night.'

'Oh, my God! Where?'

'A few miles outside Rio.'

'But . . . how . . . why?'

'They wanted to take me back to Russia.'

'And so you shot them, just like that.'

'They were trying to shoot me, at the time.'

'My God, my God, my God! They'll never stop chasing you now.'

'Clive, they have never stopped chasing me since I got out of the Lubianka. That was all but five years ago. Which is just about my entire adult life.'

'What are we going to do?'

There had been a tap on the door. 'Have breakfast.'

The dressing gown had a deep pocket, and in this she placed her pistol. 'Please don't do anything stupid,' she requested. 'I'm faster than you, and,' she smiled at him. 'I'm in practice.'

Needless to say, it was Manuelo. 'Don't you get any time off?' she asked. 'Or did you volunteer for extra duty?'

'I am here to serve you, senorita.'

'But as you can see, I have company.'

He looked past her at Clive, and his face fell. Anna signed the chit. 'There's no need to hurry back.' She closed the door and turned to the trolley, handed Clive a glass of chilled orange juice.

'You are incorrigible,' he remarked.

'Oh, he hasn't achieved his ambition yet. Nor will he, unless all else fails.' She sat down, poured coffee. 'Two lumps, isn't it?'

'But Anna . . . you realize this can't go on.'

'I don't know what you mean by 'this'. But I do know that the situation needs adjusting.' She spread marmalade and munched toast. 'Let's recap. When I left Germany, I thought, and you gave me the impression, that you and I were going to get together on a permanent basis. I quite understood that there were some matters that needed sorting out, but a year is too negative. Now, I also quite understand that after due reflection, you have decided to stick with Belinda instead of me. But I think you should have told me your decision, as soon as it was made.'

Clive drank his juice. 'Belinda is dead.'

It was Anna's turn to say, 'What?! When? How did she die?'

'She died over a week ago, of a broken neck.'

Anna laid down her half eaten piece of toast. 'Andrews did that? But a week is too recent.'

'The chief suspect is a young woman named Katherine Fehrbach.'

Anna's eyes could be colder than lumps of ice. 'I find that piece of attempted humour in excruciatingly bad taste. My sister is dead.'

'Your sister is very much alive.'

'Katherine, alive? My God!' She drank some coffee. 'You will have to explain that.'

'She turned up in my office a couple of weeks ago.'

'Your office? At MI6?'

'Bold as brass.'

'But how did she know you had anything to do with me? And where had she come from?'

'As to your first question, your old friend Laurent apparently told her I would know where you were.'

'Laurent,' Anna said thoughtfully. 'You mean she had been to Switzerland?'

'She claimed to have been in Switzerland for the last two years.'

'But that—'

'Is also impossible. Quite. Frankly, everything she told me was a pack of lies, such as how she had spent the war in Vienna, where she had regular meetings with you.'

'What did you do with her?'

'Unfortunately, I did nothing with her. She said she had become a Swiss citizen, and she was certainly carrying a Swiss passport. But . . . she made me uneasy.'

'What do you mean?'

'There was something odd about her.'

'Well, there would have been something odd about you if you'd spent two years in a Russian prison. I spent two days in the Lubianka and look at the effect it had on me. It was not an experience I will ever forget.'

'Nor, apparently, will a lot of other people,' Clive remarked.

'Ha ha. But to think that she survived . . . was she, well, damaged in any way?'

'You mean physically? Not that I could see.'

'Mama and Papa must have been over the moon to have her back. But how did she get out of Russia?'

'I have no idea how she got out of Russia, as she did not admit to having been in Russia at all. And your mother and father don't know she's alive. She refused to see them.'

Anna poured them each another cup of coffee; she had lost her appetite 'But you sent her to see Belinda. Why?'

'I did not send her to see Belinda. I told her that Laurent was mistaken and that I had no idea where you were, which at that moment was perfectly true. So she left.'

'Then how do you know she went to Belinda?'

'Belinda was killed that same afternoon by a single blow to the neck. Exactly the same way that Elsa Mayers died, seven years ago. And later that night a woman answering Katherine's description – her looks are nearly as striking as yours – boarded the Cross-Channel ferry at Dover and disappeared. It seemed too pat. But you can confirm it. Did Katherine receive any specialist training?'

'She was SD,' Anna said, half to herself. 'She was my secretary.'

'And you never told me?'

'It would have unnecessarily complicated matters. She was an enthusiastic Nazi.'

'Just how many skeletons do you still have in your closet, which you have never told me?'

Anna ignored the question. 'Why should she have killed Belinda?'

'I have absolutely no idea. Unless . . . well, you know Belinda.'

'Do I? We only actually met twice.'

'Yes, but both were pretty unusual circumstances. And after that meeting in Germany, well . . .' he paused to peer at her, flushing.

Anna was not prepared to let him off any hooks. 'And?'

'Well, she formed a considerable . . . attachment to you.'

Anna burst out laughing. 'After one night?'

'Belinda is . . . was, I suppose, very intense.'

'And you think . . .?'

'As I said, superficially, Katherine is very like you. Perhaps, if Belinda made some sort of advance . . .'

'And Katherine reacted so anti that she killed her?'

'Isn't that what you did at your training school when one of the other girls made advances?'

'I did not kill any of the other girls at training school. I broke one of their arms.'

'Because she made advances to you.'

'She tried to rape me, if you must know. I was very young, and very innocent. Very well brought up.'

'As was Katherine, I assume.'

'Yes, she was. But as I said, anyone who has spent eighteen months in a gulag can no longer be innocent, in any direction. So what happens now? To Katherine?'

'As she's back in Switzerland, there's not a lot we can do about her. We can't apply for extradition until we have a lot more evidence. At the moment, we don't have any evidence at all. Merely inside knowledge.'

'You mean this is all speculation on your part. Well . . .' The telephone buzzed. 'Excuse me.' She picked it up. 'Yes?'

'There is a telegram for you, Miss O'Flaherty.'

'Oh, thank you. Will you send it up, please?' She replaced

the phone. 'As I was saying, while I really am terribly sorry that something has happened to your lady love . . . don't interrupt,' she said as he would have spoken. 'We seem to have sidetracked the real problem, which is your inability to take care of me in any way. So I have had to strike out on my own.'

'With Andrews,' he said bitterly. 'The man who tried to kill you.'

'Correction. The man who was ordered by his superiors to have me killed, and who is very glad it didn't work out.'

'And you believe him.'

'Yes, I do.' There was a tap on the door. 'Excuse me.' She opened the door to take the envelope from the tray held by her amorous floor waiter, who gave Clive another dirty look before withdrawing. Anna slit the envelope with her thumb. I'LL BE WITH YOU TONIGHT. Breath rushed from her nostrils in relief.

'Bad news?' Clive asked.

'No. The best news I've had in a long time. Well, it's been great seeing you, Clive, and if you would like to resume a relationship I will be happy with that whenever I can spare the time, but right now I have a lot to do.'

'Anna,' he said. 'I have been sent here to take you back.'

Anna's hand dropped into her pocket. 'Tell me how you propose to do that?'

'Well, I can ask you to come without a fuss.'

'As I have tried to explain, I am going to be busy for the next couple of weeks. In fact, it may be a couple of months. And when I cease being busy, you are going to have to convince me that you can adequately protect me. And that you, personally, are prepared to treat me in the way I wish to be treated.'

'That is the damndest proposal I have ever heard.'

'Aren't I the damndest woman you have ever met? Listen, as you are here, you are welcome to spend the day with me; I may have something on tonight. But these people do indulge in a nice long siesta. However, as I'm afraid I can't altogether trust you, in the present circumstances, we are going to have to play to certain rules. I propose to have a shower and then get dressed. I can't have you hanging around here while I do that; you might get some ideas about strong-arm tactics. So you are going to have to go downstairs and sit in the lounge. I'll join you in half an hour, and we can chat and then have lunch together. You will, of course, leave your howitzer up here.'

'And if I do decide to join you for a siesta, are you going to tie me to the bed before joining me?'

'I bet you've never had that experience. It might be rather fun, don't you think?'

The phone buzzed.

'Aren't I popular?' Anna asked, and picked it up. 'Yes?'

'Excuse me, Senorita O'Flaherty,' the clerk said. 'There is a gentleman here to see you.'

'Another one? I am having a busy day. Has this gentleman got a name?'

This time the clerk put his hand over the phone and she could not hear the response, but he was back immediately. 'The gentleman's name is Gutemann.'

Shit! Anna thought. But making contact with the Nazis was her number one priority. 'Will you ask him to wait? I am just getting dressed, and should be down in fifteen minutes.' She hung up, gazed at Clive. 'I'm terribly sorry, but we are going to have to change our plans.'

'Who is the man calling on you?'

'One of the reasons for my being here at all. I don't think it would be a good idea for you and me to go down together. Also, he's quite smart, so I don't want you going down immediately in front of me either. So it looks as if I am going to have to forego my morning bath. What a life!' She took the pistol from her pocket and laid it on her dressing table, then hung up the dressing gown.

'My God!' he said. 'What happened to you?'

'I fell down a hillside.'

'While shooting Russians?'

'That too.' She pulled on her knickers.

'I thought you always wore a one-piece?'

'I've changed my dress habits. These are rather attractive, don't you think?'

'Attractive? God, Anna, seeing you . . .' He got up.

'Down, Rover. Business before pleasure.' She put on a sundress and sat before the mirror to apply make-up, grimacing at herself as she did so. She was going to have to forego the hairdresser also, at least until this afternoon. She began to brush her hair, vigorously. 'I'm going to leave you here. Please wait for half an hour before coming down, and then just walk through the lounge and out of the hotel. Please do not, under any circumstances, give any sign of knowing me, or even noticing me. This man is an old acquaintance, who knows me only as a dedicated Nazi. I would not like him to alter that opinion, right this minute.'

'Anna . . . are you a dedicated Nazi?'

She laid down the brush and stood up, turning to face him. 'That is not a question I had ever expected you to ask.'

'Because I am sure I know the answer. But since your flight, it is being asked, in certain quarters.'

'And you seriously expect me to come back to England with you?' She put on her jewellery. 'To face a multiple murder charge as well as an accusation of being a war criminal? Those men came to kill me.'

'I know that. Billy is working on getting you an exemption from prosecution.'

'Working?'

'The moment he gets it, he is sending a copy to the embassy here . . .'

Anna slung her shoulder bag, dropping the Luger into its usual place. 'I told you. I'm tied up for the next few weeks.'

'Hunting Nazis for the Americans? That's what it is, isn't it?'

'You're too smart for your own good.'

'Anna, you must know that they're using you, and when you've done what they want . . .'

'Has it ever occurred to you that I may be using them? I have to go. I told you, I'd love to get together again, when I have more time. Trouble is, I don't know when that will be. Give me a number where I can reach you?'

'I'm at the embassy.'

'Then I will call you as soon as I am free. As I said, don't panic if it's not today. I'm leaving your gun.'

'And that's all there is?'

She went to the door. 'What more there is, is up to you.'

She was actually more agitated than she had allowed herself to reveal. Quite apart from seeing Clive which was always a turn on, and one she had not expected, although she had supposed it would be inevitable that having read her ad, someone from the embassy would attempt to contact her. But Belinda, dead! And killed by Katherine?

Her memory of the Anglo-Italian woman was of those two very odd meetings, the first of which had so nearly turned out disastrously for her, the other which had so very nearly been disastrous for Belinda. And then that really unforgettable night together. Of course Belinda had known everything about her, and apparently Laurent had known that she worked for MI6, but why would he want her killed? And if he did, why or how did he get hold of Katherine to do the job? And Katherine, released by the Russians? After having been turned into a killer? Katherine, who for all her training had always been terrified of violence? Then she realized that the answer was obvious. Laurent was, as always, floundering in the middle of a situation he did not really understand. Obviously the Russians had only turned Katherine loose after brainwashing her, and targeting her sister! Anna had never actually encountered brainwashing before – if one omitted the entire German people, who had been brainwashed by Hitler – but she had read about it, and it did seem possible to point the subject at a victim, however unlikely. But why had Belinda been caught up in Katherine's mission?

Whatever had been happening, she reminded herself as the lift came to a halt, she supposed she should be grateful that Katherine had not been a part of the squad sent to get her here, otherwise she would have to add fratricide to her list of crimes.

And now it was time to concentrate. She stepped into the lobby, looked around her. She had never seen Gunther out of uniform, except in bed, but she did not think she could possibly forget him, and she recognized no one here. She went to the reception desk. 'There was a gentleman wishing to see me.'

'Oh, yes, senorita. Ah—'

'Anna!'

She turned, recognizing the voice. But . . . the SD major she had last seen not much more than a year ago had been a very typical Aryan, roughly her own height, with a shock of yellow hair, bland features, and a powerful, attractively athletic body. He had also only been a few years older than herself, and could not now be much more than thirty. But she was looking at a shrivelled body, bent so that its head was several inches below hers, leaning on a stick, its hair pure white, its features twisted and tortured. No wonder he had been reluctant to meet her in public, yesterday. 'Gunther?' she asked incredulously. 'What in the name of God . . .?'

'There is a car waiting.'

She hesitated. She had intended to receive him in the hotel lounge. But this was her chance, and she had agreed to go along with the unfortunate Schuler; if she had intended to use Jerry as a back-up that had turned out to be a damp squib. In any event, if any other of the refugees were in this sorry state she could not possibly fear being overwhelmed. Besides, to leave the hotel now meant there was no chance of them inadvertently encountering Clive.

This was another large black Mercedes – the group, or their backer, seemed to have a fleet of the things – with a driver, who made no comment as she got into the back seat and settled her shoulder bag in her lap, followed, laboriously, by Gutemann, who first handed her his stick and then needed both arms to insert himself and sit beside her with a grunt. The car immediately moved away.

'To see you again . . .' Gutemann said, 'So beautiful, so strong, so healthy . . . do you remember the first time we met, on the drive to Grozke?'

'I remember it very well,' Anna said. 'It was a car very like this one.' She decided to test the water; she had to find out how much he, and therefore his associates, knew about her departure from Berlin. 'You were taking me to Dr Cleiner. Poor old Cleiner. Do you have any idea what happened to him?'

Cleiner, she thought. An utterly hateful little rat of a man, into whose clutches she, and many other young girls – including, at a later date, Katherine – had been delivered to be trained for the SD. He had taught them all the skills she now possessed: she had been his outstanding pupil. But he had also made them all, and her in particular, as she had been a virgin in both mind and body, with a sheltered upbringing and a convent education, ashamed of their femininity, before turning them loose as programmed monsters.

Cleiner was someone she had always intended to settle with one day, the more so when she had discovered that he had become the gaoler in charge of her parents. But when she had descended upon the camp like an avenging angel to free them, and had had him at the point of her gun, she had spared his life. How foolish could you get? But at that moment, flushed with the excitement of success that she had been given the opportunity both of rescuing her parent after seven years of captivity, and of escaping Germany with them, she had wanted only to turn her back on her lethal past. So as with Birgit and Stefan, she had let him live. Now she had to find out if he, like Stefan, would come back to haunt her.

'No,' Gutemann said. 'I know he was still in charge of the camp at Grozke in March last year. But then the Russians broke through and surrounded Berlin, and we lost contact with the outside world. But you . . . I looked for you, and was told you had left the city on a mission for Dr Goebbels. And then the British put out that you had been killed . . . I did not know what to believe.'

Anna had already composed her story. 'I was lucky. Dr Goebbels sent me on a mission to Switzerland, but before I got there I encountered an American patrol, and was arrested. I was travelling under my own name, Anna Fehrbach, and in any event, they had never heard of the Countess von Widerstand. So they let me go. As for the British, while they had heard of the countess, they had no idea who I actually was, and as they could find no trace of me, they put it about that I was dead.'

'But you survived,' he said admiringly. 'You have a gift for survival. But it costs a lot of money to get to South America. I know. Did you have a lot of money?'

Anna smiled at him. 'Do you not know that it is always possible for a handsome woman to make a lot of money?'

'It makes my blood boil, to think of you having to . . .'

'It is history.'

'But coming here, and putting that advertisement in the newspaper . . . that was very dangerous.'

'I did not think it would be so dangerous. It is a year since Berlin fell, since I was declared dead. Besides, does anyone in Europe read a Rio de Janeiro newspaper?' She fluttered her eyelashes at him, the epitome of innocence.

'For a woman of your talents and accomplishments, you can be incredibly naïve,' he commented. 'What happened last night? Who was it?'

'I have no idea,' Anna said. 'Do you know what happened?'

'I wish you to tell me. We only know that you were attacked.'

'How do you know that?'

'When Schuler, and you, did not arrive by nine o'clock, we telephoned the hotel.'

'They told me.'

'They told us you had left at six. We waited another hour, then we realized that something must have gone wrong. We assumed you had had a puncture. So Bruno' – he indicated the chauffeur '– and I went to look for you, and we came to the scene of an accident. It was about eleven by then, and the police were there, crawling all over the place, so we did not stop. But we were able to see that there was a car down the ravine, still smouldering, a black Mercedes, and that there had been casualties: an ambulance was just leaving the scene. When we returned we discussed the situation, then we telephoned the hotel again to see if they knew what had happened. They told me you had come in about half an hour before, with your clothes torn, and that you had gone straight to bed. So—'

'You came looking for me this morning.' And no one had reported that second call to her, she thought.

'We're coming to the place now,' Gutemann said.

The Mercedes slowed as it approached the policeman waving his hand. There was no sign of the Russians' car, but two police cars were parked at the side of the road, and several policemen were in the ravine, combing through the bushes; if they were being this thorough, they had probably already found her shoes. The Mercedes stopped, and the policeman who had flagged them pushed his head in the front window and spoke rapidly in Portuguese, while Anna held her breath: if d'Andrade was here! The driver replied, and the policeman looked into the back seat, naturally focusing on Anna in preference to the obvious cripple beside her, then nodded, and withdrew.

The Mercedes moved on, and Anna got her breathing under control. 'What did he want?' she asked.

'Just to know where we were from and where we were going,' Bruno said. 'And to look at you, Fraulein.'

'What happened?' Gutemann asked again.

'We had reached back there when we were suddenly attacked from a car that drove up along side and began shooting. Schuler was hit, the car went off the road into the ravine, and as you saw, caught fire.'

'But you were not in it?'

'I managed to jump out.'

'And you were not hurt?'

'Not hurt?' Anna asked. 'I managed not to break anything. But I will show you my bruises, some time.'

'I look forward to that. But who were these people who attacked you?'

'I have no idea.'

'And they did not follow you into the ravine?'

She had to make an instant decision. She needed to win the entire confidence of these people. 'Two of them did. I shot them both.'

'You have not changed,' he said, admiringly. 'But the others . . .'

'They had remained on the road. Unfortunately, before I could immediately do anything about them, another car came along, and stopped. The driver got out, and they shot him. By that time I had regained the road, so I killed them. The innocent driver was badly hurt, so I took him to hospital.'

'But . . . you have involved yourself. The gun . . .'

'I was not using my Luger. It was a PPK.'

'You, were using a PPK?'

'It was a gift from a friend,' Anna explained, reverting to absolute truthfulness. 'And I left it at the scene, wiped clean of prints.'

'You are the ultimate professional. But still . . . this man you rescued—'

'He knows nothing of me. He was unconscious. Even supposing he recovers from his wound, which is doubtful, he will still only know that an unnamed woman took him to the hospital.'

'But you are still involved with the police,' Gutemann grumbled. 'You should have left that fellow to die, taken one of the cars, and come on to us by yourself.'

'Dear Gunther,' Anna remarked. 'You are thinking through a mass of cotton wool. Come on where? Schuler did not tell me where we were going. I still do not know where we are going. And wherever I went, the police would trace the car and want to know why I had not reported what had happened. It was far better to bring them in from the beginning and establish my position as an innocent bystander.'

'You think so clearly . . . but they will still want to know what happened.'

'And I cannot tell them. I was out driving with a nice man I had met while walking on the beach, when we were attacked, and my friend was shot, and then there was a regular gun battle in which some other men were shot. I escaped. And I know nothing about my friend or his background.'

'The police will know his background. That he is one of us.'

'But the police know all about you, don't they? They have no objection to your being here. They are upset that there should have been a shooting, and they will probably relate it to your Nazi background, but they can hardly blame you for not knowing why Schuler was shot.'

'The group will not like it. The Fuehrer will not like it.'

'The Fuehrer is dead.'

'We have a new fuehrer. Every group, every party, every country, must have a leader.'

'Do I know this man?'

'Probably.'

'Tell me his name.'

'I will let him do that, when he meets you.'

'Which will be today?'

'It will be when he wishes it to be.'

Anna could see no profit in pressing the matter. She would have to practise her habitual patience. And it could not be much longer, now; they were well into the foothills. 'So tell me about yourself,' she suggested. 'I mean, what happened to you.'

He grimaced. 'I was in the Chancellery at the very end, fighting for the Fuehrer. I was at the front of the building when it was struck by a Russian shell. When I woke up I was in a Russian military hospital. I suppose the reason they did not just leave me to die was that they wanted information from me. They asked me about Hitler, and Himmler . . . I did not then know what had happened to him. And do you know, they asked me about you.'

'Me?'

'They asked me if I had ever heard of the Countess von Widerstand. Well, I had to say yes. Everyone in Germany had heard of the Countess von Widerstand. But I said I had never actually known you. I was afraid that they might have found out that I was with you in Warsaw, but apparently they knew nothing of any of your companions in that business . . . except for your sister, of course. So then, as the war was over, they turned me loose. I was not even recovered from my injuries yet. I could have died. Luckily my uncle lived in Berlin, and when I sought him out, virtually on my hands and knees, I found that he had survived. He took me in and kept me while I regained my health, such as it is.'

'What a terrible experience,' Anna said, and she meant it. He might have been a member of the SD, with all that that meant, but he had been a loyal friend and faithful lover, at least until he had become afraid of her. And now, to see him in this state . . . she could only hope that he was not going to have to be included in the general destruction of his little cell. 'But you have not told me what actually happened to you.'

'Both my arms were broken, one leg, and some ribs. And I received some . . . internal injuries.'

She rested her hand on his. 'Oh, Gunther, I am so terribly sorry. Are you saying . . .'

'I am impotent, yes.'

She squeezed his fingers. 'That makes me very sad. But at least you were able to get out of Germany. That is a miracle.'

'I had friends.'

'You mean they came out with you?'

'Some. Others are still in Germany, working for the day when we shall rise again. But seeing you is a tonic. Anna, I have been thinking. Do you suppose those men who attacked you and Schuler could have been Russians? Someone at their embassy here may have read your advertisement. If that is so, then they know you are still alive, and are still determined to get you, for Warsaw.'

'That sounds very far-fetched.' She certainly didn't want this lot concluding that she might be too hot to handle, even if she was, far hotter to handle than they could possibly suspect. 'Do you really suppose they would go to all that trouble to find one woman?'

'They are a deep and devious people,' he said. 'We have arrived.'

The villa was in a very similar situation to the one in which she had romped with Jerry . . . was it only yesterday morning? . . . being perched high in the hills above the city, and similarly isolated. But there the resemblance ended. Where Jerry's villa had been all open plan, with wide, airy rooms and open windows, this was like a mini-fortress. There was no veranda overlooking the view. And when the car reached the courtyard below the house Bruno flashed his headlights and a large door opened in the apparently solid wall to allow them to drive into a concealed garage. The door promptly closed again to plunge them into darkness, but now electric light came on, and Anna saw that there were two other Mercedes parked waiting; presumably yesterday morning there had been three.

Bruno held her door for her as she got out. 'Impressive,' she said. 'Your backer appears to be worth a lot of money.'

'He is,' Gutemann agreed, slowly getting out with the aid of his stick.

'And he is that sympathetic?'

'He feels that the future of South America lies in the National Socialist philosophy.'

Which was interesting. Bruno was pressing a button let into the wall, and another door was opening to allow them into a lift. 'You will feel at home here,' Gutemann assured her. 'These are our people.'

And these are our more normal surroundings, she thought, recalling the troglodyte existence to which she, and everyone else who mattered, had been reduced during the last days of the Reich, to escape the unending bombing. But she said, 'I was sure of it.'

They were at the first floor, and the door opened. 'Countess!' said the woman standing there to greet them. 'This is a great pleasure.'

'And for me,' Anna agreed, studying her. She was quite tall, with long, dark straight hair, attractively round features, and a full figure. Anna put her down as in her mid-thirties.

'You do not remember me.'

'Ah . . .'

The woman smiled. 'There is no reason why you should. I am Trudi Ohlmann. We did meet, at an SS reception in 1941. But you were the famous Countess von Widerstand, the woman who escaped from Russia and had just returned from America, working for the Reich, while I was just a simple housewife.'

In 1941, after I came back from America, Anna recalled, I had a lot on my mind – principally having to organize the execution of Reinhard Heydrich. 'Well,' she said, 'It is a pleasure to meet you again, Frau Ohlmann.'

'Oh, Trudi, please. We are going to be such friends.'

'Then you must call me Anna.'

'Anna! It is such a lovely name. Friedrich is waiting to meet you again.'

She escorted Anna across the parquet floor of the lobby into the drawing room. Here again, although the carpets and furnishings were luxurious, the impression was that of being in a fortress. There were windows looking out over the view, but each was protected by a heavy steel shutter that could be closed and bolted into place at a moment's notice. In the centre of the room, Friedrich Ohlmann waited. Anna remembered him. He was some years older than his wife, no less tall, but running to stomach and with heavy features. He was, or had been, she recalled, a prominent industrialist, and she had encountered him, socially, on more than one occasion. 'Countess!' he said, his voice deep. 'This is an honour. The Fuehrer!'

It was so long since Anna had given the salute that it took her a moment to respond. Then she threw out her right arm. 'The Fuehrer! It is a privilege to be here, Herr Ohlmann.'

'Champagne?'

'Thank you.'

A waiter wearing a white jacket appeared with a tray. Ohlmann raised his glass. 'Your health.'

'The Party!' Anna responded. This was Bollinger!

'Come and sit down.'

Anna sat on a settee, Trudi beside her. Ohlmann and Gutemann sat opposite. 'Tell me about last night,' Ohlmann suggested. 'I am assuming you know something of it?'

'The countess was in the midst of it,' Gutemann said proudly.

'Countess?'

Anna repeated the version of events she had given Gutemann. When she was finished, Trudi clapped her hands, and was silenced by a look from her husband. 'This is very serious,' he remarked. 'The last thing we wish is to have the Brazilian police, or worse, the Brazilian press, interesting themselves in our affairs.'

'What was I supposed to do?' Anna asked. 'Stand there like a dummy and let them kill me?'

'Well, no, but . . .'

'Anyway, the police have no idea that there is any connection between me and your group.'

'The young man you stupidly rescued could be a danger. He will know the truth.'

'Of course he does not know the truth,' Anna snapped. 'He stopped his car, got out, and was hit immediately.'

'I still do not understand why you thought it necessary to take him to a hospital. You should have left him to die.'

'He is not supposed to survive in any event. And I needed his car.' It was clearly time to remind these people who she was. 'Now, Herr Ohlmann. I came here to make contact with fellow survivors of the Reich, so that we can look forward to a revival of our fortunes in the future, and perhaps even make plans for that future. Not to be lectured like a schoolgirl. I should remind you that I served eight years as Herr Himmler's aide. He had absolute faith in my judgement. If you are not prepared to do the same, then I would like to be taken back to my hotel.'

'Of course we are prepared to accept your judgement,' Trudi said soothingly. 'Fritz, some more champagne. And you will stay to lunch. Friedrich is a little tense today. This is the first time that we have lost someone since coming here.'

'I accept that the situation is unfortunate.' Anna sipped a fresh glass of champagne.

'And I apologize for my manner,' Ohlmann said. 'It is just that our leader is upset.'

'Then take me to him and I will reassure him,' Anna suggested, her heartbeat quickening.

Ohlmann nodded. 'I will set up a meeting.'

'You mean he is not here?'

'No. I will be frank with you, Countess. He had a difficult time, getting out of Germany, and then reaching Brazil. Thus he has become easily concerned when things do not happen exactly as he would prefer, and he is also very suspicious; he knows that there are a number of people, from all sides of the political spectrum, who would like to see him at Nuremberg. Therefore while he was delighted to see your advertisement, he wished to be sure that it was actually you.'

'And am I actually me?'

'I do not think there is anyone who could possibly impersonate you, Countess.'

'I'm so glad,' Anna said. 'So now I am allowed to meet him.'

'I have said, I will set up a meeting as soon as possible.'

'And now I think we should have lunch,' Trudi said.

Friends Like These

T he meal was quite convivial, full of reminiscences about the 'great days' in Berlin when Germany seemed destined to rule all Europe, if not the world. And the food was excellent, while there were even some bottles of Hock.

Trudi was ebullient throughout the meal, in some contrast to the two men, and when the coffee was served, she said, 'This has been a splendid occasion, Countess . . . Anna.'

'I have enjoyed it too,' Anna agreed. 'And now I should be getting back.'

'Do you have to? You are welcome to siesta here.' Her eyebrows arched. 'You can use my bedroom.'

Anna regarded her for several seconds. Another Belinda? Married to Ohlmann, whose ideas on sex, she has no doubt, were of the 'Brace yourself, Sheila' variety, she couldn't blame her. But from her point of view, the issue was, could she be useful. To find that out, it would be necessary both to separate her from her men folk and to establish just how fervent a Nazi she was, as opposed to just fervent. 'No, I really must get back,' she insisted. 'But I will require someone to drive me.'

'Oh, I will do that,' Trudi said. 'Gutemann is half sleep. Aren't you, Gunther?'

Gutemann grunted; he had certainly drunk a lot of wine.

Trudi gave a little giggle. 'Then perhaps I could siesta in your bed?'

'That sounds like fun,' Anna agreed, and got up. 'Well, Herr Ohlmann, that has been a most enjoyable meal. I look forward to hearing from you again, very soon.'

Ohlmann nodded. 'Tomorrow.'

'That will do very well.' Andrews would be here by tomorrow. 'Then I will say auf wiedersehen.'

She accompanied Trudi down to the garage, where Bruno looked rather put out at being told that he was not needed, then she was seated in the front beside Trudi, who drove very fast.

'I am so excited,' the German woman confessed.

'What about?'

'Well . . . at meeting you again after all these years. Of being in a car with you, alone.'

'I am flattered.'

'If you knew the stories they tell about you . . . but I suppose they are all true.'

Anna gripped the side of the door as they rounded a corner, apparently on two wheels; it would really be ridiculous if after all the work that had been done to get her in this position she were to be killed in a car accident. 'I have a terrible feeling that they probably are. You do know that there is a lot of police activity on this road.'

'Because of what happened last night? Did you really kill four men?'

'Well,' Anna said, 'they were trying to kill me.'

'Weren't you terrified?'

'I was too busy to be terrified. There they are.'

Trudi slowed to a reasonable speed, and they smiled at the policemen, who made no effort to stop them; they seemed on the point of concluding their search for any additional clues.

'Anyway,' she remarked, increasing speed again. 'You have done it before. For the Reich. Is it true that you have killed more than twenty people?'

'I'm afraid so,' Anna conceded. 'I was trained to it.'

'And . . .' Trudi's tongue came out and circled her lips. 'Is it true that you were the Fuehrer's mistress?'

'Eva Braun was the Fuehrer's mistress. He was attracted to me, yes.'

'And you slept with him?'

'He was attracted to me,' Anna repeated.

'And is it true . . . they say –' another lick of the lips – 'that you have slept with every eligible man in Berlin. And every eligible woman as well.' This time she glanced sideways.

'I did have other things to do,' Anna pointed out.

'Oh. Yes.'

She relapsed into silence, obviously uncertain how to proceed, although she had left her objective perfectly clear. But she could certainly be milked for a great deal of information. Anna remembered how Josef Goebbels had used the technique of looming sex to interrogate her the first time they had got together, and it had very nearly worked. She did not suppose this woman who had just about seduced herself with desire for so famous a figure, would be capable of very great resistance. She let Trudi ponder on the situation until they were in the suburbs of the city, then she said, 'This leader your husband wants me to meet, do I know him?'

'I'm sure you do. In fact . . .' Another sideways glance.

'You mean he could be an ex-lover? How exciting. But if he was, he wouldn't need anyone else to identify me, would he?'

'It was our job to make sure that it actually was you, and not some impostor, who could be an enemy.'

'Ah,' Anna said. 'Of course.'

They pulled into the courtyard of the hotel, entered the lobby together. Anna collected her key, checked to make sure there were no messages, and the clerk said, 'Inspector d'Andrade called to see you, senorita.'

Almost certainly about the shoes. Unless Jerry had taken a turn for the worse. 'What did you tell him?'

'That you had gone out for lunch.'

'And?'

'He said he would see you later.'

She thought it would be a hoot if he turned up in the middle of her siesta. 'Thank you, Carlos.'

'Will there be trouble for you?' Trudi asked as they rode up in the lift, gazing at each other.

'I shouldn't think so. He's a policeman, crossing Ts and dotting Is.'

'You are so calm. While I feel so . . . so . . .'

'Excited,' Anna reminded her.

'Oh, yes, as if I were on the edge of the experience of my life.'

'We must try to make it so.' They reached the seventh floor, and she unlocked the door and showed Trudi into the room.

'This is very nice.' Trudi opened the double French doors and went on to the balcony. 'And the view . . .'

Anna joined her, looked down at the now crowded beach. 'I walk there every morning, as a rule. In my bare feet. Going back to my childhood.' Which was drawing the bow a bit; there were no beaches in Vienna.

'That must be heavenly. You do know that the Metropole is one of the most expensive hotels in Rio?'

'Is it?' Anna asked. 'No, I did not know that.'

'But it does not matter to you. Have you got a rich lover?'

'Doesn't everyone?' She supposed that Uncle Sam could be classified as a rich lover.

'I don't.' Trudi wandered back into the bedroom, kicked off her shoes.

'That's an expensive house.'

Trudi grimaced. 'It's not ours.'

'Ah. It belongs to the group's benefactor.'

Trudi turned to face her. 'You know about him?'

'Poor Schuler told me, before he got hit.'

Trudi shivered. 'You speak so calmly about death. You could have been killed.'

'But I wasn't,' Anna pointed out. 'What is this man's name?'

'I couldn't possibly tell you that.'

'Why not?'

'It's a deadly secret. We are all sworn to keep it a secret inside the group.'

'But I am going to join the group, aren't I?'

'That depends on the leader. If he accepts you.'

'Of course,' Anna agreed, and having unzipped her sundress, let it slip past her thighs to the floor and stepped out of it; as usual she wore only knickers underneath. Trudi stared at her with her mouth open; her breathing had quickened.

'Those cuts and bruises . . .'

'Well,' Anna said. 'I did fall down a hill, last night.'

'And you . . .'

'I know,' Anna said. 'I take these things calmly. They have happened before. We are talking about Martin Bormann, are we not?'

'Oh. I . . .'

'I know,' Anna said. 'It is a deadly secret.' She sent the knickers behind the dress. 'Well, I am going to bed. Were you going to join me?'

The buzz of the telephone awoke Anna. She stretched out her arm to pick it up. 'Yes,' she said sleepily. She felt utterly relaxed.

'I'm sorry to bother you, senorita,' the clerk said. 'But there is a gentleman here to see you.'

She looked at her watch. Five o'clock. She wouldn't put it past Clive to have become impatient and disobey her instructions. 'It's not the gentleman who was here this morning, is it?' And then remembered that there had been two gentlemen to see her that morning.

'No, senorita. This gentleman has not been here before.'

And it could not be the policeman again; the clerk knew who d'Andrade was. 'Has he a name?'

'Excuse me, senor. The senorita wishes to know your name.'

'Look, give me that,' said an unmistakable voice.

'Oh, shit!' Anna remarked, without thinking.

'Senorita?' The clerk was alarmed.

'Darling!' Anna said. 'You were not arriving until tonight.'

'I got an early plane. Look, what the hell is going on? I'm coming up.'

'You can't. I mean . . . give me five minutes.'

'Now!'

'Fuck it!' She hung up.

'Anna?' Trudi was also sitting up, a splendidly tousled sight. 'What is happening?'

'That was my lover. I knew he was coming to Rio, but I didn't expect him so soon. Listen, he mustn't find you here. He knows nothing of my Nazi background. He'd throw a fit. You must leave. Quickly.'

'Leave? I've nothing on. I'll hide in the cupboard.'

'You could be there a long time.' Anna got out of bed and started gathering up Trudi's clothes. 'Across the hall there is an empty room. You can go in there and dress, and then leave. Quickly, now.'

Trudi also got out of bed, and stood there, uncertainly. Anna stuffed her clothes and shoes into her arms and pushed her out of the door. Down the corridor she could hear the whirring of the lift.

'Anna . . .'

'I'll make it up to you, I swear. Now hurry.' She closed the door and surveyed the room. Her own clothes were scattered about but there was nothing unusual in that. She took the door off the latch, and got back into bed just as there was a knock.

'It's open.' she called.

Andrews entered the room, closed the door, and regarded her. 'You're early,' she reminded him.

'Are you going to tell me what's going on? I have just run into a naked woman in the corridor.'

'That must have been exciting for you.'

'She had come from this room. What the hell was happening in here?'

'I was working.'

'In bed?'

'I have done some of my best work in bed.'

'But . . . a woman?'

'You really are a hidebound male. That woman is my prime contact and source of information. But I couldn't have you in here with her, because she thinks you are my slightly dim sugar daddy. Come and sit down, and I will explain it to you.'

She patted the bed, and he cautiously advanced and sat beside her; as she didn't want to distract him, she pulled the sheet to her throat. 'Have you seen Jerry?'

'I contacted our office, and they said he's in intensive care, and cannot see anyone.'

'Did they tell you what happened?'

'They don't know what happened. The police hand-out is that Jerry was innocently caught up in a gun battle between two rival criminal gangs, and got hit. But his girlfriend escaped injury. This didn't sound right to them, as they didn't know he had a girlfriend, but they felt it best to keep a low profile and accept it. What did happen?'

Anna told him. When she was finished, he gave a low whistle. 'You seem to be more important to Moscow than we supposed. So what happens next?'

'As regards the Reds? That hit squad was not local.'

'How can you tell that?'

'Because one of them was Tserchenko. Remember the female boss of the Women's Section at the Lubianka?'

'A large woman. You broke her neck. I never knew her name.'

'Her name was Tserchenka.'

'Shit! You mean . . .'

'Her brother. Because of that relationship, he appears to have been assigned by the NKVD, as it then was, to get me. He tried in Warsaw in 1944, without too much success. Then he actually did get me, outside of Berlin, in March of last year. But his orders apparently were to take me back alive to stand trial.'

'So I suppose you shot your way out, as usual.'

'I had a friend,' Anna said modestly. 'At least, he was my friend then. Your man Edert.'

'But . . . if he was your friend, why did he turn you in to us?'

'The operative word is, then. That's irrelevant now. The point is that Tserchenko has kept on looking. But he operates out of Moscow, not Rio. And there's another thing. When they were looking for me in those bushes, he was being given orders by someone else, one of the men on the road. And the orders were again, to take me alive.'

Andrews shook his head. 'Sooner or later they're going to realize that isn't on, and it'll be a sniper's rifle a mile away.'

'I think it'll be later. Don't you see, Joe? That hit squad came from Moscow, not here in Rio. I'm not even sure the embassy knew they were here. And as they were carrying no identification, the local police don't have a clue. It could be several days, or even weeks, before Moscow starts to worry about what might have happened. By which time we'll be out of here.'

'You mean you've found out where Bormann is?'

'I think I'm going to find out tomorrow. However, going on what Trudi Ohlmann told me just now—'

'Between gasps, I take it.'

'Why, Joe Andrews, I do believe you're jealous.'

'Anna—'

'Just joking. I was saying, it's not going to be too easy. Apparently he is even more paranoid than Hitler. He has at least two bodyguards with him all the time, and no one is allowed into his presence without being searched. I am certainly not going to be allowed to keep my shoulder bag.'

'Hm. You'd better leave it to us.'

'Leave what to you? I'm the only person who can lead you to him.'

'Yes, but once you've done that and leave again, we can move in.'

'Joe, you are one of those unfortunate men who always believe that everything is going to turn out just the way you want it to. Life isn't like that. I don't know what sort of a reception I'm going to get, but I suspect it is going to be wreathed in suspicion, if only because, as I told you, Bormann doesn't like me, and I'm damned sure he doesn't trust me. It's extremely likely that having seen my ad, he has decided this would be a good time to close the Countess von Widerstand's file.'

'Shit! We never thought of that. Look, we'll follow you, and protect you.'

'Jerry was going to do that.'

'With respect . . .'

'Oh, sure. You sent a kid to do a man's job. Do you know that during that shoot-out he never even drew his pistol, much less fired a shot? Mind you, I once knew a full-grown, experienced man, who didn't fire a shot, on a similar occasion.'

'You certainly know how to twist the knife. Is that going to haunt our relationship for the rest of our lives? I was following your instructions.'

'Are we going to have a relationship for the rest of our lives?'

'OK, I get the message: you want out. But you agreed—'

'Of course I agreed. No, I do not want out. I want Bormann, even more than you do. But I need protection. Can you get hold of another of those Walthers, with the same set-up?'

'Ah . . . I should be able to. You do realize that we wish Bormann alive.'

'Even if that involves me being dead?'

'Well, of course not, Anna. You are of paramount importance to us.'

'I really would like that in writing. I need the gun first thing tomorrow morning. I'm being picked up at eleven.'

'You'll have it at nine. And we'll be ready at eleven.'

'If you and your people intend to follow me, for God's sake be discreet.'

'We will be.'

'Well, then, that seems to cover everything. Now, I need a bath. Getting information out of someone is hot work.' She got out of bed, went to the bathroom, turned on the taps. Andrews watched her with sombre, longing eyes.

'That bruise, and those scratches . . .'

'I got them evading the Reds. By the way,' she said over her shoulder. 'Did you know that Belinda Hoskin is dead?'

'What?' He got off the bed, came to the bathroom door. 'You men the Reds got to her too?'

Anna added bath salts. 'If they did, they took a roundabout route. Apparently the last person to see her alive, apart from her killer of course, was my sister.'

'And you think she killed Belinda? Why would she do that?'

Anna tested the water, and turned off the taps. 'I have absolutely no idea.' She stepped into the tub and lowered herself into the water. 'Oooof! That stings. However, the point is that Katherine underwent the same training that I did, and is just as capable of breaking someone's neck as I am. That's how Belinda died, of a broken neck.'

'Good God! You mean she's being charged with murder?'

'Not right now, because they don't know where she is.'

'What are you going to do? Belinda was . . . well, as I told you, she gave me the impression that you were quite close.'

'I happened to be on hand to save her life on two occasions, and she was extremely grateful.'

'You are unique.'

'Have you just realized that?'

'You are also dangerously over-confident.'

'Actually,' Anna said, slowly soaping herself. 'I am not the least bit overconfident. I know how good I am, and I know how poor the opposition is, nearly always, because so many of them have the idea that if a large man armed with a gun confronts a woman, she will necessarily swoon in terror. But I also know that there are men who do not fall into that category. Bormann knows everything about me that is worth knowing, thus he also knows that just confronting me with a gun or even with apparently overwhelming numbers is not necessarily going to leave him standing. Everything will depend upon whether I can convince him that I am genuinely here to aid in reviving Nazism. If I can't, or if he happens to have formed a pre-opinion, he may shoot first and ask questions afterwards.'

'You can lie there and say that, so calmly?'

Anna pulled out the plug and then stood up. Andrews handed her a towel. 'What I am trying to tell you, Joe, is that if that situation looks like developing, it is I who am going to have to adopt the shoot first and ask questions later mode.'

He considered for a moment, watching her drying herself. Then he nodded. 'Point accepted.'

Anna stepped out of the bath. 'And that, should it happen, must not affect our arrangement.'

'Agreed. But Anna, we are going to be right behind you. You have my word.'

'I'm relying on it.'

'And now . . .'

She put on her dressing gown. 'And now, Joe, I propose to have supper and an early night. Tomorrow could be a long day.'

She was tempted to contact Clive, if only because her instincts were warning her that tomorrow, for all the confidence she had expressed to Andrews, might be her last on earth. But for that very reason she decided to leave things as they were. She had promised to call him as soon as she was able, but anything of the dewy-eyed variety would be a distraction. Besides, he would probably want to muscle in, with the very likely outcome that he and Joe would wind up shooting at each other. After tomorrow, now, it would be time to celebrate.

She slept soundly, stayed in bed until eight, and then ordered breakfast. Needless to say it was served by her aspiring floor waiter, delighted to find her again in a dressing gown. 'I'm expecting a parcel this morning,' she told him.

'Ah, yes, senorita. I have it here.'

He produced the box wrapped in brown paper from the lower shelf of the trolley.

'Brilliant!' It was certainly very prompt. She turned it over, but there was no sign of it having been tampered with.

'It is what you want?' Manuelo asked.

'I think so.'

'But you no wanna open it to make sure?'

'Not right now. Thank you, Manuelo.'

He hesitated, then left. Anna checked that the door was locked, unwrapped the parcel, and opened the box. The set up was exactly the same as in Virginia, again with two magazines and a silencer. After the incident with the Russians, she had become quite fond of the little gun. So, thus far Joe had been as good as his word.

She loaded the gun, showered, breakfasted and dressed, in a green sundress, the gun nestling against her groin, and added her jewellery. As she was anticipating at least a cursory search, she tucked the spare magazine into the lining of her sunhat; it made only a slight bulge, and the feel of it against her head was reassuring. Of course, if she was submitted to a proper search, both gun and magazine would quickly be detected, but as she had warned Andrews, if there was any risk of that happening she intended to start shooting first.

She telephoned for an appointment with the salon. This was for nine o'clock, and she was about to leave her room when the phone rang. 'Inspector d'Andrade is here to see you, Senorita O'Flaherty.'

'Oh, for God's sake! I have an appointment with your hairdresser in five minutes.'

'He says it will only take a moment, senorita. He has something for you.'

She knew what it had to be. 'Oh, very well. I suppose it's on the way. I'm coming down.'

He was waiting in the lobby, looking very spruce, and carrying a paper bag. 'Senorita!' He kissed her hand, and sat beside her on a settee. 'You grow more beautiful every time I see you.'

Anna reflected that might not altogether be a compliment, as the only previous time he had seen her she had been covered in mud. But she said, 'You say the sweetest things.'

'And you are fully recovered from your ordeal?'

'I'm working on it.'

He considered this for a moment, then said. 'I have something for you.' He held out the bag.

Anna opened it. 'My shoes! Oh, Inspector, you are so efficient.'

He gazed at her, waiting.

'I know,' she agreed. 'They were not where I said. You found them in the ravine below the gunman's car.'

'That is correct.'

'And I told you that I lost them when I stopped later on to see if I could help Mr Smitten. The fact is, I was so confused and upset by what happened . . .'

'Of course.' He patted her hand. 'But I would like to know what did happen.'

'I remembered yesterday. I had taken them off in the car, before we came upon the gunmen. I was carrying them in my hand. Then when Jerry got out and was hit, and I knew I had to get him back into the car, I must just have thrown them away. I was so upset . . .'

'Of course,' he said again, this time giving her hand a little squeeze. 'I entirely understand. I am sorry to have bothered you.' He released her, reluctantly.

'Have you been able to see Mr Smitten?'

'No, unfortunately. He is in intensive care. Have you seen him?'

'They won't let me in either.' She realized that either she or Andrews would have to manage that before the police could get to him.

'We will have to be patient.' He stood up. 'You still have no immediate plans for leaving Rio?'

He does not believe my story, she thought. 'No, Inspector, as I told you the night before last, I am certainly not leaving until Jerry is better.'

'Of course. Then perhaps I will see you again.'

She watched him leave then went to the salon. By this time the story of her 'accident' had permeated every aspect of the hotel. The girls fussed over her – her nails needed attention as well, as some mud had even permeated her gloves, and while she had scrubbed them clean they needed filing – chattering in

Portuguese, but, she gathered, mainly discussing the colour, quality and above all, length of her hair. There were obviously so many things they would have liked to do with it, and they were quite put out when she insisted that they leave it loose, but secured by its clasp.

Then she returned upstairs, put on her hat, and surveyed herself in the mirror, gazing into the calm blue eyes reflected by the glass. Was this the end, or the beginning, she wondered?

At ten thirty she returned downstairs, and sat in the lounge, legs crossed, staring straight in front of herself, hands still, her dark glasses dangling from her fingers. By now the hotel staff had got the message, that when Senorita O'Flaherty sat like that, she did not wish to be involved in the lightest of conversation, and so while they all clearly found pleasure in watching her, no one dared approach her.

At five to eleven Bruno the chauffeur appeared. This was disappointing: Anna had hoped it might again be Trudi. But he seemed delighted when she sat in the front beside him; happily there was not a sign of anyone watching them as they drove out of the yard.

'Is this another long drive?' she asked.

'Longer.'

'Ah.' She had to content herself with looking out of the window. It was a different road from those she had been driven over on the three previous days, and soon began to climb more steeply. Then after over an hour, on rounding a bend, they came upon a dirt track leaning off to the left. Without warning Bruno swung down this. Anna was almost nodding off, and being unprepared for the sudden manoeuvre was thrown against the side of the car, while as Bruno now increased speed over a very uneven surface, she was breathless for several seconds. Then she straightened her hat and demanded, 'What in the name of God . . .?'

'I am sorry, Fraulein, but we were being followed.'

'What?' So much for the invisible surveillance she had been promised. 'Followed by whom?'

'I do not know, Fraulein. But it is better not to take risks, eh? Or you could be shot at again.' He slowed the car, just in time, Anna considered, to avoid breaking a spring.

'But the other car . . . when they discover we are no longer on the road, will they not come back?'

'This road bends a great deal. It will take them some time to discover that we are no longer on it.'

'But they will come back, eventually. And when we return to the road, we will run into them.' Perhaps literally, she thought.

'No, no. This track is a short cut. We do not have to go back to the highway at all.'

Shit! Anna thought. So much for plans. She was now entirely on her own.

They drove for another half an hour, climbing all the time, and then peaked a hill and could look down on the main road, winding some hundred feet beneath them. They could see back at least a mile, but there was no other car in sight.

'They have turned back,' Bruno said with some satisfaction.

'So where do we go from here?' Anna was feeling quite battered from the continuous bumping.

'We have arrived.' He pointed. 'There.'

The track descended the hillside, to join the road, on the far side of which there was another track, which led into a sizeable wood. And looking more closely, Anna could detect a gleam of metal amidst the trees. A fence! The place reminded her of the internment camp in Poland where her parents had been imprisoned for several years, as hostages for her loyalty to the Reich.

'I see,' she remarked. 'I assume that fence is electrified?'

'Of course. No one can get in.' Bruno smiled. 'Or out. Unless the gate is opened for them.'

'How very reassuring,' Anna agreed. She was getting deeper and deeper into the mire, and she didn't know if she had enough fire-power, or indeed, cartridges, to get herself back out.

Bruno drove down the hill, across the road, and along the facing track. The fence was only a few yards within the tree fringe, and he stopped before a large gate which was supported by massive pillars. He got out, and used a telephone set into one of these uprights, spoke for a few moment, and then turned back to the car. 'Would you come and stand beside me, Fraulein?'

Anna raised her eyebrows, but got out and joined him.

'Now, would you look up at that box above the telephone?'

Anna obliged. 'May I ask what is happening?'

'You are looking into a camera, which is taking your photograph, and relaying it back to the house.'

'And we have to wait here while it is developed?'

'No, no. The image is received instantaneously. It is a television camera. You have heard of television?'

'Yes,' Anna said. Although she had never seen a television

screen. 'And there is one here, in the back of beyond? Oh, don't tell me. Your benefactor . . .'

'Exactly. We have all the latest equipment. At this moment, your every movement is being shown up at the house, and your voice is being heard.'

'Whatever will they think of next?'

'Ah! We are admitted.'

The gates were swinging in. They got back into the car and drove through, and the gates closed behind them. The drive wound through the trees for about five minutes, then they came to a ranch-house style building, all on one level, which formed an inverse U, stretching away from them. Outside the flat portico facing them were two men, armed with tommy guns, and two Rottweilers. Once again Anna's memory returned to the internment camp in Poland, which had presented exactly the same picture, except that there had been several houses instead of just one, and the dogs had been Alsatians. She supposed it was reassuring that these people's lack of imagination made them always act in exactly the same way.

'Are you afraid of dogs?' Bruno asked as the car stopped.

'No.' Anna opened her door.

'These are very fierce,' he warned.

'Ah, but you see, dogs are afraid of me.'

She got out and the animals came forward, growling, teeth bared.

'Get back in the car,' one of the men shouted. 'I will chain them.'

Anna ignored him and walked forward, projecting unrelenting hostility from her brain into her muscles and her arteries, while keeping her right hand close to her side zip. She knew that while dogs, like most animals, could smell fear in human sweat and would thus attack, they could also smell confident hostility, and would never take on such an enemy, certainly when larger than themselves.

The dogs ceased their advance, and sat down, wagging their tails. Anna went up to them and stroked their heads.

The guards arrived. 'That is amazing,' one said. 'I have never seen them do that before, with a stranger.'

'You have not studied nature,' Anna pointed out.

The man swallowed. 'You are to go in.'

'Thank you.'

She went up the short flight of steps. The front door was opened for her, by Trudi. 'Anna! How nice to see you again.'

Yesterday afternoon might never have been. But this was not

the Trudi of yesterday either; this woman was trembling, and not actually looking at her. 'It is nice to be here, at last,' she agreed, stepped forward, and was plunged into blackness.

A large sack had been dropped over her head. Instinctively, even as her knees buckled, she reached for her side zip, but before she could find it the sack was drawn very tight, pinning her arms to her side, and she found herself on her knees.

Shit! she thought. Shit, shit, shit! She had been taken completely by surprise, by people who had acted with even more immediate determination than herself; she had expected at least a confrontation with Bormann before having to go into action.

Now . . . it was difficult to think as she was forced forward on to her face on the floor.

'Be careful,' Trudi said. 'She must not be hurt. Now.'

When I get my hands on this bitch, Anna thought. But for the moment her hands weren't going anywhere. Someone was pressing on her back to hold her on the floor, and other hands were feeling beneath the sack, two pairs, finding her wrists and pulling them back, and then forcing them together. She felt the touch of steel, and then heard the click as the handcuffs were closed. She was helpless.

And, she realized, in the most dangerous position in her life. In all her previous tight situations she had had some form of back-up available, a perpetual Plan B, whether it had been an accessible concealed weapon, an actual partner, or even the mere fact that she was a member of the SD, the most feared organization in the Reich. And in the last resort, there had been her beauty and her sensuality. That was what had saved her even from Lars Johannsson, who had assumed that she was entirely at his mercy, and had not secured her arms before raping her.

But here, if Bormann was indeed in command, she was, to all intents and purposes, in the hands of the SD. And if she had a concealed weapon, it was no use to her until she could get rid of the handcuffs, before she was subjected to a body search. That seemed an unlikely scenario. While her back-up had disappeared, and was presumably charging up and down the road wondering what had happened to her.

Her only chance was an arrogant bluff. The hands were dragging her to her feet, and the sack was pulled from her head, taking with it her hat and dark glasses, which had in any event come off, and also her clasp, freeing her hair which was scattered everywhere, including across her face.

'You are a mess,' Trudi remarked, and pulled the strands from her eyes.

'Just what are you playing at?' Anna inquired, at her coldest.

'I am obeying orders, my dear. Bring her along.'

The two men holding her arms forced her forward, while Bruno, who had also taken part in the assault, walked beside her, carrying the hat. Well, she thought, she had never really taken to him.

But Gutemann . . . he was waiting in an inner doorway, which she noted was made of steel, leaning on his stick. 'I am sorry about this, Anna,' he said.

'You should be,' Anna snapped. 'Kindly instruct these goons to release me.'

'I cannot do that. But perhaps . . . come inside.'

One of her captors pushed her, and she nearly tripped; Bruno caught her arm to keep her up, and escorted her into the large room, comfortably but rather sparsely furnished, with the usual heavy shutters over the windows. Because of the trees that clustered round the house, there was not a lot of exterior light, but the room was illuminated by various strip lights high on the walls. Standing in the centre of the room were Ohlmann and Martin Bormann.

He did not seem to have changed at all since last she had seen him, presented the same nondescript appearance, chunky, unremarkable features, the same chunky, unremarkable body, of medium height and medium build, clad in a not very well made brown suit. It was difficult even to tell from his expression whether he was pleased or sorry to see her; but he must have caused this to happen.

'Well, Herr Bormann,' she said. 'Is this how you greet an old comrade?'

'Has she been searched?' His voice, like the rest of him, was a featureless monotone.

'She is not armed,' Trudi said.

'You are a foolish woman,' Bormann remarked. 'And you know nothing of this woman. Strip her!'

Anna opened her mouth to protest, and then closed it again; protests were not going to work here.

'Fool! Do not release her,' Bormann snapped as one of the men produced a key for the handcuffs. 'Tear the dress.'

The two bodyguards grasped her arms, while Bruno threw the hat on the floor, stood in front of her and dug his fingers into the bodice of her sundress. He would not meet her gaze, but she could almost see him salivating. He tugged, violently, and the material ripped right down to her waist. The watching men caught their breaths.

Bruno continued tugging, and the last of the material ripped, leaving the dress hanging in two halves from her shoulder straps, which were feeling as if they had been driven into her flesh.

There were more sharp intakes of breath. 'And you thought she wasn't armed,' Bormann commented. 'Get rid of that.'

Bruno stroked her flesh as he released the belt. He looked over his shoulder. 'And these?'

'Remove them as well. They will only get in the way.'

Bruno threw the holster behind the hat on to the floor and then pulled the knickers down to her ankles; she obligingly stepped out of them, losing one of her sandals in the process.

'I assume you have a reason for this ridiculous behaviour,' she said. 'If you wished me to undress, why did you not say so? There was no need to destroy my dress.'

'I hope you will die as arrogantly,' Bormann commented. 'But before you do that, you are going to have to tell me what I require to know. Put her in that chair.'

The two men holding her arms pushed her to the straight chair he had indicated, and made her sit.

'Keep holding her.'

Their hands moved to her shoulders, pressing down.

'Now secure her legs,' Bormann commanded.

Bruno knelt before her, and was handed a length of cord by Trudi. With this he tied her left ankle to the appropriate chair leg. Anna was very tempted to kick him, but that would accomplish nothing more than a probable beating. Her task was to remain as fit and alert as possible, until . . . She had no idea what might turn up, but she had to be ready to take advantage of it.

Trudi provided another length of cord, and Bruno pulled Anna's legs apart to secure her right ankle. She decided that if ever a man deserved to die, he was the one. After Bormann. But no one was going to die unless she could get free, and that meant some kind of help. She could not see the two men holding her shoulders, but she could look around the other faces. Bruno was again almost visibly salivating as he looked up her crotch. Trudi was clearly no less excited, but not with any affectionate intent; thus yesterday afternoon had had to be a set-up, into which she had blundered with that overconfidence Andrews had criticized. Ohlmann was also looking anticipatory, but Gutemann was apprehensive, and his face was working, as he no doubt remembered making love to her. He was her best hope. But he was a cripple.

Bormann was, as always, showing no emotion at all. And he remained her first problem.

'I assume,' she said, 'that you are going to tell me what this outrageous game is all about.'

'Game,' he agreed. 'Oh, yes, it will be a game.' He moved another straight chair into a position immediately in front of her, with its back to her, and then straddled it, so close that his knees actually touched hers. 'Why are you here, Countess?'

'I assumed I was coming to lunch with friends. I had no idea there were going to be silly games first.'

'Countess, you really do not wish to try my patience too far.' He stretched out his hand and grasped her left breast, not squeezing, but just holding it. Despite herself, Anna could not prevent a sudden quick breath, nor, to her disgust, could she prevent the nipple from hardening into his palm. 'Otherwise,' he said, 'I might just cut this off. And apart from the pain and the humiliation, where would the Countess von Widerstand be without her tits and her ass and her legs? Tell me why you are in Brazil.'

Anna got her breathing under control, but she wished he would let go of her. 'I am here because I was advised that this was the best place for me to be.'

'Who advised you of this? The American boyfriend you claim to possess?'

'No. He knows nothing of me. I met a man in Switzerland when I was on the run last year.'

'Would that be Laurent?'

How on earth could he know about that? Anna wondered.

Bormann actually smiled at her flitting expression. 'After Himmler deserted the Fuehrer, we had access to his files.'

Oh, the fool, Anna thought, to flee without destroying his files. But hadn't she always known that, for all his attempts to portray the ruthless policeman, her erstwhile boss had been a very foolish man? For one thing, he had always trusted her!

'He was condemned to death, in absentia, by the Fuehrer, for desertion. But then so were you.'

'I was given permission to leave Berlin by Dr Goebbels,' Anna said.

'Do you expect me to believe that?'

'It happens to be the truth.'

'Because you were his mistress?'

'Perhaps.'

'The doctor did not reveal this to the Fuehrer when your disappearance was discovered.'

'I am sure he had his reasons.' He had told her that he was sending her out into the world because he was sure that she would continue to spread death and destruction even after the Third Reich was history. Well, he had not been too far wrong. But then being a man who could not even trust his own judgement, he had betrayed her to the Russians, just to make sure that she too did not just disappear into history . . . at least without a sensational trial which he hoped would go far towards perpetuating the Nazi myth. But she did not suppose Bormann would appreciate that.

To her relief he at last released her, but remained sitting only inches away, staring at her. 'You are still sentenced to death.'

'By a dead man?'

He rested his hand on her knee, and slid it up to her thigh. Her muscles instinctively tensed, bur for the moment he did no more than grasp the flesh. 'The Fuehrer's decrees are eternal. But you have not answered my question. Did the man Laurent send you here?'

It was a convenient line to adopt. 'He did not send me anywhere. He suggested it would be the safest place for me to go.'

'With all of Himmler's stolen money?'

She had no doubt that he was using the word 'stolen' as regards the German government rather than the victims from whom it had been taken. 'That money is in a numbered Swiss bank account,' she said, with absolute truthfulness.

'To which you have access.'

'I might,' she agreed. Was this a possible lifeline?

'And Laurent also suggested that it might be possible to contact your, as you put it, old comrades here.'

'He did not. He merely told me that certain of my old comrades had already taken this route.'

'Including me.'

'He did not mention you.'

The hand on her thigh suddenly squeezed, very hard, the fingers seeming to eat into her flesh. Again she could not restrain a gasp, this time of pain. 'And he financed you to come and find me. Or did you use this numbered account?'

'No,' Anna panted.

'Then whose money are you using?'

'I . . . I told you. I have a friend.'

The grip relaxed, and she sighed in relief. The flesh on her thigh was even paler than usual where the blood had been driven away. 'This so-called American millionaire.'

'Yes.'

'Who sent you here. Why?'

'He did not send me anywhere. He knew that I wanted to get out of Europe, and he asked me where I would like to go. I said Brazil.'

'Why?'

'I have told you. I hoped I could find some old friends.'

'And the American knew of this.'

'No he did not. He knows nothing of my background. Only that I am a fugitive from Germany and a Displaced Person.'

His hand moved forward again, and she watched it as if it were a snake about to strike. Now his fingers moved round the back of her neck, under her hair, for the moment caressing her skull, but she braced herself for another agonizing squeeze, which, in that position, might well render her unconscious. 'But he followed you here.'

'He regards me as his possession.'

'And you would like to end that relationship.'

'I do not like being possessed.'

The fingers were stroking up and down the nape of her neck and her muscles remained tensed 'Who are these people who have been following you about, trying to kill you?'

'I do not know.'

The hand left her nape and came slowly round her neck, then the fingers slipped down, hooked her crucifix from between her breasts. 'Do you pray to your God every night?'

'No.'

The fingers left the crucifix, and instead moved to her breast again. This time the thumb and forefinger closed on her right nipple, again squeezing as hard as they could. Now she could not contain a little cry of agony.

'I think,' Bormann said, 'that everything you have told me has been a lie. I believe that you were sent here to find me. If you wish to live, you will tell me who sent you, and what he, or they, are planning.'

He paused, expectantly. 'I have no idea what you are talking about,' Anna said. She did not suppose there was any point in attempting to lie further, or indeed in telling him the truth; he was going to kill her no matter what she said, in which case her best course was to let him get on with it and keep worrying about who might be lying in wait for him.

And that would be the end of Anna Fehrbach, Countess von Widerstand, the most desirable as well as the most dangerous woman in the world. But she would still be beautiful when she died.

'Defiant to the last, eh?' Bormann asked. 'Do you really suppose it is going to be a matter of a bullet in the back of the neck and oblivion? No, no. I am not going to kill you, Anna.' Her head jerked, and he smiled, the most evil thing she had ever seen. 'I am going to destroy you, as a woman, before your own eyes. Bruno, bring that can of petrol I told you to have ready.'

The fingers released her nipple, and Anna could get her breath back. But her nerves were stretched to breaking point. She would not turn her head, but remained staring at her tormentor, while she listened to Bruno's feet on the floor, going and then returning with the jerry can of petrol, which he placed on the floor beside her chair.

'Now,' Bormann said, 'As I told you, it is possible that you may not die. In fact, I would prefer you to live. But the Countess von Widerstand will cease to exist, certainly as the world's most beautiful woman.'

He snapped his fingers, and Trudi unscrewed the cap and poured some of the petrol into it, handing it to Bormann. 'Only a little, you see,' he explained, and carefully emptied the contents of the cap on to Anna's stomach, just below the navel. The strong-smelling liquid trickled down her groin and into the pubic hair, and beyond. 'Now, you see, when I strike a match, you will ignite. We will burn out your sex, eh?'

Anna found that she was breathing very hard, as she thought, how the wheel does turn: five years before she had threatened an Abwehr agent with this same fate. But she had not done it. Bormann intended to.

'With respect, Herr Bormann,' Gutemann protested.

Too little, too late, Anna thought. But he had never really had anything to offer.

'Be quiet, you miserable cripple,' Bormann said. 'Enjoy the view.'

He took a box of matches from his pocket . . . and the lights went out.

Death in the Dark

'What the shit?' Bormann demanded.

The dogs were barking, and Anna realized with a surge of euphoria that someone must have cut the electrified fence. Now there came a burst of sub-machinegun fire, followed by another, and some shouts.

'My God!' Ohlmann yelled. 'We are under attack!'

Joe! It had to be Joe! He had come good after all. But was he going to be in time?

'That is impossible,' Bormann snapped. 'It is some intruder. Ohlmann, Bruno, go and see what it is.' Bruno hesitated, and Bormann smiled. 'I promise that I will wait for you to come back before I burn her.'

The two men left the room, and Bormann tuned back to Anna, taking a match from the box. 'Now, where were we?'

'You will not do it,' Gutemann said.

'I told you—'

'He's got a gun!' shouted one of the men holding Anna, at the same time releasing her shoulder to draw his own weapon.

Anna was looking past Bormann at Gutemann. And watched his face contort as he squeezed the trigger. Although he had stood beside her when she had engaged the Russians in Warsaw, this was the first time she had ever seen him actually fire a gun, and she realized instantly that he was not very good; the bullet all but struck her as it passed beside her head to hit the guard, who gave a cry and dropped his weapon with a clatter.

Trudi uttered a shriek. Bormann slipped from his chair and turned on his knees. The other guard released Anna's shoulder, but obviously was making no move to draw his gun as Gutemann's pistol moved to and fro.

From outside there came another burst of firing, and more shouts. But the dogs had ceased barking. Bormann ignored the noise. 'You're mad,' he declared. 'Put down that gun and come and help Hans.'

'You are not going to torture the countess,' Gutemann said.

'If she is guilty of betraying us, betraying the Reich, then she must die. But it must be a clean and quick execution. And you have not yet proved her guilt. Until then . . .'

The door burst open and Ohlmann staggered in; his shirt front was stained with blood. Trudi gave another of her shrieks and ran forward. 'Friedrich!'

'We are overrun,' Ohlmann gasped, sinking to his knees 'There are men everywhere. Tommy guns . . .'

'Where are the guards?' Bormann snapped. 'The dogs?'

'Dead,' Ohlmann groaned. 'All dead.'

'Bruno?'

'Him too.'

Damnation, Anna thought; she had intended to deal with Bruno herself.

'Albrecht,' Bormann snapped. 'Close and bolt that door.'

Albrecht ran to the door. Hans was still lying on the ground, moaning. Trudi was kneeling beside her husband, her arms rounds him. 'Friedrich,' she sobbed. 'Friedrich!'

Bormann rose to his feet, gazing at Gutemann, who had lowered his gun, clearly uncertain what to do, but when Bormann turned back to Anna, he levelled the weapon again. 'Touch her, and you're a dead man.'

As he spoke there was a clang on the steel door. Bormann hesitated for a moment, then ran for the inner door, Albrecht behind him. 'Wait for me!' Trudi shouted, deciding to abandon her husband and scrambling to her feet.

'Bitch!' Ohlmann muttered, but she ignored him and ran behind the two men, reaching the door just before it closed.

'Get me out of these handcuffs,' Anna snapped.

Gutemann limped forward and knelt beside Hans, who had stopped groaning and was either unconscious or dead. Gutemann fumbled in his pockets, found the key, turned to Anna and inserted it into the lock. She heard the click and the gunshot at the same time.

Ohlmann was now lying on the floor, but he had drawn his pistol, and Gutemann was on his back, arms flung wide, shot through the chest. But Anna's arms were free, even if her hands were a mass of prickling returning blood and her ankles were still tied to the chair legs. She flung herself sideways, as there was another shot, the bullet missing the chair to smash into the wall. Then she was on the floor beside Hans. And beside him lay his pistol. A Luger!

Another shot whined over her head. She realized that Ohlmann was now barely conscious, but he could still fire his gun. She peered round the chair as he was levelling the weapon again, and shot him through the head.

Then she could sit up and release her ankles and get to her feet. Men were still banging on the steel door, but she didn't want Joe taking over at this stage; she had too much to do. Too much she wanted to do.

There were three of them to settle with. She checked Hans' magazine; it contained six cartridges. She laid it down, checked Gutemann's; it had seven. She gazed at his face, contorted in the last agony of life. Poor Gunther, she thought. At the end he had sacrificed himself for her. But in view of what he had said, had he lived, he would have had to die with the others.

She went to Ohlmann, who was lying on his face in a pool of blood, extracted the pistol from his lifeless fingers. He was down to three unspent cartridges, but every one was useful.

Just to be sure, she picked up the discarded Walther as well, strapping the belt round her waist; the spare magazine was still in the lining of her hat. She put it in the pocket of her dress. Now she felt up to engaging in a gun battle, which she had to assume was very likely.

There was no time to lose. Someone was firing a tommy gun into the steel door, and from the twanging noise the metal was starting to disintegrate. She added Gutemann's and Hans' pistols to her pockets, carried Ohlmann's in her hand, and went to the inner door. This was closed and had been locked, but it was made of wood, and two shots shattered the lock. She dropped the all but empty gun on the floor, drew Hans' Luger, and cautiously pushed the door inwards.

The corridor was empty, but in the distance she could hear sound. She presumed that as they had realized the front of the house was now controlled by their assailants, they would be seeking another way out, nor could she doubt, in view of the elaborate security system, that there was such a way, with, she suspected, another car available.

But the corridor led between four en suite bedrooms, each of which had to be checked, and it was several minutes before she reached the end and a staircase leading down. She didn't know if they had heard the sound of her shots forcing the door – there was such a racket coming from behind her where the steel door was still resisting her rescuers – but she was certain they would have heard nothing of her since, as her bare feet were making no sound.

She knelt at the head of the stairs. Whatever lay beneath her was in virtual darkness because of the electricity failure, but she could hear movement, and a voice said, 'Hurry up!'

This was followed by a clang, and she deduced that they were loading a vehicle. Carefully she took the first step, crouching, the Luger thrust forward, staring in the gloom, suddenly terribly aware of the whiteness of her body; she had always been very proud of that.

After a few seconds she could make out that she was in another underground garage that contained a single car. The boot was raised, and Albrecht was loading suitcases and boxes into it. Bormann stood beside him, making no effort to help him. Trudi was holding one of the rear doors open, clearly anxious to get in, but now she looked up and saw Anna.

'Aaagh!' she screamed. 'She's there!'

Anna fired, and Albrecht went down with a shriek. The next shot was intended for Bormann, but he had dropped to the floor of the garage and she lost him in the gloom. Knowing that she was exposed, she grasped the banisters and swung herself over, just in time as a bullet smashed into where she had been a moment before; he had clearly armed himself since leaving the lounge.

The drop to the floor was further than she had estimated, and she felt a sharp and intense pain in her left leg. Shit! she thought. I've broken something. And Bormann was still alive.

She lay on her stomach, and discovered that the floor was extremely cold concrete. And there was a lot of rubbish between her and the car. With an effort she pushed a large, heavy cask to one side, and was rewarded by a bullet smashing into it beside her head, to be immediately followed by a gush of warm liquid over her shoulders; she licked her arm and discovered it was a quite passable red wine.

Trudi was still screaming, but now there was a crisp slap, and she gasped. 'Get behind the wheel, you stupid bitch,' Bormann commanded.

'But Albrecht—'

'Albrecht is dead.'

Anna cautiously raised her head. Her eyes were now attuned to the gloom, and she could see Trudi getting into the front of the car. But Bormann was on the other side; presumably he could control the garage door by means of the headlights. But he wasn't going to get away now. She levelled her pistol at the rear tyre, and was about to fire when she heard voices from above her.

'Anna! Anna?'

It was Clive!

And he was starting down the steps. 'Keep back!' she shouted, even as Bormann fired. The bullet struck the steps and ricocheted, and Anna emptied Hans' gun, no longer seeking Bormann but, to take his eye off Clive, sending the five shots into the rear of the car, which was just starting to move. The petrol tank exploded with an enormous whoosh! the confined space doubling both the noise and the blast.

She crouched behind the wine cask, arms over her head. The cask fell apart, and she was soaked, while the reverberations roared back and forth around her. When they slackened, she raised her head.

The car was a blazing wreck. Much as she had intended also to settle with Trudi herself, she could only hope that the woman had died in the explosion, otherwise she would be burning to death. And Bormann? Cautiously she stood up, grunting in pain as she put weight on her injured ankle.

'Anna?' Clive called. 'For God's sake, Anna! Are you all right?'

A bullet whined past her head and smashed into the wall behind her. The bastard was alive! She dropped Hans' pistol and drew Gutemann's, sending an initial couple of shots into the flames just to keep him busy and then hobbling to one side to take shelter behind some more wine casks, now clearly illuminated by the blaze. Two shots followed her and more wine was expended.

She realized that he must have at least two pistols. But she also had two left, and she was behind the still burning car. The flames were throwing lurid shadows up and down the walls and across the ceiling, actually making visibility more uncertain than in the previous gloom. And for the moment all was quiet; even Clive had stopped shouting, uncertain what might have happened in the explosion.

But although she could not see him, there was only one place Bormann could be – crouching on the left-hand front side of the car, where he would have been partially sheltered from the exploding petrol tank. And now he had stopped shooting. He had either run out of ammunition or he was re-loading.

It had to be now. She stood up and emptied Gutemann's gun in turn, sending the seven shots into the gloom in nine seconds, then limped forward, drawing the Walther as she did so. The heat was intense, but as she drew abreast of the car, stepping over Albrecht's body, she saw her target, slumped against the wall. He actually was reloading one of his guns – the other lay beside him – but his hand was trembling to the extent that he could not force the fresh magazine in.

He looked up and saw her, and his face, already twisted with pain, became yet more contorted. Anna stood above him, pistol levelled. 'The Third Reich ends here,' she said, and shot him through the head.

She returned round the car, and saw Clive halfway down the steps, Browning pistol thrust forward. Behind him were two other men, armed with tommy guns.

'Anna?' he asked. 'Oh, Anna!'

She holstered the Walther and was in his arms. He kissed and hugged her, and then held her away from him. 'Are you all right?'

'Not entirely.' She looked past him at the other men. 'I must apologize for my appearance. But I would have looked a lot worse if you guys hadn't turned up.'

'But that smell,' Clive said. 'And your face?'

'Part petrol, part wine. They were going to torch me. I need a bath. And I think I've broken my ankle.'

'Christ almighty!' He peered at her leg. 'But . . .'

'You turned up. So now you can carry me. Let's get out of here. But you'd better have your chaps use those extinguishers over there, or the whole building may go up.'

'You heard the lady,' Clive said.

'Yes, sir. Ma'am.' One of the men unhooked a fire extinguisher from the wall and began playing it on the flames.

'But what about all of these corpses, Mr Bartley?' the other inquired. 'They should be reported.' He peered at Anna, gulping as his eyes became accustomed to the gloom and he realized she was naked save for the tattered remnants of her dress.

'To whom?' she asked.

'Well . . . the police?'

'Are you out of your mind? Look, they're all dead. They'll be found eventually. But we don't want to be anywhere near here when they are.'

'Miss Fitzjohn is right,' Clive said. 'We have broken every law in the Brazilian book. We can't risk getting involved. But Anna, tell me one thing: these people . . . we know they were a Nazi cell, but were they important?'

'The man behind the car, the one I have just shot, was Martin Bormann.'

'My God! And you were acting for the Yanks? They sent you in here, alone . . .'

'Today I was acting for myself,' Anna said. 'I'll explain when we're on our way, and when you've told me how you got here.' And Andrews didn't, she thought. 'Now will you please give me a hand? This thing is hurting like hell.'

Clive lifted her into his arms and picked his way through the rubble and up the stairs, leaving his two partners to deal with the still blazing car. 'I have got to have a bath,' Anna said, 'I won't be long.'

'Your ankle . . .'

"You can have a look at it while I get rid of this muck,' she suggested 'In here will do.' He carried her into the first of the bathrooms and sat her on the chair before turning on the taps. She took off her belt and holster. 'If you hunt around out there you should find my knickers.'

'And this?' He held up the torn sundress Anna had just discarded.

'It would be nice if you could find me something else. Try the wardrobes.'

She used her arms to get into the bath and sank into the warm water, biting her lip; the pain was now considerable. She found a bar of soap, and washed vigorously. As always after an event of this nature she felt mentally exhausted, just wanted to curl up in a ball for a couple of hours. But also as always, she was not going to be allowed to do that. And the ankle promised to be a nuisance; it was the first time she had been incapacitated since being shot by Hannah Gehrig, seven years ago.

Clive returned. 'There are a couple of dressing gowns.'

'Damn!' She had hoped some of Trudi's clothes might be available. 'Ah, well, I suppose the hotel is getting used to it.' She extended her left leg clear of the water. 'How does it look?'

He held it, tenderly. 'Horrendous. It's swollen.'

'That figures. Can you move it?'

'If I do that . . .'

'It'll hurt like hell. But we must find out if it's broken.'

Tongue between his teeth he cautiously turned the foot in his hands. Anna sucked air into her lungs at the pain, but it remained dull rather than sharp, and there was no sound of grating bone. 'Aaagh!' she sighed. 'It's not broken. Help me out and then go find something to strap me up.'

'Your hair . . .'

'Oh, shit!' But he was right; it was soaked in wine. 'Hold on.'

So much for the girls' efforts, she thought, as she soaped; they'd have to do it all over again. 'OK.'

He lifted her from the tub, sat her on the chair with a towel, wrapped another round her head, and then hurried off, returning a few minutes later with a first-aid box. 'All mod cons.' He knelt before her and began passing a roll of Elastoplast round the ankle.

'Tight as you can,' Anna instructed. 'Now tell me how you got here? Or was it a miracle?'

'You need to remember I was a detective before joining MI6. You were here, working for the CIA. At what? It could only be sniffing out Nazis. Our embassy in Rio have a pretty good idea of which Nazis are here, and where. They weren't doing anything about it, because our government hasn't decided what to do about it, apart from making representations to the Brazilian government. There were two main addresses they had, so I had them both put under surveillance. And you, of course.'

'You are a bastard.' The strapping was finished, and the pain, if still severe, seemed to be under control. Anna stood up, towelled herself. 'But thank God you're a bastard. And today?'

'When you left the hotel, we followed. We had to keep out of sight of Andrews, who was also following you.'

'He was supposed to be looking after me,' Anna said. 'But he lost me.'

'I figured that. We passed him coming back. They didn't recognize us. We had no idea where you were, but then we got a radio call from one of our two stakes-out that you had just entered this property. So we came on here, considered the situation, and decided on executive action.'

'Even if you knew I was doing something for the Yanks?'

'Call it a gut feeling. There were three men in the car with Andrews. That is not ordinary surveillance. That is a back-up squad. So they were expecting you to run into trouble. Then there was that shoot-out, night before last. It seemed to me that you were operating in pretty dicey conditions. I was sent here to bring you back on two legs, not in a box.'

'And thank God for that. You mean Baxter approved this?'

'Baxter doesn't know about it yet.'

'Ah! And how did you get through that electrified fence?'

'We had to cut it. That was the most tricky part of the entire operation.'

'And that's when the lights went out.' She put on the knickers he had found. 'Show me these dressing gowns.'

He helped her into the next bedroom. 'Now you tell me exactly what you were doing here.'

'I'll take the green,' Anna decided. 'I told you, I was locating Bormann.'

'The CIA sent you to kill him?'

'No. They wanted him in Nuremberg. I was grinding my own axe.'

'And now . . .'

'Yes,' she agreed. 'We have some things to sort out.'

'Senorita?' The reception clerk peered at Anna; Clive's two assistants had dropped them off before disappearing – only two, for all of Ohlmann's hysterical exaggeration. 'Oh, senorita!'

'I know,' Anna agreed. 'Another accident. I seem to be prone.'

'Anna?' Joe Andrews had been seated on the far side of the lobby. 'What the sh— hell is going on? Where have you been? In a dressing gown? And . . .' He gazed at Clive.

'Just protecting my property, old buddy.'

Two other clerks had by now turned up behind the counter, intrigued by the exchanges.

'I don't think it is something we need to discuss in public,' Anna said. 'And I need to lie down.'

Andrews peered at the bandaged foot. 'You're hurt!'

'Nice of you to notice. We'll go up to my room.' She turned to the clerks. 'Senors, I have not had any lunch. Kindly have a full meal, for three, sent up. And two bottles of Freixenet. No, make that three.'

They rode up in the lift, Andrews glowering, Clive smiling, and Anna still trying to work out how to handle the situation. 'This room,' she announced, as the door closed behind them, 'is becoming an absolute haven of peace and tranquillity. I aim to keep it that way.' She discarded the borrowed dressing gown, and then the gun belt as well. 'I'm becoming quite fond of this little chap.'

'You mean . . . Bormann . . .'

Anna lay on the bed with a sigh. 'Bormann is dead. I warned you that might happen. He is dead along with . . .' She looked at Clive.

'There were only the two chaps outside and one inside. And the dogs, of course. Pity about the dogs. There was another chap, but he got through the steel door. Did you . . .?'

'Yes,' Anna said. 'Along with eight of his cohorts, Joe. I think you can say that this particular Nazi cell has been wiped out.'

'You . . . nine men?'

'Of course not. One was a woman. And I was only responsible for four. Two were internal affairs. And Clive's lot did for
the other three. And the dogs. As you say, Clive, sad about the
dogs, they were splendid animals.'

'Fuck the dogs,' Andrews shouted. 'I want to know what
happened.'

Anna got up and put on her own dressing gown, peered at
herself in the mirror. If there was still a faint aroma of petrol
and wine, at least she did not seem to have accumulated any
new bruises, apart from her ankle. What she really felt like was
a couple of aspirins to ease the pain, but as that might also dull
her brain, she supposed it would have to keep. 'Well, then, sit
down and I'll tell you.'

She was in the middle of her account when lunch arrived, a
four course meal distributed over three trolleys, with the required
three bottles of wine. Marshalling the three waiters was Manuelo,
whose eyes as always rolled as he discovered Anna in her dressing
gown, although he was distinctly disgruntled to discover that she
was intending to share the meal with two men while in such a
state of dishabille.

'Isn't he sweet?' Anna asked. 'Let's eat. And drink.'

Which they did while she finished her story. 'You realize you
could be in deep shit,' Andrews remarked when she had finished.
'Your instructions were to locate Bormann. Nothing more.'

'I warned you that there might have to be more,' Anna reminded
him. 'And what was I supposed to do, sit there and let him burn
my pussy?'

'From what you have just told me, you were going to be
rescued anyway.'

'I didn't know that, did I? And even when I knew someone
was there, I couldn't be sure they'd get to me in time. It was
Gutemann set the rescue ball going, from my point of view.'

'Why don't you admit it, Anna? From the very beginning you
were determined to kill Bormann, regardless of your instructions
from us.'

'Well,' Anna conceded, drinking wine. 'I did have that in mind.
But he made my mind up for me.'

'And like I said, you have probably landed us all in the cart.'

'Not if we act promptly,' Clive pointed out. 'Those fellows
kept themselves so much to themselves that I would say their
bodies are unlikely to be found for a day or two, and it's going
to take the local police a lot longer than that to connect what

happened to us, if they ever can. I have a plane standing by at the airport; Anna and I can be out of here tonight. I recommend you do the same.'

'You've lost the plot,' Andrews remarked. 'Anna works for us.'

'She has carried out this highly dangerous assignment for you. With no help from you. Be satisfied.'

'I don't think you understand the plot at all,' Andrews said, and looked at Anna.

'You remind me of two schoolboys squabbling over a toy,' Anna commented. 'Only you are grown men, and I am not a toy. However, Clive, you must understand that when I realized I had to leave England, Joe was my only way out, and he is right to say that I did take on a commitment.'

'You did not have to leave England, Anna. You could have come to us . . .'

'And you would have protected me from the law? Do you think you could possibly have done that?'

'Well . . . we would have done our best.'

'Not good enough, with my life at the end of it. And whatever your intentions, had I come to you I would have had to face a trial . . .'

'You shot those men in self-defence. Didn't you?'

'Yes, I did. But I would still have had to stand trial, and while I was doing so the MGB would have known exactly where to find me. '

'We would have protected you.'

'In a society where you are not allowed to shoot first, even if you know the other guy is a killer on the job? You weren't too good at protecting me in London in 1940, as I recall. I had to take care of those three Gestapo thugs myself.'

'We let you get away with it.'

'Because you were already at war with Germany. Unfortunately, you are not at war with the Soviet Union. Or do you have plans for that?'

'Touché,' Andrews commented. He had been following the exchange with amused interest.

'So you are turning your back on England,' Clive said bitterly. 'And me.'

'The last thing I want to do is to turn my back on you, Clive. England, now, they are going to have to prove that they haven't turned their backs on me.'

'And your parents?'

Anna frowned. 'Just what are you saying?'

'Don't get agitated. Their safety is guaranteed. But if you're not coming back to England, you won't be able to see them.'

'I'll have to make arrangements for them to join me when I'm settled somewhere else.'

'You mean somewhere in America.'

'That seems likely.'

'Working for the CIA.' His tone was more bitter yet.

'I'm afraid so,' Anna said. 'When the second half of our initial agreement is completed. I hope you remember that, Joe.'

'Sure I remember that. Just as soon as it can be done.'

'Uh-uh. The deal was, I deliver Bormann, you help me complete my private business.'

It was Clive's turn to look from face to face. 'I seem to have missed something.'

'Nothing to do with you, old buddy.'

But Anna had been thinking, during the discussion. She still could not bring herself entirely to trust Joe, and certainly his employers, who, as he had suggested, might well take the view that she had exceeded her instructions. Whereas Clive, whatever the limitations imposed on him by Baxter and Baxter's bosses, was at bottom, she was certain, one hundred per cent on her side. So she said, 'It's a small matter of ten million dollars I'm keen on reclaiming.'

Clive stared at her in consternation. 'What? You have . . .?'

'Now wait a minute,' Joe protested. 'We agreed—'

'That you would give me all the assistance I need to get that money, providing I agreed to work for you, and handed over the rest. However, if you haven't already guessed, it's not something you and I can do on our own. So I'm recruiting.'

Clive was still trying to get his facts straight. 'You have ten million dollars waiting to be picked up? You mean in that Swiss bank account? I hadn't realized it was that much.'

'The money in that account doesn't belong to me. This is something different.'

He gazed at her for several seconds, then snapped his fingers. 'The gold reserves. You know where they are.'

'I put them there.'

'Holy hell! But only ten million?'

'That's my share. And that is somewhere else. As you will have gathered, I need help to get it. Once we've done that, I'll tell you where the main body is.'

'Now, hold on,' Joe said. 'That was a deal between you and Uncle Sam.'

'No,' Anna said. 'That I'd find Bormann was the deal with Uncle Sam. Recovering my nest egg was a deal between you and me. Well, I've found Bormann for you. Now I want my half of the deal.'

'Half? What about the rest?'

'So I agreed to work for the CIA. I won't renege on that. But the contract doesn't begin until I get my money.'

He looked at Clive, who grinned at him. 'There are those who would say the contract has been rendered void by bringing in MI6.'

'I'm not bringing in MI6. I'm bringing in Clive as my back-up. I've an idea he may be slightly more useful than Jerry Smitten.'

Joe grimaced. 'I'm going to have to clear this with Washington.'

'No way. This is a private deal.'

'They already know of it. I had to tell them.'

'And they gave you the go ahead, providing I got Bormann. Now they have to deliver their side of the bargain. I'm not asking them to help, except maybe in smoothing the ground. I don't want them getting involved.'

'And you think the three of us can pull it off?'

'That depends. Are either of you any good at underwater stuff?'

'You are saying that the bullion was dumped under water?'

'Only my share.'

Again Joe looked at Clive.

'I can raise a couple of divers.'

'Who'll want a cut.'

'Who will be employed on a contract,' Anna said. 'To recover certain items from the bottom of a river.'

'And you don't think, when they discover just what these items are . . .'

'No,' Anna said, 'I do not think they will try anything. I hope they do not.'

Joe gulped. 'The guys who originally put it there . . .'

'Are both dead.'

'And the guys who helped you put away the main stuff?'

'Are also dead.'

'Holy shit! You did all of that?'

'I had a little help.'

'And?'

'He is also dead.'

'Great God Almighty.'

'But I did not kill him,' Anna said. 'He was shot by the Russians when we were trying to escape from Berlin.'

'He wasn't Edert, then.'

'Joe, you tell me that Edert is still alive.'

Joe again looked at Clive. 'You happy with all this?'

'What he means,' Clive said, 'is, are we going to be alive after we have recovered your money?'

'You're my partners,' Anna said. 'My lovers. But we'll need a little more help than a couple of divers. I'll tell you when we're on our way.'

They wheeled the trolleys out.

'What happens now?' Joe asked.

'You give me time to get dressed and pack, and then I think we should get out of here. We want to be well out of the country before anyone calls on that villa. I assume you have transport standing by?'

'I came down by scheduled flight,' Andrews said.

'Then I think your best bet is to come with us.'

'Seems to me you guys are calling the shots,' he complained.

'As of now, I am calling the shots,' Anna said. 'I assume this plane of yours will get us back to Europe, Clive?'

'It will. By a somewhat roundabout route.'

'That's right,' Joe said. 'We have to go via the States first.'

'No chance,' Anna said,.

'I have to report on this Bormann business.'

'Joe, until, you arrived here yesterday, you had no idea how close I was to getting to Bormann. All you, and therefore your superiors know is what was in my telegram, that I had lost contact with my target. No one can expect me, and therefore you, to have picked up the trail again so rapidly. You can be back in the States in another week, and explain what happened then. I'm sure Clive won't object to your getting the kudos.'

'Be my guest,' Clive said. 'I'm not supposed to be here, anyway.'

'So let's move it. I'll be ready in half an hour. There isn't that much to pack. You owe me two complete new outfits, one dinner gown and one sundress.'

'You didn't lose that fur?' He was anxious.

'No I did not. So if you gentlemen . . .'

'No packing,' Clive said.

'What?'

'From what you told me, the police aren't entirely happy with your account of what happened the other night. And again from what you told me, they ascertained that you would be here for at least the next few weeks. If you check out now, you can bet your bottom dollar that the hotel staff will feel obliged to inform them.'

'But who will pay the bill?'

'If that really bothers you, you can send them a cheque.'

Anna looked at Joe, who shrugged. 'Makes sense.'

'But . . . you mean, abandon all of these new clothes? Abandon my sable? I've only ever worn it once, on the flight down here.'

'Shit!' Joe commented.

'Anna,' Clive said patiently. 'When we get hold of your money, if it really is ten million dollars, you will be able to buy yourself a dozen sable coats. Now, I think we get out, while everyone is having a siesta.'

'Lavrenty,' Josef Stalin said, regarding his chief of police from benevolently sleepy eyes. 'How good of you to come up to see me, at such short notice. I know how busy you are, but I need your help. I do not understand this report. I would be so grateful if you could explain it to me.'

Beria lowered himself into the chair before the desk, situated in the Premier's private office in the Kremlin. Although he would have admitted it to no one, he was apprehensive. He regarded himself as indispensable to his master, and even a friend: he had stayed with him at his dacha in the Crimea, had taken tea with him and his children in an atmosphere of the utmost relaxed geniality. But he also knew that this man, after no doubt a pleasant interview, had condemned one of his predecessors to death by simply ringing a bell. Just as he knew that the kindly old gentleman now smiling at him had similarly condemned something like ten million people to death during his twenty-odd years of power, and that did not include those killed, or executed, or simply worked to death, during the recent war. Stalin's views on humanity were expressed in one of his own sayings, that one death is a tragedy, a thousand is a statistic.

Thus it was necessary to choose his words with care. 'I have to confess that I do not understand it myself. I am still seeking answers.'

'From Major Kovotnov? Or the embassy?'

'Both. But they are as confused as I. Kovotnov piloted the plane that took Kamarov and his squad to Brazil. He was instructed to wait for them until they were ready to come home, but that they would not be longer than three days. When the third day had elapsed and he had heard nothing from them, he approached the embassy. But as the mission was entirely secret, and, frankly, illegal, we had not advised the embassy of it, only that the aircraft was on a goodwill visit to Brazil. They had actually arranged for the crew to be entertained by the Brazilian air force. However, when Kovotnov returned there on the third day, he felt obliged to confide in the ambassador, whereupon the ambassador virtually ordered him to leave Brazil immediately. It seems that he had been visited by the police, who were investigating the mysterious deaths of five men on a lonely road outside of the city.'

'Five men?' Stalin queried. 'But Kamarov only had three with him.'

'Quite. I do not know who the fifth man was.'

'But the police were able to identify Kamarov. How did that happen? You told me he was one of our best men.'

'He was. And the police could not identify him, or any of his squad; they carried no documents. But I'm afraid he was careless. The pistols they carried were identified as of Russian make, and there were Russian labels on their shirts and shoes. Thus the police approached the embassy to see if it could shed any light on the matter. Of course the embassy could not, but they felt the best thing the air crew could do was leave before any investigation led back to them.'

'And what of the fifth man?'

'No identification at all was possible; he was almost entirely consumed in the fire which destroyed his car.'

'So you do not even know if Kamarov was able to trace the countess.'

Beria sighed. 'He traced her all right. All five men had been shot. The police are convinced there was a sixth person present, who did most of the shooting and just about all of the killing. They are naturally assuming that it was a man. However, my knowledge of the countess and her methods . . .' He paused: Stalin's expression was no longer benevolent.

'What knowledge?'

'According to what the embassy learned from the Brazilian police, four of the bodies died from a single shot to the head. This includes the man in the burning car, and that bullet had exited. Nor does it make sense for the countess to have shot him, if she had been in that car. But the other three bear the countess's trademark, and the fifth man was also shot in the head, after being hit in the body. If we add that to the fact that Kamarov was sent specifically to find her . . .'

'Your best man,' Stalin remarked, quietly. 'What does that make now?'

Beria swallowed. 'Twenty-five.'

'Twenty-five. Do you know, Lavrenty, that I have entertained the countess to tea, in this very room? Such beauty, such charm, such sheer animal magnetism. Had I been even ten years younger, I would have made her my mistress. I actually considered doing that. And all the while she was just awaiting orders from Berlin to assassinate me. It ruins one's faith in human nature. If a woman like that cannot be trusted, who can?'

His gaze became speculative, and Beria licked his lips. 'I promise you, Josef, I will get her if it is the last thing I do.'

He paused, realizing that he might have made a mistake, as Stalin continued to regard him for several minutes. 'I am sure you will,' the Premier said at last. 'But at this rate we may wind up with a depopulated country. Do you think she is still in Brazil?'

'No.'

'Why not?'

'Because the visit to Brazil was for a specific, limited purpose.'

'The British claim she fled England to escape their justice.'

'We have no means of knowing whether or not that is true. What is true is that she went to Brazil, and then put that advertisement in the newspaper. Now why did she do that?'

'I am sure you have a theory.'

'The gold reserves, Josef. She knows where they are, because she put them there. But obviously, she cannot reclaim them all by herself; we are talking about a hundred tons of solid gold. She has to have help, and where is the Countess von Widerstand going to obtain help, except from the ranks of her old associates, her fellow Nazis? That is why she went to Brazil, and that is why she put that advertisement in the newspaper.'

'Is that not all the more reason for her still to be there?'

'No, because I believe that she did make contact. The moment we knew of her being in Rio de Janeiro, I put the embassy staff on to it. I did not, of course, tell them that a hit squad was on its way, just that I wanted all the information they could gather on her. They made contact with a member of the staff at the Metropole Hotel, a floor waiter, where she was staying. The results were very interesting. She was there for a week, doing absolutely nothing save walk on the beach. Then she suddenly started looking at property. I do not know why, although it may have been some kind of contact. But then strange men started appearing at the hotel, asking for her, even eating with her in her room. On the night Kamarov made his play, having been keeping her under surveillance, she left the hotel in the company of one of these men. This man was driving a large Mercedes, and from his accent our contact is certain that he was a German. Now, the burnt-out car was a Mercedes, and later that same evening the countess returned to the hotel, her clothes torn and covered in mud. I believe that this man, this German, was taking the countess to a rendezvous with other Nazis when Kamarov made his play.'

'That is an ingenious deduction,' Stalin agreed. 'It is a pity Kamarov did not simply follow them instead of taking immediate executive action.'

'Well, his instructions were to seize her and bring her back here. He obviously thought that a lonely country road was his most favourable opportunity.'

'A sad lack of judgement.'

'Indeed. But that does not alter my theory. I believe that the countess did make contact with other Nazis. But after the Kamarov incident she knew she would be under investigation by the Rio police. She would have left the country as soon as possible.'

'To go where?'

'If she wants to reclaim that bullion, she has to come back to Europe and gain entry to Germany. And as Germany is now divided between us and the Allies . . .' He paused.

'I know,' Stalin agreed. 'It is something I have under consideration. You were saying.'

'Her plan must be to enter Germany clandestinely, recover the gold, and escape again.'

'And we have no idea where the gold is.'

'No. But we do know that removing it is going to be a large operation. Not even the Countess von Widerstand can conceal a hundred tons of gold in her handbag. Depending on where the gold actually is, it will take very careful planning, from a safe but adjacent base. There is only one such base available to her: Switzerland.'

Stalin stroked his moustache. 'Isn't she also wanted for murder in Switzerland?'

'Our information is that the Countess von Widerstand is wanted in Switzerland for murder. But apart from the name and a rather indistinct description of her, they really know nothing about her.

I believe that she could come and go without arousing suspicion. She could be there now. If not, I believe she soon will be.'

'But we don't know when, where, or how. So how are we to obtain possession of her?'

'I believe there is a simple solution to that as well. What do you do when you are in possession of a large amount of gold bullion, which will almost certainly be in ingots? You cannot simply walk into a restaurant, plunk an ingot of pure gold on the table, and say feed me and take it out of that. You cannot even walk into a bank, show them an ingot, and say, I wish to open an account with whatever that is worth. Too many questions would be asked. So what the countess has to have is someone who can take over the gold and market it for her.'

'And we have no idea to whom she will go,' Stalin commented, gloomily.

'But we do, Josef. The man Laurent. The man to whom Katherine Fehrbach went the moment she was free. A banker, with contacts all over the banking fraternity. He is clearly an old friend of the sisters. It is my estimation that not only will the countess go to him for help in this matter, but that she will go to him to set the wheels in motion before she attempts to return to Germany.'

Stalin continued to stroke his moustache. 'It is a long shot. Handling a hundred tons of gold is, as you say, no easy business. Even if there were considerable profits to be made, do you seriously suppose this man would take the risk, in order to help a wanted war criminal?'

'Very simply, Josef, because they are, or certainly were, lovers.'

'You have proof of this?'

'I have proof that on several occasions during the war, the countess and Laurent shared a bedroom in the Lakeside Hotel, Lucerne.'

'But is he not now living with her sister?'

'The decadent West, eh?'

'But if they are, or were, lovers, would he betray her? To us?'

'With some pressure, yes. The important point is that the countess would not have been able to make regular visits to Switzerland, with the war at its height, without the permission of her then boss, that is, Himmler. Which makes it seem very likely that she was carrying out some mission for him, something in which Laurent was involved, or at least, acquiescent. That means that he was, at the very least, a Nazi sympathizer, or, indeed, actually a Nazi agent. I do not think that a respectable investment banker would like that fact to be known, in the present political climate. I think it will be a simple matter to persuade him to co-operate with us.'

'You are a very devious fellow, Lavrenty.' Stalin's sleepy eyes came alive for a moment. 'Do you know, Lavrenty, I sometimes dream of her?'

'Sir?' Beria was alarmed. He was not going to all this trouble to bring the countess back to Russia simply to have her taken to bed by his boss.

'I dream of her sitting in that chair, naked, with her hands bound behind her back, entirely at my mercy.'

It was the turn of Beria's eyes to gleam. 'What would you do to her, were that dream to come true?'

'I would make her scream, and beg for mercy.' He stroked his moustache again. 'Implement your plan, Lavrenty. And this time, make sure that nothing goes wrong.'

Closing In

Henri Laurent rode down from his office in the lift to the underground car park. He felt pleasantly relaxed; it had been a successful day, with an important new account, and he was looking forward to the evening. He always did, for the past few weeks.

This lift always reminded him of the first time he had met Anna. It was not a day he was ever likely to forget. He had known he was to receive a courier from Berlin, bringing funds to be deposited in Himmler's numbered account, an account that still remained untouched, because he had not yet dared touch it. But he had not expected anything more than a straightforward business transaction, involving some unimportant and uninteresting messenger.

Instead there had walked into his office the most striking woman he had ever seen, tall, elegant, wearing a black full length coat, her hair totally concealed beneath a black cloche, her face the epitome of beauty, as had been her soft blue eyes and her equally soft, slightly accented voice. He had thought then, what a fortunate fellow Himmler was, to have such a treasure in his employ, without in any way anticipating what had been about to happen.

She had, he recalled, been in something of a hurry, as she had a train to catch. And thus he had been taken aback when, the money having been counted and receipted, she had asked if she could use his toilet before leaving. She had disappeared for five minutes, with that shoulder bag he was to come to know so well, her trademark; at that time he had had no idea what it contained.

And then she had returned. But the tall, elegant woman who had left the room, had disappeared, together with the sombre coat and hat. In her place was a tall, utterly beautiful, utterly charming girl, wearing a pink frock with a sufficiently low neckline and sufficiently high hem to set his heart pounding, the whole illuminated by the long, dead straight, silky golden hair. That she could be a day older than eighteen had been inconceivable, while the fact that her eyes had now been concealed by dark glasses only added to here allure.

He had fallen in love immediately, had offered to drive her to the station himself – thus they had ridden down in this lift, gazing at each other . . . And she had, only a few hours before, shot and killed two men, and spent the night in her room with their dead bodies, in the arms of her lover, that detestable Englishman! And yet, despite eventually learning that, he had willingly become her lover himself. Or, at least, her bed-mate when she wished it. Because Anna Fehrbach had that effect on men. But had she ever loved anyone?

When he had realized that she certainly had never loved him, but had been using him as a means to get her parents out of Germany, he had determined to hand her over to the police, less out of outraged ego than to safeguard himself against any implication in her many crimes. Bartley had prevented him from doing that, but she had in any event disappeared from his life forever.

And yet, in the strangest possible manner, she was back, waiting for him in his apartment, a poor imitation, perhaps, but close enough to be enjoyable. And more importantly, she was his, on his terms, not vice versa. If Katherine clearly possessed enough of her sister's intensity, and perhaps, even, he sometimes thought, some of her ruthlessness, to be interesting, she was also utterly alone in the world, and thus utterly vulnerable, dependent on his protection . . . and she knew it. And even if she could not match Anna for either looks or sensuality or intellect, she could be a most stimulating companion. His principal pleasure was having her relate her experiences in the gulag, how she had been forced to submit to beatings and sexual harassment by the guards, and to gang-rape by her fellow in-mates. The exciting thing about her stories was the angry hatred she revealed towards all humanity. But not to him.

The lift stopped and he stepped into the underground car park. It was deserted, and although there were electric light bulbs at regular intervals, it was gloomy. And as, because of the new account, he had worked later than usual to get all the paperwork finished, his Mercedes was one of only two cars left in the various bays. This was not unusual, but as he walked to his car he heard the sound of a door opening, and turning, saw that two men had got out of the other car and were approaching him.

They both wore topcoats and slouch hats, and were heavily built; he did not like the look of them, but he was too far from the lift door to regain it without running, and that would have been humiliating. Besides, what possible reason could there be for two entirely strange men to wish to harm him? So he stood his ground, and was relieved when one of them raised his hat, courteously enough. 'Herr Laurent?' He spoke German with a foreign accent.

'I am he. May I do something for you?'

'We would like to talk with you.'

'Ah. Well, I'm afraid I'm in rather a hurry. I suggest you ring my office tomorrow morning and make an appointment.'

'I'm afraid it must be now, Herr Laurent. It will not take long.' He gestured towards the waiting car.

'Where are we?' Anna asked, waking up as the plane dropped from the sky. Once they had been airborne, she had finally taken aspirin to combat the persistent throb in her ankle, and, being able to relax completely for the first time in several days, had gone into a deep sleep.

Clive was seated beside her. 'Just coming in to Dakar.'

'Dakar. That's in French West Africa, isn't it?'

'Correct. We've just crossed the South Atlantic. Now we have to refuel. Don't worry, they're expecting us, and we'll be away again in a couple of hours.'

Anna looked out of the window. It had been dusk when they had touched down at Belem, and they had been flying all night; the dawn was just coming up in front of them. 'Dakar,' she said thoughtfully. 'French. I don't think we need to hurry on for a day or two.'

'What?' Joe had been seated immediately in front of them; he turned his head to echo Clive's comment.

'I think my ankle needs a couple of days to settle down; I'm not going to be much use to anybody hopping about on one leg. And I only have the clothes I'm wearing, save for a spare pair of knickers in my bag. If this is a French city, there'll be some dress shops. And hairdressers' salons. I'll also need a coat and some decent shoes. And some stockings. It can be chilly in Germany in April.'

'Don't tell me you want another fucking fur,' Joe complained.

'I'll settle for cloth for the time being. But you'll have to lend me the money to buy it. And the rest.' She smiled at him. 'I'll pay you back. As soon as we've done the job.'

'It's the job we need to talk about,' Clive said. 'Not your wardrobe. You haven't told us yet where we're going.'

'Or what precisely we are going to do when we get there,' Joe pointed out.

'What you don't seem to appreciate,' Clive added, 'is that this aircraft belongs to the RAF, and was loaned to me simply to go to Rio, pick you up, and take you back to England.'

'I assume that was Baxter's idea.'

'We discussed it.'

'And he, and you, supposed that it was going to be a matter of arriving in Rio, going to my hotel, tapping me on the shoulder, and we'd be on this plane in an hour.'

'We are on this plane,' he reminded her.

Anna's eyes suddenly became glacial.

'Relax. I'm not going to let you down. I'm just trying to make you understand that this plane must go home.'

'Surely not even Baxter can expect you back in less than a week. But I agree that you have to go back. You have to get those divers. So when I've kitted myself out, you can drop Joe and me in Switzerland, and join us there as quickly as you can with your team.'

'If I go back to England, I'll have to report to Billy.'

'Just so long as he doesn't try to muscle in.'

'Did you say Switzerland?' Joe asked.

'That is the most convenient jumping off place for a foray into Germany.'

'Where in Germany?'

Anna smiled. 'I'll tell you that when we're ready to go. But

I can tell you that it is in the Soviet-controlled area. So we may need some fire power.'

'Oh, shit!'

'Did you think it was just going to be a matter of picking the stuff up?'

'I didn't reckon on having to start a war.'

'Hopefully it won't come to that. It's only a few miles over the border from Hessen. That's in the US sector right? Joe, you'll use your CIA clout to get us into position. We cross the border on foot and get to the location. There we recover the gold. We'll have to steal a truck to get it out.'

'Jesus, Jesus, Jesus.'

'I've done it before,' Anna pointed out.

'Just across the border from Hessen,' Clive said thoughtfully.

Damnation, Anna thought. She had forgotten how well Clive had known Germany before the War. 'Once we get it out,' she went on, 'we drive it down to Switzerland.'

'Why this harping on Switzerland?' Joe asked. 'If we can get it back into the US sector . . .'

'Joe, we are talking about four hundred fifty-pound ingots. We can't just carry it into a bank and say we want to open an account. They'd lock us up for a start.'

'And you don't think they'll do that in Switzerland?'

'Not if we go to the right place.'

'If you're thinking about Laurent, you have got to be stark raving mad,' Clive said. 'The moment he lays eyes on you he'll call the police. Besides, I promised him you'd never trouble him again.'

'You always seem to be making promises you can't keep,' Anna pointed out. 'It's a bad habit. As for Henri, he isn't going to hand me over to anybody. We can still blow his business apart. And we can make it worth his while.'

'Who the hell is this guy Henri?' Joe inquired. 'Have I met him?'

'Not yet.'

'And you reckon he can handle ten tons of gold?'

'He can handle anything where there's money involved.' The seat belt light came on. 'So here's the programme,' Anna said. 'We spend two days here in Dakar, while my ankle picks up and I get some clothes. You'll have to square that with the pilot, Clive. Then we fly on to Geneva. Joe and I will leave the plane. We are both American citizens and have the passports to prove it. I will wear my hair up and be totally nondescript.'

'Do you seriously suppose that you could ever be nondescript?'

'You say the sweetest things. But I can be sufficiently nondescript to get through airport immigration. I have only ever been in and out of Switzerland by train, except for last year when you and I and Mama and Papa left, in an RAF plane, and no questions were asked. You will then fly on to London, make your peace with Baxter, recruit your two divers, and return to Geneva, where we will be waiting for you. By that time we will have set up Henri, Joe will have accumulated what we need, and be ready to go.'

Clive looked at Joe, who shrugged. 'She seems to have it all worked out.'

Anna stood in front of the mirror in her hotel bedroom, and gave a little twirl, as best she was able virtually standing on one leg. But the ankle was healing nicely, and the dress, in her favourite pale blue linen, was both cool and comfortable. Of course it was very hot in the West African seaport, and she had no idea what the weather was going to be like in Central Europe, but the coat she had bought was warm enough, and she had also bought a pair of slacks and a thick shirt to wear on the actual recovery, as well as several pairs of stockings and a pair of heavy lace-up shoes. These were all temporary expedients, and then . . . but she hardly dared consider what lay ahead. All, or nothing. But it was going to be all!

There was a tap on her door. 'Come,' she said, wondering which of them it would be.

It was Clive. 'How do I look,' she asked.

'Stupendous, as always.' He closed the door behind himself. 'We leave in an hour.'

'I'll be ready.'

'Anna . . .' he came further into the room. 'You know this idea is crazy.'

'Are you opting out?'

'Would you be happier if I did?'

She sat on the bed. 'What makes you say that?'

He sat beside her. 'While you're waiting for me in Geneva, what will you be doing?'

'You mean apart from making contact with Henri? Keeping a very low profile.'

'With Joe?'

'He's our partner.'

'And you feel like a change of bed-mates.'

Anna's eyes were cool. 'Right now, I don't have a bed-mate to change. But it's nice to know you're jealous.'

'When this is done, if we manage to pull it off . . .'

'We'll talk about the future.'

'But you tell me that you're committed to working for the Yanks. Even if you do happen to be a multi-millionairess.'

'I gave Joe my word.'

'For how long?'

'That's something I will have to discover.'

'And you really think that they will ever let you just walk away from them?'

'Clive, in my position, I have to take each day as it comes, and hope that there is a tomorrow. I have some plans, but they are pretty nebulous at the moment. You are welcome to share in those plans. I really would like that more than anything else in the world. But you can't do it unless you give up your world and enter mine. I can't give mine up, you see. They, whether they be the Reds, the Yanks, or HM Government, won't let me. Unless, one day, I can get out completely. And I mean, completely. Disappear. Ten million dollars will help me to do that. But once I go down that route, I can't ever come back. Nor can anyone who accompanies me.'

He regarded her for several moments. 'Do you really think you can do it?'

'I intend to.'

Another consideration. 'There is something I should tell you.'

'Please do.'

'I know our ultimate destination.'

'I thought you might have some ideas. But you cannot possibly know where my ingots are lying. No one living knows that, except me. All you know is that it is at the bottom of a river. There are quite a few rivers in the Thuringian Wald.'

'Of course. But as I understand it, Joe, and the CIA, are going along with you because they want to get their hands on the main store of bullion.'

Anna frowned. 'So? I don't propose to tell them until after I'm safely back in Switzerland.'

'And you don't think they have someone on their staff capable of working out that a hundred tons of gold that has totally disappeared in Erfurt can only have been concealed in the old salt mines some miles south of Eisenach?'

Anna got up, limped to where her shoulder bag lay on a chair.

Would she use it? On Clive? Please, she thought, oh please convince me that I should never have to do that.

'I'm not going to betray you, Anna. I love you too much.'

She turned to face him. 'Did you say love?'

He flushed. 'It's been growing on me since that Scottish debacle.'

She was in his arms and kissing him with more passion than she had ever revealed in bed. Then she pulled her head back. 'Does that mean . . .'

'As you always say, business before pleasure. I just want you to keep your eyes open, just in case someone makes that point to Joe before you're ready. Now, we have a plane to catch.'

'You really trust that guy?' Joe asked, as they sat together in the back of the taxi to ride from Geneva airport to the hotel at which they had made reservations.

'I told you, he's the one man who has never let me down.'

'You keep rubbing my nose in it. But you do appreciate that he was sent to collect you.'

'And I talked him out of it.'

'Let me see, his brief was to return you to England. Well, he seems to have got you more than halfway there without too much effort.'

'Joe, you really are a snarling dog. He happens to have just saved my life.'

'Well, I imagine he is required to bring you back alive.'

'Bastard! We also happen to have been flying in his plane for the past three days.'

'I also imagine he's as interested in that bullion as anyone. You won't forget that the location is promised to us, no one else.'

'I have given you my word, Joe, that I will reveal the location of that gold to no one but you. I always keep my word.'

'I guess you do,' he said thoughtfully. 'So what's the programme? A quiet supper and then . . .'

'A quiet bed. I have a lot to do tomorrow. But so have you. I'll outline it over dinner.'

'Miss Fehrbach is here, Mr Laurent,' Rudolf announced.

Laurent looked at his watch. 'Already? We're supposed to be meeting for lunch, after she finishes her shopping. I suppose she's run out of money. Well, send her in.'

'Ah,' Rudolf said.

Laurent raised his eyebrows.

'This is . . . well, not the Miss Fehrbach.'

Laurent leaned back in his chair. 'I have no idea what you are talking about, Rudolf. Do you mean . . .' he sat bolt upright. 'Oh, Jesus Christ!'

'Sir?' Rudolf had never heard his boss blaspheme before.

'Is this lady . . .?'

'She is very like Miss Katherine. Save that . . .' He hesitated. 'She is better looking.'

'Well, sir . . . she could be her sister.'

She is her sister, you buffoon, Laurent thought. What to do? Call the number he had been given? But while the two Russians had terrified him, they had not been able to convey the subtle menace that Anna could suggest. And they had not told him how they intended to manage the matter. Kidnapping Anna was not something that could be undertaken on the spur of the moment, certainly not with him in the middle. And one never knew just how much back-up Anna might have tucked away.

'Shall I send her away, sir?' Rudolf asked.

Laurent licked his lips. 'She is alone, is she?'

'Oh, yes, sir.'

'Then I suppose I had better see her. But Rudolf, leave the door open, will you.'

'Certainly, sir.'

Rudolf turned, and Laurent said, 'Rudolf, is the lady carrying a shoulder bag?'

'Yes, sir, she is.'

'Shit!'

'Sir? Would you like me to search her, or at least require her to leave the bag outside?'

'No. I don't think that would be a good idea.' Not if you intend to collect your pension, he thought. 'Just show her in, but as I said, leave the door open.'

'Certainly, sir.' Rudolf opened the door and stood in the aperture. 'Mr Laurent can see you now, Miss Fehrbach.'

'Thank you,' said that unforgettably liquid voice. And there she was. Laurent goggled. The three years since he had first seen her might have dropped away. Except that both the coat and the cloche were pale blue instead of black, he might have been looking at the same woman who had entered his office on that July day in 1943, equally with her hair tucked entirely out of sight, and now taking off her dark glasses. She smiled at him. 'I do assure you, Henri, that I am not a ghost. Or would you prefer it if I were?'

'I . . . ah . . .'

Anna turned to the petrified Rudolf, 'You may close the door.'
'Ah . . .'

'Close the door!' Anna's voice suddenly became a steel trap, closing.

'Yes, ma'am.' Rudolf gave his boss an apologetic glance and backed from the room, closing the door behind him.

Anna advanced to the desk and sat down, crossing her legs. 'You're looking well.'

Laurent had been patting his brow with his handkerchief. Now he restored it to his pocket. 'As are you, as always. You have not changed at all since the first time I saw you.'

'Well, it was only three years ago. Actually, I have changed quite a lot in those three years, even if perhaps it doesn't show.'

'But to come back here, where . . .'

'I am wanted for murder?'

'Well . . .'

'But things have changed there as well, in the past year. Those men were Gestapo, regarded today as the last dregs of humanity, and I killed them in self defence. I have an eyewitness.'

'Bartley.'

'Quite. Whereas your transactions with Himmler are on file.'

'Set up by you. You were SD.'

'But you're not in a position to reveal that fact, without admitting how you know it. I have not come here to settle old scores, or to issue you with a summons to appear at Nuremberg. At this time, anyway. I am here on business.'

'Business,' he muttered.

'Your business. Which is handling and disposing of money, is it not? Now concentrate. When I left Germany, last year, it was in rather a hurry, as I am sure you appreciate. I therefore had to leave certain items behind. I am now on my way back to reclaim those items.'

'You mean to return to Germany?' Just as the Russians had said she would do!

'Why else would I be here? You should know that I am doing this with the full support of both the British and American governments, and am in fact being supported by an Anglo-American team of experts. You should bear this always in mind. However, for reasons which need not concern you, they wish this operation to be clandestine. That is, top secret. Do not forget that. Your business is to dispose of the goods when I deliver them to you in a few days' time. We will make it worth your while.'

Now he was using the handkerchief again. 'These goods . . .'

'Will consist of four hundred fifty-pound ingots of pure gold.'

'Four . . .' His mouth opened and shut like a fish just taken from the water. 'Fifty-pound . . . that is ten million dollars!'

'I believe so. Can you handle that amount of bullion?'

'I . . . well . . .'

'I'm sure you can. Now, if we agree that it is worth ten million dollars, then each of the bars is worth twenty-five thousand. You may keep four of them for yourself. Another ten you will set aside for disposal in a separate manner. I will tell you how this should be done when I return. The proceeds from the remaining three hundred and eighty-six ingots will be placed in a numbered bank account in the name of Anna O'Flaherty.'

'That is . . .'

'Me, yes. I have a passport to prove both that and that I am an American citizen.'

Think, God damn it, he told himself: while the Russians had made it clear that they wanted Anna, they had not mentioned ten million dollars: did they know of it? But coherent thought was next to impossible when he was impaled upon those huge blue eyes and could remember what lay beneath the blue dress. These were weapons Anna had used throughout her career, just as effectively as her gun or her hands or her speed of thought and reaction. And ten million dollars . . . it made far more sense to wait until she brought the money back, and then . . .

'Something disturbs you?' Anna asked.

'I was thinking . . . if you are in a hurry, I may not be able to get the best price for the gold, immediately. After all, there seems to be a great deal of it, and it is illegal money, is it not?'

'It is far more legal than anything you handled for Himmler. And I am not in that much of a hurry. I quite understand that you may need to handle it in small amounts. However, when I deliver it, you will give me a receipt, and you will keep me informed as to your progress in disposing of it. What you need to remember is that I am operating under the auspices of both MI6 and the CIA, each of whom are far more deadly that the SD, and far more powerful. A betrayal of me, this time, would be a catastrophe for you.' She stood up. 'It has been so nice seeing you again. When I return, we must have a meal together and talk about old times.' She went to the door, stopped, and turned. 'Oh, by the way, I don't want to put you to any trouble having me followed about the place. I am staying at the Imperial Hotel, under my new name of Anna O'Flaherty, in the company of a Mr Joseph Andrews. He is my CIA controller.'

Laurent tried to pull himself together. 'I would have thought it would be Bartley.'

'Oh, yes, ' Anna said. 'He is joining us in a day or two. Ciao.'

Laurent remained staring at the door for some time after it had closed behind her. A nightmare, returned to haunt him? Or a dream, returned to life? When he remembered . . .

Of course she would have to be destroyed, both to remove her from his life and to get the Russians off his back. Therefore . . . he stretched out his hand to the telephone, and then withdrew it again. Ten million dollars! She was taking her life in her hands in any event by returning to Germany, but she clearly felt that when she regained Switzerland she would be safe. So, think rationally.

If she were to run into the Russians while trying to regain her money – he wondered where it was? Surely not even Anna would dare attempt to return to Berlin? – she would either be killed on the spot or carted off to a gulag. Going by what Katherine had told him, there would be no possibility of her getting out of there unless she also were to be released, and he did not see any chance of that. And there would be the end of the matter; she would cease to be either a dream or a nightmare and become only a memory.

While if she were to pull it off, and return with the money, a simple phone call would similarly end her bloodstained career, and he would be left ten million dollars the richer. As she obviously had no idea that the Russians had worked out exactly what she would do, neither could her associates. He did not doubt the Reds would be happy to dispose of them also.

So, wait for her to come back. If she came back. That determination suited his reluctance to make irrevocable decisions.

And Katherine? Why, Katherine would never know anything about it.

Baxter had been smoking so vigorously as he listened to Clive's report that he was surrounded in a fog. 'You took out Bormann?' he asked.

'No, I did not. Anna did that. But I helped her eliminate a Nazi cell. That can't be bad.'

'You had no authority.'

'Be real, Billy. Isn't, or wasn't, he the most wanted man not at Nuremberg? And if I hadn't acted as I did, we'd have lost Anna.'

'If I understand what you have been telling me, we've lost her anyway.'

'I have an idea I can get her back, if the government will play ball. Have you got that exemption yet?'

'No.'

'You mean . . .?'

'No. I do not mean that they have closed the door. They are still considering the matter.'

'What a shower. Apart from trying to turn the entire country into a government-run corporation, and pack up the empire at the same time, their idea seems to be that if they make no decisions each problem may go away.'

'Have you read your terms of employment recently? I suggest you do so now, when you will be reminded that we are not allowed to take political sides.'

But the fact that he continued to speak quietly indicated that he agreed. 'There can be no law, in a free country, against holding opinions,' Clive pointed out. 'Are you saying that, strapped as they are, they won't even be interested in the Nazi gold reserves?'

'Which you tell me they will have to share with Washington.'

'They will have to share with more than that,' Clive said. 'If I am right about where the gold is, it is not going to be gettable without the co-operation of the Soviets. But at least we should be able to do a deal, as they don't know where to look. They don't have Anna. You can't stop this now, Billy. The Yanks are dead keen and they're moving. If we don't move as well, we're out in the cold.'

'I'll have to—'

'No, you will not. No referring the matter upstairs. They'll still be discussing it this time next year. Neither Anna nor the CIA are going to wait that long.'

Baxter regarded him for several seconds. Then he sighed. 'Tell me what you need.'

'Well?' Anna asked, as they sipped an aperitif before lunch. 'Is everything arranged?'

'In so far as it can be.' Joe had just returned from a hasty visit to the American sector, just north of the Swiss border. 'Part of what you require will be here tomorrow; the rest will be waiting for you in Germany.'

'And no problems?'

'A magic formula, CIA. They understand that we are undertaking a clandestine mission into Soviet-controlled territory, and may be coming back out in a hurry. If we can get back to the border, they'll look after us.'

'I could kiss you.'

'Be my guest.'

'Later.'

'That, of course, is supposing we have something to come back out with, or for. What about Clive?'

'He'll be here this afternoon.'

'And how did your morning go yesterday?'

'As I expected,' Anna said. 'He will handle the transaction.'

'And you trust him?'

'Good lord, no. I gave up trusting people, most people, long ago. But I have grown to understand a little of human motivation; there are only three that matter: love, fear and greed.'

'You wouldn't include hate?'

'Hate is merely an aspect of fear. We only hate the things we fear.'

'And thus you hate no one.'

'Not right now. Which is not to say that there are a few people I believe the world would be a better place without.'

'And Laurent?'

'He comes under the heading of all three. He cannot forget that once we were lovers; it is obvious in his eyes every time he looks at me. But he also hates me, because he is afraid of me, and he knows he has good reason to be afraid. Those two emotions largely cancel themselves out, in that while he may wish to be rid of me in his more lucid moments, he cannot suppress the hope that one day, perhaps, we might be able to get together again.'

'Anna, you are a lot deeper than most people suspect. I guess that's because most people find it difficult to look past a pretty face. But in my book, what you have just said about Laurent doesn't make him the least reliable.'

'Ah, but you see, with love and hate cancelling each other out, that leaves only greed. And that is irresistible, to a man like Laurent.'

'But when he gets the money . . .'

'He will still love, and he will still be afraid. With good reason. He knows that if I happen to need his know-how to complete this business, I still haven't forgiven him for trying to turn me in last year.'

'Because forgiveness isn't part of your scheme of things. It's a good old Christian principle.'

'There hasn't been a lot of time for me to be a Christian, Joe.'

They gazed at each other. 'But you'll forgive me for being interested,' Joe said. 'As regards you, I have never had only either hate or greed. Only love.'

'Desire.'

'Love. This caper could turn out badly. I'd hate one of us to die with any angst between us.'

Again Anna regarded him for several seconds, then she reached across the table and squeezed his hand. 'So would I. Come to my room after lunch, and we'll . . . consider the matter.'

'This came in from Geneva this morning, Comrade Commissar,' Litovsky said, laying the paper on Beria's desk.

He was an eager man, tall and thin and intense, with a long face and excited eyes. Having just been promoted to take Kamarov's place he was desperate to please. No one knew for sure what had happened to Kamarov, but that was the pattern in Stalinist Russia: people just disappeared.

Beria studied the brief entry. 'A tall, elegant, very handsome woman. Hm. Walking with a slight limp?'

'She could have had an accident.'

'Hm. It does not mention her hair. That would establish her identity beyond a doubt.'

'She apparently had it concealed beneath her hat.'

'This says Laurent did not report this mysterious visit.'

'There has been no contact with Laurent. Geneva wishes to know if we want anything done about him.'

'Why should something be done about him at this time?'

'Well, Comrade Commissar, it could well be that he is setting up to betray us.'

'Litovsky, things are going exactly as I foresaw and as I planned. If this woman is the countess, then she is in Switzerland, and has made contact with her old business associate. That can only be because she wishes to use his money-laundering facility. Now she has to get the money to deliver to him. That means she is about to enter Germany. A part of Germany that we control.'

'We do not know that, sir. The money could be in Allied-controlled territory.'

'Litovsky,' Beria said patiently, 'There can be no doubt, from the way they have been protecting her and concealing her, that the countess works for the British. And in view of the way Andrews contacted her in Scotland, and then disappeared with her, I have a growing suspicion that for all their fine words and promises, she is also now again working for the Americans. If the money were in their controlled territory, she would simply go there and pick it up. There would be no need for this cloak-and-dagger stuff. Now listen carefully. If it is the bullion, or even part of the bullion, we are talking about, she will need both support and transport. My guess is that she will have a squad with her, and that they will enter our sector clandestinely and on foot, intending to steal transport when they have reached their goal. You will go to Germany and oversee this business person-ally. You have carte blanche to control our people in Germany. Double all border patrols, but they are to keep entirely out of sight and not interfere with the countess or her team in any way, until they actually recover the gold.'

'Ah . . . would it not be simpler to arrest them the moment they cross the border, and . . . persuade her to tell us where the bullion is stored?'

Beria smiled. 'You dream of having her stretched naked before you while you amuse yourself. Well, I agree, that is a very attract-ive prospect. And we may still be able to achieve it. But there are two strong caveats to attempting such a plan. One is that there is no guarantee that we would be able to take her alive, and if she were to die in a shoot-out, the secret of the bullion's location would go with her. The other is that even if we were to succeed in taking her alive, I very much doubt that she would give in to torture.'

Litovsky looked sceptical. If he had read the file on the countess, and understood that she could be deadly, she was, after all, only a woman. He could not avoid the disquieting thought that his boss had become obsessed with her, and in so doing had also become afraid of her.

'When they have recovered the gold,' Beria continued, 'you may move in and arrest them. I would still like her to be brought back here alive, but once we have recovered the gold, that is no longer a pre-requisite.'

'It is a large area to cover,' Litovsky pointed out. 'Certainly if our surveillance has got to be unsuspected.'

'I am sure you will do very well, but we have the comfort-able fall-back position, that if by any chance she does manage to evade you, we know exactly where she will be going after-wards. Back to Switzerland. Back to Laurent. That is why he must not be touched until we have her, one way or the other. Now go and do your duty.'

*　　*　　*

'Petty Officer Harris, Royal Navy,' Clive explained, as they gathered in the hotel courtyard.

'Ma'am.' Harris, short and heavy-featured, with a mop of black hair, shook Anna's hand, while his gaze drifted up and down her body; she was wearing slacks, canvas ankle boots, a shirt and a jerkin, carried a waterproof coat and had her hair totally concealed beneath a headscarf; her jewellery was stored in the hotel strong room.

'Petty Officer.' She squeezed the fingers.

'Sergeant Riddick, SAS.'

'Ma'am.' Tall and thin, but with powerful shoulders.

'Sergeant. SAS?'

'Stands for Special Air Services, ma'am.'

Anna looked at Clive.

'It's a specialist unit created to work behind enemy lines during the war.'

'Brilliant.'

'Both of these fellows are trained frogmen.'

'You've lost me.'

'Divers, ma'am,' Harris said. 'We were told you need divers.'

'I do indeed. And this stuff . . .?' She gazed at the pile of equipment, what looked like gas cylinders and masses of black rubber.

'That's our Self-Contained Underwater Breathing Apparatus, ma'am,' Harris explained. 'Together with our wet suits.'

'Do you think you could possibly manage that again?'

'It's called Scuba gear,' Clive said. 'It was developed during the war for clandestine attacks on enemy shipping, planting limpet mines on their hulls and that sort of thing. Using those lungs and their breathing apparatus, they can stay under water for an hour at a time.'

'There's an awful lot of it,' she pointed out. 'We're travelling on foot, at least on the way in.'

'We can manage the cylinders, ma'am,' Riddick said. 'The rest is pretty light.'

Anna looked at the two Americans, who were waiting patiently beside the truck with US Army markings. Joe shrugged. 'From what you told us, we're gonna need these guys.'

'Yes,' Anna said thoughtfully. 'And this gentleman?'

'Staff Sergeant Maynard, ma'am. United States Marine Corps.'

'And your function is?'

'Motors, ma'am.'

'If it can work, he'll make it,' Joe said.

'Well, welcome all of you. I'm sure we'll make a great team. Now, you know what we're about?'

'We're gonna lift some dough from inside the Soviet Zone,' Maynard said.

'Correct. You understand that the Soviets may object to us doing this?'

'Yes, ma'am,' the three men answered together.

'Right. So we will be picking up some additional gear this evening.' She looked at Clive. 'You've explained the terms?'

'As this is a secret, unofficial assignment, each man will be paid fifty thousand dollars danger money. In case of death, the money to be paid to next of kin,' Clive said.

'That is, of course, providing any of us gets back. With the money. There is just one thing: I am in command of this operation, and I expect my orders to be obeyed instantly and to the maximum of your ability.'

She looked from face to face, and the men looked at their officers.

'That's the way it is,' Joe said. 'And just in case any of you guys has any reservations because of the fact that she is a lady, I think you should know that the Countess has accumulated a body count of . . .' he looked at Anna.

'I'm afraid it's sixty-five,' Anna said.

The men stared at her in disbelief, than looked at Joe, and then at Clive.

'Fact,' Clive said. 'Of whom twenty-five were Russians. So when it comes to confronting an enemy, any enemy, there is no one in the world, male or female, that you'd do better to have standing beside you.'

The men gazed at her, and she smiled at them. 'He says the sweetest things.' She looked at her watch. 'Eight thirty Let's move it. We want to be in position by dusk.'

She sat in the front, between Maynard and Joe; Clive shared the back with the two other Englishmen. He wasn't too happy with this arrangement, but it was an American truck, and they were about to enter American-controlled territory. They crossed the border at Basle, Joe's CIA identification wallet seeing them through the US checkpoint, then it was a drive of something more than three hundred miles to the little town of Bad Hersfeld, which Anna had chosen as their starting point. The roads were still under repair from the wartime ravages, as were many of the towns and villages through which they passed. With a stop for lunch in Mannheim, it was five thirty and the afternoon was drawing in when they reached their destination, but they could see the hills of the Thuringian Wald in the near distance.

An MP lieutenant was waiting for them. 'Holford, sir. We spoke on the phone.'

'Yes, we did. You ready for us?'

'Yes, sir.' He looked past him at Anna. 'Say, is that—'

'This is a woman, yes,' Joe said. 'She is coming with us.'

Holford looked into the back of the truck, obviously counting. 'You said you wanted six tommies . . .'

'That's right. One each.'

'But—'

'One is for the lady, yes. She feels naked without a tommy gun. Time is passing, lieutenant.'

'Yes, sir.'

He had a jeep waiting, and led them out of the town.

'I guess you run into this kind of thing all the time, ma'am,' Maynard ventured.

'I'm afraid I do, Sergeant.'

'And that guy doesn't have any idea who he's dealing with.'

'Which is how I like it. It would be a good idea for you to remember that.'

'Yes, ma'am,' he said fervently.

A couple of miles outside the town they came to an army camp, commanded by a captain. He also had been previously contacted by Joe, but he also had to go through the double take routine, especially when Anna took off her headscarf and shook out her hair, at the same time pocketing her dark glasses. 'Captain Roberts, ma'am.'

She squeezed his hand. 'My pleasure, Captain. Where's the border?'

He pointed. 'That stream marks it.'

'May I have a look?'

After a week she walked with only the slightest of limps, although she had no idea how her ankle was going to stand up to twenty-five miles. Joe and Clive accompanied them through the trees, leaving their three companions to unload the truck.

'Where is the bridge?' Anna asked.

'Three miles upstream. But it's a check point.'

'So we'll only be using it on the way out.'

'On the phone, Mr Andrews,' Roberts remarked, 'you said something about needing a diversion. What exactly did you have in mind?'

'Just cover at the bridge. We'll be defectors, see.'

'No problem. But what about getting in? This border is constantly patrolled.'

They had reached the last of the trees, some thirty yards from the water, and Clive gave Anna a pair of binoculars. She studied the far bank, and the trees, which began again close to the water. 'They must be having an early dinner.'

'Eh?'

'I don't see any movement at all.'

Roberts took the glasses, also studied the far bank. 'Well, I'll be damned. You guys could just wade across now. That stream ain't all that deep.'

'They could be watching us from those trees,' Clive suggested.

'Ain't likely. You know what the Reds are like. They normally parade up and down.'

'But if they knew we were coming . . .'

'How can they possibly know that?' Anna asked.

'Laurent! I never did like that character.'

'Clive, you're into the Reds under the bed mode. Laurent can't possibly have betrayed us, for the simple reason that he doesn't have any idea where we're headed.'

'No one does, except you,' Joe pointed out.

'Which makes the odds on a betrayal astronomical, wouldn't you say? But we won't take any risks. If it's all right with you, Captain, we'll eat now, and stick to our plan of crossing when it's good and dark.'

'Coming back when?'

'I'll show you.'

She spread the large-scale map on the table while they ate in the command house. 'We are here. We cross the stream tonight, and head north-east.'

'You mean we're making for Eisenach?' Joe asked.

'We're going to by-pass Eisenach. We're making for the River Horsel. Here. That's twenty-five miles from the border, to cover which, carrying all of this diving gear, we have to allow eight hours. We must be there by dawn. The area is wooded, and we'll lie up there for the day.'

'You guys aim to walk twenty-five miles through Russian-controlled territory? Even at night, that's taking a big risk.'

'Not if we have those uniforms I requested,' Joe said.

'I have them. But even so, if you're challenged . . . you guys speak Russian?'

'I do,' Anna said.

He scratched his head.

'As I was saying,' she went on, 'We'll sit tight for the day and start work at dusk tomorrow night, depending on what, if any, activity there is around us.'

'What exactly are we diving for, ma'am?' Harris asked.

'At the bottom of the river, at a place I selected when I was there last year, are four hundred fifty-pound ingots of pure gold.'

There was a brief silence. Then Riddick asked, 'And only you know the exact location of this stuff, ma'am?'

'That's why I'm here, Sergeant.'

He peered at the map. 'But it's not marked.'

'It's in my head.'

Riddick and Harris exchanged glances.

'Relax,' Clive said. 'The Countess has a photographic memory.'

'As well as . . . you're saying she's a raving genius.'

'Why, yes,' Anna agreed, modestly. 'I am a raving genius. Or so they tell me.'

'The point is,' Joe put in, 'that without her we're not going to get anywhere. You guys need to remember that.' He prodded the map. 'What's this area here, a couple of miles this side of Eisenach? Looks kind of bleak.'

'Those were once salt mines,' Anna said, and glanced at Clive, but his face remained expressionless. 'They're no longer worked. I think either the RAF or you people brought the whole mountain down in a raid.'

'Boy, those guys sure were meatheads,' Maynard commented. 'Loosing a load of bombs on a load of salt.'

'Yes,' Joe said thoughtfully.

'A lot of wars have been fought over the rights to gather salt,' Clive pointed out.

'Now,' Anna said. 'Transport. I reckon we should have retrieved the bullion in about six hours. Allowing two extra, if we start at six we'll be ready to move by two. By then you, Maynard, will have secured us a truck. Your best bet is Eisenach. How good is your German?'

'Like a native, ma'am.'

'That's why I chose him,' Joe pointed out.

'Right. Now he should have some papers?'

'I prepared them,' Joe said. 'Gottfried Ehrmann, from Dresden.'

'Gottfried?'

'It's a good old German name.'

Too good, she thought. It brought back too many memories. But she said, 'Then it should do. So, we will wear the Russian uniforms, and you, Sergeant Maynard will be a German civilian, under arrest. Now, gentlemen, please listen very carefully. If we are challenged on the way in, leave the talking to me.'

'But you're a woman,' Harris objected. 'Won't they smell a rat?'

'There are quite a few women in the Red Army. We will have been on a secret mission into the American sector, and are now on our way back with our prisoner, Gottfried Ehrmann. Maynard will accompany us until dawn – there will be a curfew – and then he will make his way into Eisenach. You are looking for work. You spend the day in Eisenach, sizing up the situation, and tomorrow night you will make your play. Don't move before midnight; it is only five miles from the city to where we will be.' She prodded the map. 'You'll take this road; it runs beside the river. One of us will be on the road to stop you.' She looked around their faces. 'Any questions? Then let's get changed and get started. Captain Roberts, where are these Russian uniforms?'

The fit was not very good, but they wore them over their own clothes, and Anna was able to tuck her hair out of sight beneath her steel helmet, while the tightly laced boots provided support for her ankle. 'You are the prettiest damned soldier I ever did see,' Joe observed.

'Do you know, the last time I had to wear male uniform, our friend Edert said the same thing. Captain, we'll be back just before dawn the day after tomorrow, driving a Red Army truck.'

'We'll be waiting for you, ma'am.'

The Goal

'**R**eport,' Litovsky said.

The MGB colonel cleared his throat. 'The woman identified as possibly the Countess von Widerstand left her hotel in Geneva yesterday morning at zero eight thirty. She was accompanied by five men, and a considerable amount of equipment, some of which was identified as what appeared to be gas cylinders, and rubber suits. They were driving in a truck with US Army markings.'

'Yesterday morning,' Litovsky commented. 'Go on.'

'They drove north, crossed the border at Basle, and entered the US sector. It was not possible for our surveillance team to follow them further.'

'What? You mean you have lost them?'

'As I say, Comrade Commissar, it was not possible to follow them further without being discovered.'

'When Comrade Beria learns of this . . .'

The colonel refused to be disconcerted. 'However, just after dark last night, six men were observed to cross the border into Erfurt, twenty-five miles south-west of Eisenach. As you instructed, the border guards did not interfere with these men, but they were followed, surreptitiously. They were on foot, and continued on foot, but again they were carrying a considerable amount of equipment. In the dark it was difficult to be sure what this was, but some of it was certainly metal, and one of the observers is convinced that they were wearing Russian uniforms. As were your instructions, our people still did not interfere with them. Merely continued to track them from a distance. Now—'

'Your people are wasting their time, Comrade Colonel,' Litovsky said. 'We are looking for five men and a woman, not six men. It is not conceivable that a woman like the countess would hand over the quest for her gold to others. You had better just arrest these people and keep looking.'

'With respect, Comrade Commissar, is it not possible that the countess is dressed as a man? She would hardly undertake a mission of this sort in a frilly skirt.'

Litovsky regarded him with a frown, and he realized that his sarcasm might have been misplaced. He hurried on. 'My people continued to follow them. They walked all night, with only short breaks, and when they reached the River Horsel, they followed the bank, as far as these woods. I have marked the place.' He spread the map in front of his boss, and prodded it. 'They entered the wood just before daybreak, and are still there. With one exception.'

'Explain.'

'One of them detached himself from the others, as they reached the wood, and walked away from them, back in the direction of Eisenach.'

'One of them. It could have been the countess.'

'No, sir. It was daylight by now, and my people were able to watch him through binoculars. It was definitely a man.'

'The countess is supposed to be a tall woman,' Litovsky pointed out.

'Yes, sir. But still a woman. This man moved like a man. And besides . . .' He could not resist another attempt at humour. 'Did you not tell me that the countess is a beautiful woman? There was nothing beautiful about this man's face. I specifically asked my sergeant about this.'

Litovsky stroked his chin. 'If you are right, Malinov, they obviously mean to remain in that wood all day, and then move on when it again gets dark. Although why they should have detached one of their number is a mystery, unless he lost his nerve and pulled out.'

'I do not think that is the case, sir. The countess's record does not indicate that she allows people to pull out. And I should add, as it was daylight, it was possible to ascertain that the man who left the group was not wearing Russian uniform, but was dressed as a civilian.'

'Well, then, what is your theory as to what is going on? You must have a theory. And I must warn you that it had better be right. This business has the personal interest of Commissar Beria.'

'Well, Comrade Commissar, I believe that they are at their destination, and not just waiting for another night before proceeding.'

'Your reasons for assuming this?'

'There are two, sir. One is that if those containers hold oxygen, as, in view of the other gear they have with them seems likely, I estimate that they need to dive to recover the gold, and they are now camped virtually on the banks of the Horsel. The other point is that they can only have sent the sixth man away in order that he can steal some transport. You tell me that they are seeking to recover a large amount of gold bullion. They cannot hope to walk back to the border carrying that kind of weight. And as stealing a car or a truck will necessarily be discovered within a few hours, there would be no point in attempting to do so until they are ready to make their move. In my opinion, that would be tonight.'

Litovsky continued to stroke his chin. 'That is a very good analysis of the situation, Colonel. What are your dispositions?'

'There is only one road through the wood. I have twenty men watching the exits, five on the eastern side and fifteen on the west. If they have to move the gold by truck, they have to use the road, and as their aim must be to regain the border just as rapidly as possible, it would seem certain that they will drive west. The other five are just a back-up in case I am wrong. We will be in a position to move in the moment you give the word.'

'It cannot be until after they recover the gold. As we do not yet know exactly where it is, if you merely kill them it will be lost forever.'

'But if we manage to take at least one prisoner . . .'

'Commissar Beria is certain, from what he knows of the countess, that she will have confided the exact location of the bullion to no one.'

'But if we managed to take the countess herself . . . after all, a woman is hardly likely to take any part in a shoot-out, and once we have her, well . . .'

'Your mouth is watering,' Litovsky pointed out. 'Unfortunately, you are not in possession of all the facts. Do you know how many of our people the countess has personally killed?'

'A woman has killed our people?'

'Twenty-five at the last count.'

Malinov stared at him with his mouth open.

'And even if, by any strange chance, you managed to take her prisoner, well, eleven of those twenty-five had done just that, taken her prisoner. And they still died. In any event, Commissar Beria, who seems to know more about her than any of us, is of the opinion that she would suffer death by torture rather than tell us anything she did not wish us to know.'

'Twenty-five,' Malinov muttered. 'A woman!'

'Not a woman,' Litovsky corrected. 'An angel from the deepest pit of hell.'

Malinov swallowed. 'What do you want me to do?'

'You have two objectives. One is to obtain possession of that gold. The other is to obtain possession of the countess. If you can do this and return her to Moscow alive you will be commended. If you cannot, or are in any doubt about it, kill her. However, we will need proof of her death. But obtaining that gold has priority.'

Malinov licked his lips. 'You said, 'we' will require proof. Won't you be there, sir?'

'No. I will be in Switzerland, just in case she slips through your fingers.'

Malinov considered this for a few moments. Then he asked, 'And the man detached to go into Eisenach?'

'He is under surveillance?'

'Of course.'

'Then dispose of him. That will make one less of them, eh?'

'This is all we need,' Clive remarked, sitting beside Anna and offering her a slice of Spam to put on her biscuit, and watching a drop of water splash on to it.

Anna sat with her back against a tree and her waterproof cape over her head. 'Can't be all bad,' she said. 'Rain keeps people's heads down. Just keep thinking, this time tomorrow you'll be soaking in a hot bath.'

'Your idea of heaven.'

'Close.' She munched her food, thoughtfully.

'So how are your feet? Mine are never going on a long walk again.'

She smiled. 'My ankle's sore. But it's done its bit. And when we finish this job, you won't have to, ever again.'

'If I play my cards right.'

'There's always that.'

He finished his own brief meal, looked at the other men. They were sitting, or lying, most already half asleep, so exhausted even the rain wasn't bothering them. But Anna seemed surprisingly wide awake. Or was it surprising? He couldn't doubt that she was the toughest of them all, even including the SAS sergeant. And he had known her long enough to understand that when she was in the middle of an assignment her brain turned into an ice-cold computer, impervious to either. Yet he could not stop himself asking, 'You reckon we're going to make it?' And then immediately correcting himself. 'I'm sorry. That was stupid. If you didn't think we were going to make it, you wouldn't be here.'

'Good thinking.' She finished her meal in turn, took a sip of water from her canteen, and slipped down the tree, eyes shut.

'But afterwards . . . Anna, do you trust me?'

Her eyes opened. 'As much as I trust anybody.'

'I'll accept that. Then I just want you to know that no matter what happens, I'm in your corner, now and always.'

She squeezed his hand, her fingers wet with the dripping rain. 'I'm glad of that. Now get some sleep.'

The rain stopped in the middle of the afternoon, the sun came out, and it warmed up, although the wood remained very wet. The men jumped up and down to assist the process. Anna walked through the trees to survey the road, on the other side of which was the river, and the little tributary with the separate copse she had committed to her memory: she was just a few yards away from ten million dollars. Supposing it was still there! But now was not the time for doubts.

She heard the rumble of an engine, and flattened herself against a tree to watch the truck pass by. It was marked with the red star of the Red Army, and contained several men, sitting and chatting, their rifles between their legs. There was nothing unusual in that, certainly this close to the border, but yet she could feel the tension creeping up the backs of her legs. Or maybe it was just the cold; for all her waterproof cape she was wet through.

She turned, and found Joe behind her. 'You reckon that's a problem?' he asked.

'Routine.'

'Don't you ever feel fear, or even apprehension?'

'I can't afford to, when I'm working. Neither can you, Joe, when you're working with me.'

'I guess not. Anna . . . I never had the chance to tell you what a fuck-up I feel at losing you that day in Brazil.'

'One of those things.'

'Then you forgive me?'

'No. But it's history.'

He brooded for a few moments, then asked. 'You reckon Maynard got into Eisenach?'

'That comes under the heading of fear and apprehension, Joe. If he didn't, we may have a problem.'

'Which you are confident you can solve?'

'I'll work on it, when the time comes. If the time comes. But you chose him.'

'Yeah. He's as good as we have. Anna . . . shit, there are so many things I want to say to you.'

She squeezed his hand, and led him back through the trees. 'I would save them, until we're on the other side of this hump.'

Harris and Riddick had already tested their underwater lamps, before it grew dark, as Anna had not wanted any passers-by or Russian patrols noticing flashing lights in the wood. Now, as the evening drew in, they became restless, walking to and fro. Anna reckoned neither Clive nor Joe were much less nervous; none of them had her experience at clandestine operations.

The time certainly dragged, as she waited for complete darkness before moving. At seven she called them together. 'The location is marked by two isolated trees on the edge of the copse. It is only a couple of hundred yards from where we now are. At that place the river is about eight feet deep, and there is a layer of soft mud over the bottom. When I was here last year I tested it with the branch of a tree, and it was about eighteen inches thick, over a fairly firm bottom. The ingots will be in that mud, but they should be close together as they were all dropped from the same spot. Questions?'

No one seemed to have any.

'Joe, you will be with me on the bank to stack them as they are brought up. Clive, I want you to act as lookout. There may be some traffic from time to time, but this is a lonely spot. And as long as no one shows any sign of stopping, ignore it.'

'And you're expecting Maynard about two.'

'Not before then. He's not supposed to make his play until after midnight. Now, weapons. Clive, you'll take one of the tommies. We'll keep the other five. Check anything else you happen to have.' She took her Luger from the shoulder bag and placed it in the deep pocket of her uniform; the two spare magazines she put in the other pocket; as she had not relished the idea of walking twenty miles with the Walther rubbing into her groin she had left it at the US camp. 'All set? Then let's move.'

The two divers picked up their gear and she led them across the deserted road. It was now utterly dark and quiet, save for the whisper of the river moving slowly by. She took them through the copse to the marker trees. 'There you go.'

Harris and Riddick pulled on their wet suits, then strapped on their lungs and spat into their goggles.

'Happy hunting,' Anna said. 'Clive.'

He nodded, and receded into the darkness to wait by the road. The two divers were ready, and now they went in. A moment later their lights became visible as they began to search the bottom of the stream.

'What happens if it isn't there?' Joe asked, standing beside her on the bank.

'Joe,' she said, 'I put it there. Only just over a year ago.'

But she couldn't resist a prickling feeling as the minutes ticked by and she watched the lights moving to and fro, distorted by the water, but seeming to cover an increasingly wide area. Then Riddick's head broke the surface and he took off his mask. 'It sure is mucky down here, ma'am,' he remarked.

'Have you found anything?'

'How about this?' He held up, in both hands, an oblong object. It looked like solid mud, but then he moved it to and fro in the water and suddenly it gleamed in the darkness.

'Oh!' Without meaning to, she hugged Joe.

'Are there any more?' he asked.

Harris also surfaced, carrying an ingot. 'A whole lot.'

They handed up the gold, and then crawled out of the water to sit on the bank and take off their lungs.

'Ah . . . what about the rest?' Anna asked, her stomach tying itself in knots.

'Well, ma'am, we only have an hour's capacity in these lungs, and like I said, there's one hell of a lot down there.'

She couldn't believe her ears. To have come so close . . .

'You mean you can't get the rest up?' Joe asked.

'Oh, that's not a problem, Mr Andrews. Now we know where they are and in maybe nine feet of water, we'll free dive.'

Anna felt close to tears.

The two men worked with relentless efficiency, and the pile of ingots on the bank slowly grew. They paused every half-hour for a breather, and then resumed. Clive came back every so often to see how they were getting on, reporting always that it was as quiet as a mouse out there.

By midnight there were two hundred and fifty ingots, neatly piled on the bank. 'I reckon we're getting on top of it,' Riddick said, sitting beside them and breathing deeply.

'But there's still some more down there?' Joe was anxious.

'A hell of a lot more, Mr Andrews. But less than there is up here.'

'You are two of my favourite people,' Anna said. 'From now on.'

He grinned at her. 'I thought we were before.'

The minutes and then the hours ticked by, and still the pile grew. Joe checked his watch. 'One thirty. Maynard should be on his way.'

'I hope he's not,' Anna said. 'Or he'll be too early. Once he gets out of the city, it's only a ten-minute drive.'

But he was now becoming agitated, looked at his watch every few minutes. 'Two o'clock,' he announced. 'He should be here. And we have three hundred and eighty bars. We'd better pack it in and get ready to move.'

'He's not here yet,' Anna said. 'And there are still twenty bars down here.'

He considered this, waited for Harris next to surface. 'Any left?' he asked, as he took the ingot.

'A few.'

'Well, then . . .'

'Another fifteen minutes will do it.'

He submerged again, and Joe added the ingot to the pile and then stamped up and down, taking each bar as it was handed up.

'Relax,' Anna said, doing the same. 'Only ten to go.'

'He should be here by now.'

'And here he is.' The sound of an engine drifted through the night.

'Thank God for that. Leave the rest,' he told Riddick. 'We have enough.'

'I beg your pardon,' Anna said. 'Just—'

There was a shout, and then a shot, followed by a fusillade of tommy gun fire.

'Jesus Christ!' Joe cried, and dropped to the ground.

Riddick followed his example, and Harris, just emerging, threw his ingot ashore and joined them. Anna had realized immediately that the shots had not been aimed at them, in which case . . . 'Clive!' she shouted.

'Get down!' he replied, and a moment later crashed through the bushes to join them. 'A bloody truckload of Reds. I thought it was Maynard, and signalled it to stop.'

'Shit!' Joe said. 'How the hell—'

'Questions later,' Anna recommended. 'Is everyone armed?'

'Yes, ma'am,' Harris and Riddick answered together.

'Countess!' a voice called in German. 'You are surrounded. If you and your people come out with your hands in the air you will not be harmed.'

'How these people do like to talk,' Anna remarked.

'What's he saying, ma'am? Riddick asked.

'He wants us to surrender. You don't want to do that, do you?'

'Not unless I have to, ma'am.'

'Anna,' Joe said. 'If we are surrounded . . .'

'Joe, as you once told me, we're living in the real world now. If we surrender, we're dead. So we may as well see how many of us can come out of this alive. You're sure there is only one truck, Clive?'

'As far as I saw, or heard.'

'Then we're talking about maybe twenty-five men.'

'Twenty-five,' Joe muttered.

'Five each. That shouldn't be a problem. There's just one thing. As it seems that Maynard isn't going to deliver, we need that truck, intact and working, to get the gold out of here.'

'Jesus Christ!' Joe said. 'You're not still thinking of getting away?'

'Give me another reason for being here. But listen. We're going to need at least an hour to load it, so there cannot be any survivors. You with me?' She looked around their faces, just visible in the gloom.

'We're with you, ma'am,' Riddick and Harris answered together.

'Of course,' Clive said.

'Joe?'

He sighed. 'You call it.'

'Right. Now—'

'Countess!' the voice called. 'You have one minute to come out, or we will burn the entire copse.'

'I guess that means they have a flame thrower or two,' Anna said. 'So, follow me. I would say they're pretty spread out. On your bellies, and when you have to shoot, make sure the target stays dead.'

She wriggled forward on her stomach, using her knees and elbows so that she could hold the tommy gun in both hands in front of her, remembering that crawl along the embankment in Brazil. More mud. But at least her hair was tucked up under her steel helmet.

She reached the edge of the bushes and saw the truck, and four men, who were standing in the glare of the headlamps, tommy guns levelled at the copse. When will they ever learn? she wondered. Then she heard the roar of the flame-throwers, further to her left; she could smell the scorching foliage and turning her head saw the trees and bushes glowing, but not really catching fire; they were still too wet from the rain. 'Careful now,' the voiced shouted. 'They will make a break for it.'

'Nobody shoot,' Anna said: the men could not be hit by tommy gun fire without endangering the truck. She laid her gun on the ground and drew her Luger. Holding it in both hands, she levelled and fired. Before the first man hit the ground the second was dead. The other two loosed off their guns, but they had no target, and a moment later they were also both dead.

'Holy Jesus Christ!' Harris commented.

'Wow!' Riddick said.

Neither Joe nor Clive spoke; they had known what was coming. She led them out of the bushes.

'They're coming out by the truck!' someone shouted.

'Joe, you're OC truck,' Anna said. 'Drive it through those bushes and park next to the bullion.'

'The copse is on fire,' he objected.

'No, it's not. It's too wet to burn.' And in fact the flames were already sizzling out. 'Go!' She gathered up the scattered tommy guns dropped by the dead Russians and passed them around, so that each man had two weapons. 'Now we have enough firepower to take on an army. Just remember chaps, we need all these people.'

Their expressions indicated that they understood. Joe engaged gear and drove the truck into the bushes. Anna realized that the other Russians had not heard the sound of her Luger above their flame-throwers, but now they heard the sound of the truck engine. Three of them came running back along the road, and were met by a hail of fire. There were shouts from further away. 'Into the copse,' Anna commanded. 'Harris and Riddick, give us your weapons and get to the truck. Load those ingots. We'll cover you.'

They obeyed, so that now she and Clive had four tommy guns each. 'Take cover,' she said.

The knelt together in the first of the trees 'Shoulder to shoulder,' Clive said. 'What a way to go.'

'We're not going anywhere,' she said, 'Until that gold is loaded. Listen! We don't have to worry about running out. When they move towards us, just blanket them and keep firing, using gun after gun.'

'Yes, ma'am.'

She squeezed his hand, and peered into the darkness. The Russians had gathered in a group by the dead bodies, chattering at each other as they tried to work out what had happened. In the gloom it was impossible to see exactly how many there were, but she estimated about twelve. That meant there were perhaps another nine knocking about somewhere, but this lot had to be dealt with first.

She watched two of them move towards the copse. After a moment the others followed. 'Flat,' she told Clive, and lay beside him. As she had anticipated from men who were already nervous, they opened fire, but with nothing to aim at and no knowledge of the whereabouts of their enemies, the only damage they did was to the trees.

The firing stopped, and a voice said, 'That will keep their heads down. Reload, then we go in. You three to the left, you three to the right. The rest follow me.'

They heard the clicking of the drums being replaced. 'Before they separate,' Anna said, 'Now!'

She rose to her knees and opened fire, Clive joining her. She emptied the entire drum of her first gun, dropped it, picked up the next, and continued firing without a break. The dark figures in front of her fell about, screaming and shouting; a couple tried to run and were brought down by the seeking bullets.

'Hold it,' Anna said. There was no one standing in front of them, although there were several still writhing on the ground, groaning and moaning. She stood up, and there was a burst of firing from behind her, and a cry of pain. 'Shit! You finish those off,' she told Clive.

He swallowed, but went forward. Anna picked up two of the unused tommy guns and pushed her way back through the bushes to the truck, listened to a voice calling out in German. 'Surrender or die.'

Cautiously she advanced, making as little noise as possible, saw a man standing with his hands up, and another, obviously Joe, climbing down from the truck, also with his hands up. Facing them were six men, all armed with tommy guns. 'There were five of you,' the man said. 'Where are the other two?'

Anna's brain raced. If he knew there were five of them, then they had been tracked since entering the Russian sector, and if they had been tracked since entering Erfurt, then he would know there had been six originally, which meant that he now knew that Maynard would not be coming back. Poor Maynard. And equally, if he was now confronting three of them, but she could see only two standing, another one was down. Shit, she thought. Shit, shit, shit!

'I do not know where the others are,' Joe was saying. 'I think perhaps they have been hit.'

'Then find the bodies,' the commander said, reverting to Russian, and thus obviously addressing his own people. 'It is the countess we want.'

Anna saw four of them move into the bushes. That left two in front of her.

'All of this gold,' the commander said, again speaking German. 'You must be very pleased. The rest is still down there, eh?'

'That's all there is,' Joe said.

'Do not lie to me, Comrade. There is much more than this. But we will find it, now we know where to look.'

'He isn't lying, Comrade,' Anna said, and opened fire.

Both men went down, 'Get their weapons,' Anna snapped. 'There are the other four.'

They had heard the shots, and were coming back through the bushes, making a good deal of noise. Anna dropped to her knees behind the truck and opened fire, spraying the area with bullets, but now there was an additional burst from behind them, and screams of pain. Clive! she thought.

He stood above her. 'You all right.'

She got up. 'One of your people is down.'

It was Riddick. 'Stone dead, Mr Bartley,' Harris said.

'Damn.'

'Do you realize,' Joe said. 'That between you, you have just killed twenty men?'

'More like twenty-two, I think,' Anna said.

He wiped his brow, 'So what happens now?'

'We load the rest of this stuff and then get the hell out of here.'

'Just like that? After this racket? The whole goddamned country is going to be up in arms by now, looking for us.'

'I don't think so,' Anna said. 'There's a lot going on here that we don't know about, yet. But we can guess. Look at these uniforms. They're all MGB men. Not a single regular amongst them. That means it was an undercover operation. In their own territory? That has to mean whoever instituted this action has his own agenda. And that means the military in Eisenach have been told to keep away. They may take a different attitude when these bodies are found tomorrow, but by then we have to be back on your side of the border.'

'And how are you proposing to do that?'

'Why Joe, exactly how we said we would, across the bridge in a truck with Red Army markings. That's what Captain Roberts is expecting.'

'But without Maynard.'

She sighed. 'I'm afraid not.'

'And Riddick?' Clive asked.

'We can do nothing for him,' Anna said. 'And we have no time to lose. Say a prayer, if you like, and then let's get this stuff loaded.'

'There is a telephone call for you, Comrade Litovsky,' said the anxious clerk in the Russian Embassy in Geneva. 'Moscow.' He lowered his voice to an awed whisper. 'Comrade Beria, personally.'

'Is this line scrambled?'

'Of course, sir.'

Litovsky took the phone. 'Good afternoon, Comrade Commissar.'

'Tell me what is happening.'

'Well, sir, at the moment I am waiting to hear from Colonel Malinov. He should have apprehended the countess and her group by now. We know they left Geneva three days ago. But he was under orders, as you wished, not to interfere with them even after they crossed the border, until they had started to recover the gold, and thus indicated its exact location. Depending on how far they had to go, it may have taken them a day or two.'

'Why were you not with Malinov?' Beria's voice was deceptively calm.

'Well, sir, I thought it best that I should remain here, as a back-up, just in case she slipped through Malinov's fingers and returned here with the bullion. Given her reputation, I had to allow for that possibility.'

'I see. Well, I sincerely hope you are right, because you are not going to be hearing from Malinov.'

'Sir?'

'His body, and that of his entire squad, was this morning found in a small wood only a few miles from Eisenach.'

Litovsky's stomach seemed to fill with lead. 'But . . . but . . . that is impossible. He had twenty-one men with him.'

'That appears to be correct. There was another body on the site, but he appears to have been one of the countess's people. And a man was killed in Eisenach, apparently by MGB people, the night before last, while trying to steal a truck. He may have been connected with the countess. You knew nothing of this?'

'I . . . well . . . well, at least we know that she is in Germany. I will—'

'She is not in Germany. Yesterday morning there was a border incident, in which a Red Army truck was driven across a bridge from Erfurt into Hessen, refusing to stop when challenged. Our people opened fire, but were unable to stop it, and some fire was returned from the American side. The incident is being investigated, and we are making the strongest possible protest. But the whole affair is just too much of a coincidence for it not to have been the countess. Thus we must face the fact that despite your best efforts and all the information at your disposal, she has entered our territory, collected what she wanted, and once again escaped, leaving another twenty-two of our people dead.'

'Sir—'

'The Premier has not yet seen this news, Litovsky, but when he does I do not feel that he is going to be very happy about it. I do not know if you ever pray, and who you pray to, but I strongly suggest that you do so now, and hope that the countess does indeed return to Geneva, and that you manage to correct the situation. I look forward to hearing from you.'

'How do you feel?' Clive asked.

'Better than I did,' Anna said. 'A few dozen more aches and pains.'

'You mean you slept?' Joe asked.

The three of them sat together in the cab of the truck as they drove south. The markings had been altered to US, and the bullion was entirely concealed beneath piles of sacking.

'Like a log for twelve hours. Didn't you?'

'Not really. I kept thinking of how many lives this little caper has cost.'

He was driving. Anna squeezed his arm. 'I'm sorry about Maynard, believe me. And Riddick, Clive. I feel like absolute shit about that. Listen, I'll double their shares, and it'll go to their next of kin.'

'And Harris?'

'His too.'

'He sure must trust you,' Joe remarked. 'Taking off like that.'

'I never let down anyone who is on my side,' Anna pointed out. 'Although I'm sorry he left without even saying goodbye.'

'His leave was up,' Clive explained. 'And you were sleeping like a baby, so I told him not to disturb you.'

'I hadn't realized he was on so short a leash.'

'Talking about not letting people down,' Joe said. 'You have your share, but you haven't delivered the goods yet.'

'This job isn't finished yet.'

'And you think I might still do a nasty on you? I hope you haven't forgotten that you're still working for us.'

'I haven't forgotten that, Joe, but as I said, there's still work to be done. Such as finding out who betrayed us to the Russians.'

'Eh?'

'You don't suppose that MGB unit just happened on us by chance? And took a wild guess at what we were doing?'

'Shit! I hadn't thought of that.'

'I have,' Clive said. 'It has to be Laurent.'

'You mean the guy who's going to handle the money for us? That doesn't make sense. Wasn't he picking up a hundred grand for the deal?'

'Yes,' Anna said quietly. 'Maybe some things are more important than money.'

'Son of a gun. What are we going to do? Why are we heading for Switzerland, if there's no point?'

'We are getting out of Germany, Joe.'

'But we were in the US Sector.'

'Don't you think this whole business is going to cause a certain diplomatic stir? So your people, on your say-so, helped us get into Erfurt and back out again, by stopping the Reds chasing us across that bridge. While they're trying to sort that out, somebody is going to come across those twenty-odd dead bodies and put two and two together.'

'Sure they are. But this whole thing was condoned by the CIA. Once you tell us where the rest of the gold is, you're absolutely in the clear.'

'I'm sorry. Joe. My experience of governments who guarantee you immunity for services rendered is a little negative. Would you agree with that, Clive?'

He sighed. 'You have a point.'

'So, I reckoned things would have gone like this. We would have shacked up some place in the US sector while we found someone to handle the bullion. However, within days, probably by now, the Russian bigwigs would be in touch with your bigwigs raising a stink. Your bigwigs would feel obliged to place us under arrest, if only as window-dressing, while the matter is investigated. Once that was done, they would definitely find the bullion. Then all hell would break loose. By this time, of course, you will be in touch with Washington shouting help. And they will of course promise it. But hold on, they will say, has she yet told you the location of the main body of the bullion. Once I have done that, their past record suggests that they may well say, this damned woman is more trouble than she's worth, and write me off. Even if they do not, we will have been in custody for several days, and I cannot bring myself to believe that the gold would still be around by then.'

'You've just worked out all of those possibilities?'

'I'm alive,' she reminded him.

'And you still think you can take on the world, and win.'

'I'm pretty sure I can make a better job of that while I'm footloose and fancy-free.'

'So what is our plan?'

'For starters, see how the land lies in Geneva.'

'Welcome back, Fraulein,' said the reception clerk. 'Did you have a pleasant trip?'

'It had its moments,' Anna acknowledged. 'Tell me, do you have lock-up garages?'

'Of course, Fraulein.'

'Oh, good. I'd like to rent one for a couple of days.'

'I'll look after it,' Clive said, and took the keys.

'So what happens now?' Joe asked, as they rode up in the lift.

'I don't think we want to lose any time,' Anna said, 'as the Reds are definitely too interested in our activities. I am going to have a much-needed bath, then I am going to get dressed, and pay a call. You gentlemen are welcome to come with me, if you wish.'

He looked at his watch. 'Six o'clock. It'll be seven before you're ready. Laurent will have gone home by then.'

'That,' Anna said. 'is the general idea.'

The address was in the phone book, and was an apartment. Anna bathed and rebound her ankle, which was slightly swollen, strapped on her Walther and then put on a frock, brushed her hair and added make-up, checked her Luger to make sure it was loaded and that there was still a spare magazine, slung her shoulder bag, then went downstairs to reclaim her jewellery; she put some on, stored the rest in the bag; where she went it went. Both men were waiting for her. 'We'll take a taxi,' she decided.

'How are you proposing to handle this?' Clive asked.

'We'll play it by ear. It's just possible there may be nothing actually to handle.'

They rode up in the lift of the very plush apartment building. Anna rang the bell, while Clive and Joe, each from years of training and practice, stood against the wall to either side of her, out of the line of vision of anyone opening the door. Anna felt pleasantly relaxed. She did not know what, if anything, Laurent was trying to pull, but she was prepared to deal with it, and she did know that she had gone into Germany and come out again, with ten million dollars. Thus she was taken completely by surprise when the door opened.

But so was Katherine. 'Anna! Oh, Anna!'

'Katherine?' They embraced. 'I don't understand,' Anna said. 'What are you doing here?'

'Oh!' She flushed, and released her. 'I . . .'

She looked over her shoulder, and Laurent came across the living room to stand behind her. 'Anna?'

'You almost sound surprised to see me.'

'But . . . you mean . . . you . . .'

'I don't think it is something we want to discuss in the corridor.' She looked at Katherine. 'And we seem to have rather a lot to discuss. Aren't you going to invite me in?'

'Of course.' Katherine stepped back, carrying Laurent with her. 'It is so good to see you. And looking as beautiful as ever . . .'

'You say the sweetest things,' Anna said, stepping through the doorway. 'Do you mind if my two friends come in as well?'

'Your—?'

'Oh, shit!' Laurent said, as Clive appeared, followed by Joe. Katherine stared at them, and then pointed. 'That man . . .'

'Of course,' Anna said. 'You have met. This is Mr Joseph Andrews. He works for the Central Intelligence Agency. That is Uncle Sam's latest equivalent of MI6, only I believe it also incorporates their equivalent of MI5. You could call it a very far-reaching organization, with virtually unlimited powers.'

'And they have arrested you, and brought you here?' Katherine was aghast.

'I think . . .' Laurent ventured, but was ignored.

'I said, they're my friends, and my partners,' Anna said. 'And if you can explain exactly what happened between you and Belinda Hoskin, I may be able to persuade them not to arrest you, for murder.'

'She said you were a traitor to the Reich, a double agent for the British. She said . . .' Katherine glared at her. 'My God! She was telling the truth! You were betraying the Reich. For this . . .'

'That is history,' Anna said.

'Bitch!' Katherine screamed, and hurled herself at her sister.

Clive stepped between them and endeavoured to catch Katherine's arms, only to be struck a flailing blow across the side of the head that sent him to the floor with a crash.

'Holy Jesus Christ!' Joe said.

Katherine's arms swung back to Anna, but here she was out of her class. Anna caught the first swinging hand with her own left, and swung her right in turn, a scything blow which sent the edge of her hand into Katherine's ribs. Katherine gasped, choked, and fell to her knees, vomiting.

'My God!' Laurent cried. 'You have hurt her.'

'She'll recover.' Anna dropped to her knees beside Clive, who was shaking his head. 'Are you all right?'

'Jesus! That kid—'

'Was SS trained. As was I. You were careless. Now . . .'

The hall door burst open. Joe swung to face it and had a pistol thrust into his ribs. Anna turned her head, and found a gun muzzle pressed into her temple. 'I have permission to kill you, Countess,' Litovsky said, speaking German. 'But I am sure you would rather live, at least for a while.'

Anna took deep breaths. On her knees, and with both her hands holding Clive's head, she had been caught as much off guard as she had been on entering Bormann's villa. And there was no back-up waiting outside to come to her aid. Clive was only half conscious, Joe has been pushed against the wall, a pistol still in his ribs, Laurent seemed petrified, and Katherine was still retching.

And there were four men in the room, each armed with a pistol. Again, in normal conditions, this should not be enough. But these were not normal conditions. Although the Walther was nestling, unsuspected, against her pubes, this dress did not have a side vent, and there were now two men standing, one on each side, and each with a pistol pressed to her head; she could bring one down with a scything blow to the legs, but the other would certainly kill her.

'Now, Countess,' Litovsky said. 'We know all of your little tricks. Do not attempt to get up. Stay on your knees, and take off the shoulder bag. The famous shoulder bag, eh? Move slowly.'

Anna carefully lifted the strap over her head and laid the bag on the floor. The other man kicked it across the room.

Katherine stopped retching and gasping for breath. 'Fucking bitch,' she growled, and then seemed to realize that they had additional company. 'These men—'

'Are your old friends the MGB, my dear,' Laurent explained. 'I was going to telephone you,' he assured Litovsky, 'as soon as the countess returned. She took me by surprise, but—'

'Shut up,' Litovsky said. 'You have not carried out your instructions. I will deal with you in a moment. Now, Countess, you may get up, very slowly.'

The two men moved away, but their pistols were still levelled. Thus far they had totally ignored Katherine, but now she suddenly shrieked, 'Russians!' reached her feet, and hurled herself at Litovsky. He turned and fired, and she went over backwards with another shriek, but both men had been distracted. Anna threw herself sideways, rolling across the floor but at the same time dragging her dress to her waist to reach the Walther. The two men turned back again, and died before they realized what was going on. Anna kept on firing.

The man by the door fired, but his bullet was wide and he was dead before he could focus. The man holding Joe against the wall had also turned, and went the same way.

Still holding her pistol, Anna knelt beside her sister. But Katherine was also dead. Clive pushed himself up. 'Anna . . .'

'Poor kid,' she said. 'Poor mixed up kid.'

Joe carefully stepped over the man at his feet; he was trembling.

'Anna,' Laurent said. 'I can explain.'

Anna looked at him. 'You can't you know. I still have one bullet.'

'Anna!' he wailed.

Anna fired.

'I think,' Clive said, 'that we should get the hell out of here. Someone is sure to have heard those shots.'

Anna was again looking at her sister.

'We can't take her with us,' he said. 'And she'll get a decent burial. And if you're here when the police come . . . you're already wanted for murder in Switzerland.'

She holstered the Walther and straightened her dress, picked up her shoulder bag and they went outside, closing the door behind them, although the lock was in any event shattered by the Russians' charge. There were people gathered in the corridor, chattering at each other. 'Call the police,' Clive suggested. 'There's been a tragedy in there.'

They hurried to the elevator, while behind them a woman screamed. Then they were on the darkening street.

'What a fuck-up,' Joe said.

'The hotel is that way,' Anna said. Her brain still felt numb. To have found, and then lost, her sister in a matter of moments . . . even if Katherine might have got no more than she deserved.

'The taxi rank is down here,' Clive assured her. They got into the first cab. 'The airport,' Clive instructed.

The car moved away.

'But . . . what about the truck?' Anna asked. 'We have to get the truck.'

'It's not going to do us a lot of good now that Laurent is dead,' Joe pointed out. 'That was a pretty silly play, Anna.'

'I know,' Anna said. 'I lost my head.'

'You, lost your head?'

'But we can't just abandon it. Ten million dollars!'

'The truck,' Clive said, 'is across the border and into France, by now.'

'What?' Anna and Joe shouted together.

'I had a notion this was going to turn out badly. Harris didn't have to rejoin his ship. I had him follow us by car, and when you told me to garage the truck this afternoon, I simply gave him the keys and told him to get out of Switzerland.'

'But . . .'

'Relax, my dearest girl He is absolutely trustworthy. I also have an RAF plane waiting for us at the airport, and we will be in Paris in an hour. I also,' he added, 'know of a totally reliable broker who will handle the bullion for you. In Paris.'

'Clive Bartley, I could love you.'

'You already do,' he reminded her.

'Lucky for some,' Joe commented. 'But there is still some unfinished business. Such as the rest of the bullion.'

'It's in those defunct salt mines you spotted on the map. The RAF didn't blow them up. I did. With a little help.'

'But . . . that's in Soviet territory!'

'Joe,' Anna said. 'The deal was that I tell you where it is. I never claimed that getting it out was going to be easy.'

Epilogue

'*D*id they ever get it?' I asked.

'*I think they did some kind of a deal with the Reds,*' Anna said.

'*Then that must have got them off your back.*'

She sighed. '*Unfortunately, bears appear to have even longer memories than elephants. I had by then, with some help from time to time, been responsible for the deaths of fifty-one of their people. Then, of course, I was still under contract to the CIA, who thought of me in only one capacity.*'

'*Did you ever encounter Jerry Smitten again?*'

'*Yes, I did. He still had a lot to learn,*' she added, enigmatically.

'*And you mean you and Clive didn't manage to sneak off and live happily ever after, spending your loot?*'

'*Not right then. We had our moments. But I was about to find out just how cold the Cold War could get.*'

'*So tell me, did you ever come face to face with Beria?*'

Anna Fehrbach smiled.